# THE UNTITLED BOOKS

## The Glass Library
### Book 3

# C.J. ARCHER

*To Mum and Dad.*
*Thank you for your unwavering support and the sacrifices you made along the way.*

# CHAPTER 1

## LONDON, SPRING 1920

There can be no doubt that the most enchanting way to spend a wet day is indoors with a cup of tea in one hand and a book in the other. In my case, it was more than one book. I sat on the attic floor, surrounded by them. Large ones that required two hands to lift and small ones that could fit in my palm; leather-covered tomes and unbound manuscripts; texts I could read and others written in foreign languages.

I didn't mind the dust and musty smell of the Glass Library attic. Indeed, the attic felt welcoming, once I cleared away some of the cobwebs.

I set the teacup on the floor and picked up my notebook. Positioning it near the gas lamp for better light, I transcribed the details of a slim volume written in an Arabic script as best as I could before setting it aside. There were at least two dozen more to be cataloged. They'd been stored in the wooden trunk decorated with cutwork brass and studs that Professor Nash had placed near the back of the attic after returning from Egypt with them many years ago. The trunk had remained closed all that time, gathering dust, along with several others he and his friend collected. It was going to take months to catalog everything, and even longer to have them translated.

At some point in the afternoon, the downpour eased and the rain became a light patter on the roof. I hardly noticed when it happened. Nor did I notice the time until the professor's head popped through the trapdoor like a jack-in-the-box.

"I've just locked up," he said.

"Is it that late already?" I closed the book I'd been cataloging and set it aside with the notepad. "I'd better go. Mrs. Parry doesn't like us to be late for dinner." My landlady was generally very sweet, but she didn't like going to the trouble of cooking for her lodgers if it wasn't necessary. I'd learned that the hard way after dining out with Daisy one night without informing Mrs. Parry. She'd scolded me the following morning over breakfast and made me wash the dishes for an entire week instead of following the roster.

I passed the teacup to the professor and extinguished the lamp before following him through the trapdoor and down the ladder to the mezzanine level of his flat. He pushed his spectacles up his nose and regarded me with a smile.

"You'd best dust yourself off before your landlady sees you or she'll think you've gone into service."

Fortunately, I'd worn gray for my foray into the attic this time. The day before, I'd worn a pretty white blouse that may never be quite as white again.

I washed the cup in the kitchen sink and turned to the professor as I dried it with a towel. "Don't get up," I said as he rose from the chair. "I'll see myself out."

"Goodnight then, Sylvia."

"Goodnight, Professor."

I headed out of his flat via the secret door hidden among the bookshelves to the library then down the stairs to the small reception area. I collected my bag and coat and was about to open the door when someone tried to enter from the other side. Finding the door locked, they banged on it. Incessantly. Either the person was rude, or they desperately needed to speak to the professor or me. I assumed the latter and hurriedly unlocked the door.

The woman standing there holding an umbrella fell into the former category. I managed to refrain from sighing with disappointment at the sight of her, but only just.

"Lady Stanhope. What are you doing here?" Perhaps it wasn't the politest way to greet a viscountess, but it didn't warrant the scowl she gave me as she regarded me down her nose.

She pushed past me, her strides purposeful. The damp hem of her black skirts tangled around her ankles and her black cloak billowed like a cloud behind her. She folded up the umbrella and held it out to me, shaking it when I didn't immediately take it from her. "Is the librarian here?"

I was about to answer when a man I'd not noticed in the gloomy light followed her inside. He did not carry an umbrella and his chauffeur's cap and oilskin raincoat were damp. The empty arms of the raincoat hung loosely at his sides and, judging by the bulge, he carried something under it to protect it from the rain. Lady Stanhope's umbrella could have done the job, but she would have to hold it over his head instead of her own and I suspected she'd claim that was beneath her.

She pushed back the hood of her cloak, revealing a face that was still striking, although a lifetime of haughtily pinched lips had formed deep lines around her mouth that now drew together in disapproval. "I asked you a question, Miss Ashe."

"The library is closed, madam. We open again at nine tomorrow."

"I am here now and what I have in my possession will be of interest to the librarian."

I should have persisted, but her claim intrigued me. "In what way will it interest him?"

"I have some magical books."

My gaze fell on the chauffeur. "I'll fetch the professor. If you'll wait here—"

"I'll wait through there." She marched off between the two black marble columns marking the entrance to the library and strode to the reading nook.

The chauffeur gave me a small shrug of apology then asked me to help remove his raincoat. I deposited the umbrella in the stand near the door and hung up his raincoat. He followed Lady Stanhope into the library carrying a cardboard box in both hands, his tall black boots *click-clacking* loudly on the floorboards.

I returned upstairs and informed the professor of Lady Stanhope's arrival. "I am sorry to bother you, but she insisted I fetch you."

He patted my shoulder as he closed the door to his flat behind him. "It's quite all right, Sylvia. I wonder what she wants."

"She claims to have magical books."

He blinked back at me. "Well, well. Let's find out why she believes that."

Lady Stanhope sat at one end of the sofa in the reading nook while her chauffeur stood behind her, his uniform and stiff stance giving him the air of a military escort. The box he'd been carrying sat on the desk.

Professor Nash bowed his head in greeting. "Good evening, Lady Stanhope. To what do we owe this pleasure?"

She signaled the chauffeur with a forward jut of her chin. He reached into the box and removed six quarto sized books bound in olive green leather covers. He placed them on the desk then stepped back.

Lady Stanhope smiled like a cat who'd caught a mouse. All that was missing was a lick of her lips. "You may look at them."

The professor waited, but she seemed to think no more explanation was required. He switched on the desk lamp. "What am I looking at?"

"Magical books made with magical paper."

I joined the professor as he carefully picked up the topmost book. There was nothing stamped on the front or spine, but the cover's corners were encased in silver protectors engraved with the initials JF. He opened it and scanned the first page. There were no publisher details, just a title and author name.

"*The Well of Wild Wood* by Honoria Moffat-Jones," I read. The words were handwritten in neat uniformly spaced capitals. "That name rings a bell. Did she write *The Little Folk of Wild Wood*?"

"She did," Lady Stanhope said with a hint of excitement in her voice. "The book sold well, but she never published another. That makes these rare. Unpublished manuscripts by a famous author handwritten on magical paper are priceless."

And yet she paid a price for them.

I read a few lines of the handwritten text over the professor's shoulder as he slowly turned the pages. It was a fantasy book written for children, complete with accompanying sketches. They were simple, with no real artistic merit, and the prose was a little overblown.

Professor Nash closed the book. "It's a novel." He studied the titles of the other books. "They're all novels, written by the same author."

Lady Stanhope's lips thinned further. "And?"

"You misunderstand the library's purpose. We house

books *about* magic, not books that contain magic. The thought is very much appreciated, however. Thank you, madam."

Her brows drew together in a severe line. "I'm not donating them, Professor. They're mine."

"Oh. Then why are you here, if I may be so bold as to ask?"

She stood and picked up the book he'd just set down. She thrust it in front of his face. "I'm here to ask you to verify they contain magic. I bought them from a reputable bookbinder on Paternoster Row, but one can't be too careful. Mr. Littleproud contacted me out of the blue claiming to have some untitled books that might interest me, and I purchased them on the proviso that they do indeed contain magic."

"You don't trust his word?"

"He claimed they're untitled, for starters, and they clearly have titles." She opened the book to the first page and stabbed a gloved finger on the capitalized text. "Perhaps he also lied about the magic to drive up the price."

"'Untitled' is a term used in the book trade to describe an unpublished manuscript." Professor Nash picked up one of the other books and opened it to the first page. It also lacked publishing details and was handwritten. "Whether these manuscripts were intended to be published by the author or not isn't clear, but I can assure you he didn't lie about them being untitled in the correct sense of the word. As to whether or not the paper contains magic, I'm afraid I can't answer that. Nor can Sylvia. Neither of us are magicians."

I hadn't told the professor that I suspected I might be a magician. It had been Gabriel Glass's suggestion after I'd easily found the stolen Medici Manuscript last week. He'd theorized that its magical silver clasps called to me, called to the magician's instinct within me. Yet I wasn't a silver magician. I knew that with certainty, despite my brother suspecting he might be, if his diary entry was anything to go by.

I stared at the books on the desk, trying to determine whether my eagerness to touch them was because they contained magic or because I simply liked old, mysterious books.

Professor Nash cleared his throat and pushed his glasses up his nose. "If you're not prepared to take the bookbinder's word, madam, then you'll have to find a magician who can verify whether there is magic in these or not. If you don't know one—"

"Of course I know one. I know several."

We'd met Lady Stanhope when she tried to dupe a young magician artist before he became aware he was a magician. We'd learned that she took lovers from among the art community, using her influence at the Royal Academy to entice them into her bed. She'd shown an uncommon interest in Gabe, suspecting that he'd inherited his mother's magic, and had befriended his fiancée in the hope of getting close to him. The moment his relationship with Ivy ended, Lady Stanhope took his side and warned him to distance himself from the Hobson family as their boot making company faced difficulties. We thought we wouldn't see Lady Stanhope again after Gabe told her he wasn't a magician, but it seemed she wouldn't be easily dismissed. Here she was again, her insatiable appetite for magic bringing her back into our sphere.

I reached for the book sitting on top of the stack, but Lady Stanhope snatched the pile out from under me before I could touch it. She shot me a frosty glare, as if I had no right to touch her possessions without permission, then jerked her head in the chauffeur's direction.

He took the books from her and placed them inside the box. He followed her to the front door where she waited for someone to open it for her. Professor Nash obliged. It was no longer raining, and Lady Stanhope strode off down the lane without a backwards glance.

The poor chauffeur had to juggle the box of books and her umbrella while I settled his raincoat around his shoulders. He raced after her, slipping on the wet cobblestones as he exited the lane behind her.

Professor Nash scratched his head. "I wonder if the book-binder is telling the truth about the paper containing magic or if he saw a way to make easy money from a wealthy woman."

"If he did, he should close his shop and leave the country immediately. Lady Stanhope won't take kindly to being duped."

He gave a wry chuckle. "Very true. She prefers to be the one doing the duping."

* * *

I DIDN'T VENTURE into the attic the following morning. I didn't want to be dusty for my outing with Gabe. He arrived promptly at ten as arranged, entourage in tow. Clearly his friend, Alex, and his cousin, Willie, weren't prepared to let him out of their sight until they knew there was no threat of another kidnapping. The two thugs arrested in Crooked Lane last week wouldn't identify the person who employed them, and until he or she was caught, the threat of another attempt loomed.

If Gabe was worried, he didn't show it. His smile lit up the library, reaching his warm eyes. There was no sign of concern for his safety in his relaxed stance, no sign that the discovery of his ability to alter time confused him, or that he felt guilt for ending his relationship with Ivy Hobson.

Yet I knew those things weighed on his mind. When he let his guard slip, he revealed a man scarred by war who was still trying to discover who he was and how he fitted into a world that had altered dramatically since 1914.

But he was a master at keeping that guard up.

Before we left, Professor Nash told them about our visit from Lady Stanhope. "She'd purchased a collection of unpublished works from a bookbinder on Paternoster Row who claimed the paper was magician-made. She thought we could verify it for her. We couldn't, of course. I was about to suggest Huon Barratt, but she assured us she could find a magician to ask."

Gabe's gaze slid to me, but he made no comment.

Alex snorted. "Barratt and Lady Stanhope...now that's a meeting I'd want to see. He's a lazy good-for-nothing and she's got as much charm as Medusa."

"The snake-haired woman of Greek mythology?" Willie asked. "The one who turns folks to stone when they look at her?"

"I'm surprised you've heard of her."

"Course I have. I ain't an idiot."

Alex gave her an arched look.

She narrowed her gaze. "I know a few people I'd like to turn to stone with a stare."

"Why not just marry them?"

She thumped his arm.

Gabe sighed. "I apologize," he said to the professor and me. "They've been spending too much time in one another's company lately. I've tried telling them I don't need nannies, but they insist on dogging my every step. It's grown beyond tiresome for everyone."

Alex and Willie stood side by side, arms crossed, and glared at Gabe, challenging him to try and order them to leave. They might bicker, but when it came to protecting him, they were united.

"It would seem Lady Stanhope is becoming a serious

collector," Gabe said as we headed along Crooked Lane behind Alex and Willie. "She's obtaining quite the reputation in the last few weeks among magician circles, ever since the opening of the Royal Academy exhibition."

Given his family's reputation among magicians, and his work as a consultant on magical investigations for Scotland Yard, I imagined he knew a lot of them, even though he wasn't magical himself.

Willie stopped inside the narrow entryway to the lane from the main street and put out an arm, stopping the rest of us from passing. She scanned left and right, checking for kidnappers.

Alex waited with barely disguised patience until she finally moved and let us through. "Next time, let me go first. Trapping me back there defeats the purpose."

"The purpose of what? You getting in my way? I want to see who's around, not have my view blocked by your fat head."

"If anyone around here has a fat head, it's you."

"Did I say head? I meant ass."

Gabe opened the back door of the black Hudson Super Six, his parents' old car that was usually driven by the chauffeur. He was nowhere in sight today as Gabe smiled and held out his hand to me. "Meanwhile, I've just been kidnapped because those two can't stop fighting."

I nodded at the only passersby in the vicinity, two gray-haired ladies walking arm in arm as they doddered along at a snail's pace. "You could probably charm your way out of a kidnapping by those two."

He laughed softly. Then he turned serious. "It's good to see you again, Sylvia."

My face heated. "It's good to see you, too, Gabe."

He looked away at his friends then back at me, smiling again. "It'll be nice to have some sane company for a while."

Oh. He hadn't meant it was nice to see *me*, just *anyone* who wasn't Willie or Alex. They were currently arguing over who was going to drive.

"I'd like to make it to our destination in one piece," Alex told her as they squared off.

"You calling me a bad driver? I drove ambulances in France during the war."

"That doesn't make you a good driver, just an available one." He thrust his hands onto his hips. "I'll drive."

She mirrored his stance with hands on hips and feet apart. "No."

"I'm driving, Willie. You crank."

"Make me."

Alex looked as though he was considering how when Gabe slid into the driver's seat. "I'll drive. One of you crank the engine, or do I have to do that, too?"

His two friends reluctantly called a truce, and a few minutes later, we drove off, heading to the last known address of Marianne Folgate.

My brother had written in his diary that he suspected he was a silver magician. He'd always been keen to know more about our family, but our mother had not encouraged questions. She wouldn't even tell us about our father. She'd instilled fear in me, about him and men in general, and I'd not been inclined to challenge her view until her influence over me faded when I moved to London after her death.

Now I wanted to know more about myself, and knowing more meant learning about my family. If my brother was indeed a silver magician, then there was most likely a connection to the only silver magician—Marianne Folgate. Gabe's parents, Lord and Lady Rycroft, had met her years ago, but she'd since disappeared. It was Gabe's suggestion that we question the neighbors at her old address. Perhaps someone remembered her.

Or perhaps this would turn out to be another wild goose chase that ended nowhere. I was beginning to think I was destined not to learn more about my family after every effort proved unproductive. Even so, I wanted to follow every clue to the very end.

But I couldn't dismiss the small voice in my head, the one that sounded like my mother, telling me it might not be a bad thing to be left in the dark.

# CHAPTER 2

*G*abe's parents had met Marianne Folgate on the front porch of her Wimbledon home, and now here we were almost thirty years later, standing on the same porch. The handsome cream brick house with the white bay window had probably been built only a decade before Marianne lived there. The notes written by India, Gabe's mother, stated that it was a big house for one person and speculated she'd lived there with another. The notes had also said she no longer lived there when they went looking for her a short while later.

Gabe's knock was answered by a maid who'd never heard of Marianne. Since the current occupants had lived in the property for only seven years, she directed us to a neighbor who'd lived next door for over forty.

The maid who answered the neighbor's door asked us to wait on the porch while she checked if her mistress was receiving callers. A few minutes later, she invited us into a sitting room that looked as though it hadn't changed since the elderly lady occupying one of the armchairs was a new bride. The green velvet curtains and carpet had faded, but the room

felt homely thanks to the dozens of family portraits deco-
rating the walls and the vases full of pink roses and frilly
peonies.

Mrs. Pullman picked up a lorgnette from her lap and
squinted through it at Gabe. She nodded, as if we'd passed
some kind of test, and motioned for us to sit on the sofa. We'd
left Alex and Willie with the motor. Little old ladies presented
no kidnapping threat to Gabe.

We introduced ourselves to Mrs. Pullman and told her we
were trying to locate her former neighbor, a relative of mine.

She tilted her head to the side. "Speak louder, young man.
Who are you looking for?"

"Marianne Folgate," Gabe repeated. "She used to live next
door in 1891. Do you remember her?"

Mrs. Pullman's wrinkles folded together in a frown. "I
recall a woman named Marianne, but she wasn't a Folgate.
Pretty little thing, but quite timid. She rarely ventured
beyond her front door."

"Do you recall Marianne's full name?" I asked.

She cupped her hand to her ear and I repeated my question. Then she studied me through her lorgnette. "If you are
her relative, why don't you know her name?" She might be
hard of hearing, but she was still sharp.

"Marianne and my mother lost touch. I've never met her,
but my mother passed away from influenza and I want to
locate what few relatives I have left."

Mrs. Pullman turned to the wall with the framed
photographs of young, smiling soldiers dressed in uniform.
Her wrinkles shifted and refolded into a picture of sorrow.
"Family is important, especially now."

"Your grandsons?" I asked gently.

She nodded and turned back to me. "I knew Marianne,
but not as a Folgate. She went by the name of Cooper."

Not Ashe. Even though I wasn't entirely convinced that

Marianne was a relative, a glimmer of hope burned inside me. If she'd been named Ashe, the same as me, it would have been proof of a connection.

Now, the glimmer dimmed. But it didn't die altogether.

"What can you tell me about her?" I asked. "What was she like?"

Mrs. Pullman settled back into her chair as if settling into the story she was about to tell. "I didn't know her very well. She was timid, as I said. They both were."

"Both?" I echoed. "She lived there with someone?"

"Her husband." She frowned. "You didn't know she was married?"

"No." We'd already checked the marriage records at the General Registry Office and there was no record of Marianne Folgate marrying. There was no record of her at all.

"I only saw him once, and not clearly at that. It was so long ago," she added, somewhat apologetically.

"What did Marianne look like?"

"Pretty. Brown hair. Small stature, very slim. I'm afraid I don't remember much more than that. They lived here for such a short time and hardly interacted with the neighbors. I invited her to tea, but she always claimed she had another engagement, although I never saw her go anywhere." Mrs. Pullman frowned. "She apologized profusely for declining. She seemed sad. Sad that she couldn't join me or invite me inside her house." Mrs. Pullman shook her head, shaking off the memory. "Perhaps I'm imagining things now, with so much time having passed."

I leaned forward, wanting her to go on. I was so desperate to hear more about Marianne that I was a little too abrupt when I urged her to continue. "Imagining what, Mrs. Pullman?"

She shook her head again, shrugging. "Don't listen to me. It's just the ramblings of an old lady."

My heart sank. Anything I'd say might sound harsh from my desperation, forcing her to retreat further.

Fortunately I had Gabe at my side. While I couldn't hide my desperation, he was a master of covering his emotions with a charming mask. He leaned forward, resting his elbows on his knees and lightly clasping his hands together. "You may have lived a handful of years longer than us, Mrs. Pullman, but from what I can see, your mind is quick."

She chuckled. "Do you think flattery will work on an old thing like me, young man?"

Gabe's lips twitched at one corner. "You see right through me."

Her whole body shook with her deep chuckle. "Very well, I'll oblige since you're trying so hard." She grew serious. "This is just my opinion, mind, and I didn't see an awful lot of Mr. and Mrs. Cooper. But from what I can recall, they were both anxious people."

"What do you mean?" Gabe asked.

"They rarely left the house. They kept the curtains closed, and I never saw or heard them in the garden. At first, I thought Mr. Cooper demanded his wife remain indoors and not befriend anyone. I thought she was afraid of him. She was young, you see, and if she'd chosen unwisely…well, some marriages are rotten from the start. I kept an eye open for Mr. Cooper, to get my measure of him, so to speak. If he seemed cruel then I would have tried to help her, be a shoulder for her to lean on. I watched every day for him, expecting him to leave for work in the mornings to go to the city, and return in the early evening. But he didn't. Whatever he did for a living didn't require him to keep regular hours. Mr. Pullman saw him leave the house after dark a few times, but I saw Mr. Cooper go out during the day only once. I remember it even now because he was so strange. He kept his hat low to hide his face and he looked over his shoulder as he walked."

"He was afraid, too," I muttered.

"I believe so, Miss Ashe."

"You say Cooper walked that day," Gabe said. "Did he keep a carriage?"

"No."

"What about other staff? A housekeeper or maid?"

"I can't recall, I'm sorry."

Gabe gave her a sympathetic smile. "It's all right, Mrs. Pullman. Thank you for your time." He rose.

I stayed seated. "Mrs. Pullman, how long did they live next door?"

"Only a few months, three at most." She frowned in thought. "They left overnight, without a peep."

Gabe and I exchanged glances. "You didn't hear the removalists?" he asked.

"No. The owner kept the house furnished so they only needed their personal belongings. Other tenants before the Coopers rarely stayed long, although usually longer than them. There were no new tenants after they left and the house was sold not long afterwards."

I sat forward, eager to hear more. "Who owned it in 1891 and leased it to the Coopers?"

"I don't know. I never did learn his name. He never lived there himself."

We thanked her and the maid saw us out. We returned to the motorcar and sat inside with the engine off while Gabe repeated what we'd learned for Alex and Willie's sakes. It allowed me time to begin to piece together what little of the puzzle we possessed. The more I learned about Marianne, the more I wanted to find out more. Mrs. Pullman had painted a picture of a mysterious couple who'd made a lasting impression on their neighbor, despite living a mere three months next door.

Willie gazed at the nice house where Marianne Cooper

née Folgate had lived. "I wish I'd taken more notice of her in Ninety-one, but I never thought we'd be looking for her almost thirty years later."

"My parents would agree with that." Gabe turned to me in the back seat and offered a small smile of encouragement. "At least we have something to go on with. I'll ask our lawyer to find out who owned that house when the Coopers lived there. Hopefully he'll still have a record of his tenants. They would have needed to provide former addresses before leasing the property."

I wasn't so sure finding the owner would help. It was so long ago. If he was still alive, it was very likely he'd not kept records dating back that far. But Gabe seemed enthused. Whether he was acting that way to keep my spirits up, or he was simply in need of something to do, I wasn't sure. I'd come to realize that Gabe needed an occupation, something to keep him both physically and mentally active. If he allowed boredom to creep in, the memories of war crept in too. Like many returned soldiers, he wanted to keep them at bay.

Any boredom he might be experiencing was soon allevi-ated, however, and in rather dramatic fashion.

* * *

DAISY ENTERED the library late the following morning wheeling her bicycle. I'd spent most of the morning cata-loging books in the attic but had come downstairs for fresh air and to ask the professor for his advice about one of the books. We looked up upon her arrival and smiled.

"Just in time for tea," Professor Nash announced as he rose. "Park your vehicle, Daisy, and join us in the reading nook."

I picked up the book and followed Daisy into the library proper as the professor headed upstairs. She removed her hat pin and hat as she walked and patted her hair. A library patron happened to wander out from between the stacks at that moment and suddenly stopped, his sharp intake of breath audible in the silence.

Daisy was caught off guard, but quickly recovered. She cast him a cheerful smile and a "How do you do, sir" before continuing on to the reading nook. The patron watched her go, until he realized I'd noticed him staring.

Daisy often elicited stares from men. She knew it, too, and rather enjoyed the attention. Even with her back turned, I suspected she knew the man admired her. It was why she kept her arms raised to her hair and swayed her hips. Wearing trousers gathered at the ankle and a white Grecian style blouse tied at the waist, she cut a fine figure from behind.

She was still smiling when she sat. "You should have come to the Buttonhole with me last night, Sylv. It was such fun." She kicked off her left pump and rubbed her toes. "My feet are on fire today after all the dancing, but it was worth it."

She'd asked me to attend the nightclub with her, but I'd declined. I had to work today and Daisy liked to stay out late. She didn't have employment, although she was auditioning for roles in the moving pictures. "I told you not to go alone."

"What was I supposed to do? You wouldn't come. Anyway, I met people I knew there. Actors, writers, artists...I move in very artistic circles now. Oh, and that fellow Huon Barratt was there, the professor's ink magician friend."

"They're hardly friends. The professor traveled with Oscar Barratt, but he doesn't know his nephew very well."

Unlike his adventurous and enterprising uncle, Huon was a wastrel with no employment and no desire to find any. He lived alone in his father's London townhouse and seemed to spend much of his time drunk or asleep. His parents let him be, unsure how to deal with a son who'd come back from the war alive but now wanted to lose himself in a dissolute lifestyle. The horrors of war manifested itself in the returned servicemen in many different ways. Gabe needed to keep busy, while Huon preferred to numb his senses with alcohol.

"He asked after you." Daisy smiled slyly. "I think he likes you."

"I'm not interested in Huon."

"Why not? He'll be a challenge, I grant you, but you could be good for him. You're steady and reliable, which is something he needs right now."

"Just what every man desires—a steady and reliable woman."

She rolled her eyes. "You're not dull, Sylvia. That's not what I meant."

"I'm not interested in Huon Barratt. Not even a little bit."

She sighed. "Pity. His family has money. And of course, there aren't many options anymore. We need to snap the available men up when they're keen or we risk staying spinsters forever."

It wasn't something I liked to voice when there were so many horrid outcomes from the war, but she was right. Many men our age had died. In ten years, it wouldn't surprise me if the spinsters of my generation outnumbered the spinsters of all other living generations combined. But I couldn't bring myself to encourage Huon's interest; not even to capture that rare commodity, an eligible bachelor.

The patron who'd admired Daisy came to tell me he was leaving and that he'd return tomorrow. He'd been in every day this week to research magic for a book he was writing. We didn't allow patrons to borrow the books so he read them here. I accompanied him to the front desk where he signed himself out. As he left, he passed Gabe, Alex and Willie arriving.

"Have you heard from your lawyer already?" I asked.

"That's not why I'm here." Gabe's ominous tone had me eyeing him carefully. "We need to speak to you and the professor."

I led the way to the reading nook, more than a little concerned. That concern was alleviated somewhat when Willie clapped Daisy on the back and greeted her with enthusiasm. She wouldn't be that cheerful if there'd been another kidnapping attempt on Gabe. She'd have locked the door behind her and searched every inch of the library before relaxing.

"Hello, Willie, Gabe. Alex," Daisy added, as if he were an afterthought. While she met Willie and Gabe's gazes, she did not look directly at Alex when she greeted him.

She'd got it into her head that he disliked her, that he thought her silly and spoiled. I didn't agree. That was her own opinion distorting her perception. She might appear confident to the world, but she doubted herself. Growing up in a privileged household meant she'd never had to fend for herself, never had to save every penny, never needed to work. On the surface, she seemed spoiled, yet she was sweet and kind and never put herself above others. She saw me as her equal, despite our vastly different backgrounds. Indeed, I'd go so far as to say she thought herself beneath *me* because she lacked my education and common sense. It wasn't her fault. She'd been brought up never having to apply herself to get what she wanted. She'd been blessed with an inheritance but only a limited education, which prepared her for marriage to a gentleman of good breeding but not gainful employment. It was the reason she was pursuing careers that didn't require an education, merely a vibrant personality. She had that in abundance.

She tucked her shoulder-length strawberry blond hair

behind her ear in a self-conscious move and resumed her seat on the sofa.

Willie dropped onto the cushion beside her. "Had any more auditions, Daisy?"

"Just one. It's for the part of a duchess."

Willie thumped her on the arm. "I can see you as a duchess."

Alex leaned closer to me. "It doesn't require a great stretch of the imagination."

If he would only stop teasing her, they might get along swimmingly. It raised her hackles and made her either want to tease him back or ignore him altogether.

She must not have been able to think of a good retort because she chose to present him with her shoulder. She smiled at Willie. "You should have come to the Buttonhole last night. The music was jazzed."

"I've been busy." She jerked her head at Gabe.

"Oh, yes, of course. He needs protecting."

Alex crossed his arms over his chest. "I can take care of him on my own."

Willie wrinkled her nose and pretended to think about it. "Nope. You need me. You ain't ruthless enough."

"You mean I won't shoot first and ask questions later."

Daisy laughed but tried to hide it with a cough. She didn't want Alex knowing she thought him amusing.

Gabe glared at his cousin and friend in turn. "I can take care of myself, something I've proved time and again. You should both go to the Buttonhole with Daisy tonight. You need to get out."

"And deprive you of my sparkling company?" Willie shook her head. "I can't do that to my favorite cousin."

"I thought my father was your favorite cousin."

"My favorite cousin under thirty." Willie nudged Alex's foot. "You should go with Daisy. You like to dance.

You're real bad at it, but everyone'll be too drunk to notice."

Alex looked caught. Teasing Daisy was one thing, but he didn't want to be blatantly rude to her, yet it was clear he didn't want to go out alone with her either. It would be an unequivocal statement that he liked her. "Ah, Professor Nash! It's good to see you, sir."

The professor approached carrying a tray. "Thank you, Alex. It's good to see you, too. Let me put this down and I'll fetch more cups."

"We can't stay," Gabe told him. "We came to see you and Sylvia about Lady Stanhope's visit."

The professor sat on the spot Daisy vacated for him. "When she brought the magician-made untitled books to us?"

"Untitled?" Willie asked.

Professor Nash explained that the term referred to unpublished manuscripts in industry circles. "She told us she purchased them from a bookbinder. He claimed the paper held magic."

"Was his name Adolphus Littleproud?" Gabe asked.

The professor pushed his glasses up his nose. "Yes. How do you know his name? I don't recall mentioning it to you."

"My father told us," Alex said. "Littleproud is dead. Murdered the night before last."

I gasped. "How awful."

"Do you have to be so blunt about it?" Daisy said as she reached for the teapot.

Alex shrugged. "Just stating a fact. The victim's wife found Littleproud's body yesterday morning and notified the local constabulary, who quickly realized it was murder." Alex cleared his throat and glanced at Daisy. "Suffice it to say, it was obvious the death wasn't natural."

Gabe took over the story. "Cyclops was assigned to the case. Last night, when Alex and I dined with his family,

Cyclops told us about it in passing. It immediately piqued our curiosity. It seemed too much of a coincidence to hear about a bookbinder in Paternoster Row twice in one day. I wasn't entirely sure it was the same man until now."

"Will you consult on the case?" I asked.

Gabe nodded. "Now that we know there's a link between the victim and Lady Stanhope's magical purchase, Cyclops will see it's arranged." The mention of magic would necessitate the involvement of Gabe, Scotland Yard's consultant detective on all cases magical in nature.

"We need to question her," he went on. "But first, what more can you tell us about her books?"

The professor and I exchanged glances. We shook our heads. "There's nothing more to tell," I said. "She was going to get the paper verified by a magician, but we don't know who."

The professor absently accepted a teacup from Daisy. "You don't think she killed him, do you?"

"No," Gabe said at the same time that Willie said, "Everyone's a suspect until they're not. Even you."

The professor's eyes widened. "Me?"

Willie chuckled. "The look on your face is priceless, Prof."

"Were there any witnesses?" I asked.

Gabe shook his head. "No one saw or heard anything. Time of death was around midnight. Mrs. Littleproud entered her husband's shop on Paternoster Row yesterday morning at seven after he didn't come home."

It would have been a dreadful discovery for the poor woman.

"We'll speak to her after we check the crime scene," Gabe went on. "I doubt Cyclops missed anything, but fresh eyes can't hurt." He picked up his hat from where he'd left it on the desk. "Do you want to come, Sylvia?"

I blinked at him. "Me? Why?"

"Mrs. Littleproud will be upset. Having a woman in the interview might help."

Both Alex and Willie narrowed their gazes at him but didn't say anything. I expected they were thinking the same as me. Gabe required no help questioning upset widows.

"Go on." Professor Nash gave me a nod of encouragement. "It'll do you good to get out and about."

"To a crime scene?" Daisy asked. "That's not my idea of a good day out."

"You weren't invited," Alex said. Realizing it sounded somewhat nasty, he tempered it with, "You wouldn't want to see the shop. I'm sure it's unpleasant."

Gabe put his hat on his head. "Sylvia can stay in the motor for that part."

Willie gave a grunt of amusement. I shot her a little smile. She understood the meaning behind it perfectly. Given the shaky start to our acquaintance, it was the friendliest gesture we'd exchanged.

The professor followed us to the front door, teacup and saucer in hand. "May I just confirm...I am not a suspect for the murder, am I?"

Willie threw her arm around him. "I was only joking, Prof. Of course you ain't. If you were going to kill someone, it would be in self-defense with a gun or knife. You wouldn't torture a man then watch him bleed to death."

"Willie!" Alex scolded. "The ladies."

It was Professor Nash who'd gone pale, however, not Daisy or me. She wrinkled her nose, while I pulled a face.

"Who would torture and kill a bookbinder?" I murmured.

No one had an answer to that.

I collected my purse and hat and waited to exit the library behind Daisy. She wheeled her bicycle out, following Willie who'd gone ahead to scout the vicinity for potential kidnappers.

"So did you get the part of the duchess?" she asked Daisy.

Daisy put a foot on the pedal but didn't mount the bicycle. "No. The director offered me a part as a sales assistant instead."

"At least you got a part. Many don't."

"I'm only in one scene and all I do is wrap up a tie or something equally dull. I don't even look at the camera. I'm supposed to just be in the background, along with a dozen other girls."

"You'll get a good role sooner or later. You can't be this pretty for nothing." Willie patted Daisy's cheek.

Daisy giggled. "Thank you for saying that. You are sweet. Isn't she sweet, Alex?"

Alex regarded Daisy first then Willie, a deep frown scoring his brow. "That is not a word I'd ever use to describe her." He watched Willie stride off to the lane's exit. When Daisy went to mount the bicycle, he grasped the handlebars to steady it for her even though she was capable of balancing it herself since her toes could reach the ground.

She waited, but when his mouth opened and closed without uttering a word, she said, "May I leave or are you going to just stand there?"

"I, uh, just wanted to say…" He cleared his throat. "You would have been an excellent choice to play a duchess."

She stiffened. "I heard you the first time."

"No, I meant he made a mistake. The director, that is. You'd be great on screen."

"There's no need for sarcasm." She glared pointedly at his hand.

He let go of the bicycle and stepped back, folding his arms over his chest as he watched her ride off.

Gabe clapped him on the shoulder. "Better luck next time."

"I was trying to be nice."

"I know."

"I don't really care if she doesn't want to accept my friendship."

"If you say so."

Gabe watched as Alex strode off along the lane.

I fell into step alongside him as we followed. "You need to coach him on how to talk to women."

"I'm not sure the man whose engagement failed should be giving anyone relationship advice."

"You're being too hard on yourself. What happened between you and Ivy wasn't your fault."

He walked on, his strides purposeful.

I quickened my step to keep pace. "Many relationships forged during the war have ended in peacetime. Yours wasn't unique."

When he didn't slow down, I caught his arm to stop him. I wanted to get my point across. But he simply stared back at me through eyes that had lost their spark.

"What you needed when you didn't know if you would come home again is different from what you need now. Don't blame yourself for that, Gabe. It's natural."

His face remained impassive, unreadable.

I suddenly felt foolish for speaking sentimentally when I'd never even been courted by a man. I was far less qualified than him to give relationship advice. I didn't even have my parents as an example to follow. I let go of his arm. "So I hear, anyway. I'm not an expert."

He huffed a cynical laugh. "It seems neither of us are equipped to interfere in Alex and Daisy's relationship, if that's what their little dance can be called."

I smiled, relieved he was making light of my bumbling attempt at giving advice.

He caught my hand and gently squeezed. "Thank you, Sylvia. I appreciate it." He let go and indicated I should walk ahead of him through the narrow exit to the adjoining street.

My heart lifted. My attempt may have been bumbling, but he understood my message. Hopefully one day he'd believe it.

# CHAPTER 3

*G*abe protested only once when I said I wanted to join them in the bookbinder's shop. I didn't need to protest a second time. Willie did it for me. Her lecture on equality for women was met with a groan from Alex and a shrug from Gabe. It must be a variation of a lecture she'd given before.

After a word with Gabe, the constable guarding the front door disappeared inside. He emerged a moment later and held the door open. "Detective Inspector Bailey says to go in. Mind the blood."

Only Willie noticed my shudder. "Don't spill your breakfast or I'll never hear the end of it from Alex. Now, buck up. We're women. We've seen worse."

She might have, but I hadn't.

There was less blood than I expected, however. Droplets were splattered on the floor near the door, but there weren't pools of it.

Cyclops greeted us gravely. He took my presence in his stride, even steering me by the elbow around the dried blood, as if civilians at crime scenes was entirely natural. "Everything is more or less as we found it."

I looked past him and my heart sank to my stomach. A table in the center of the small shop had been overturned. Several books lay scattered nearby, some open, face down, their hand-stitched spines straining. I resisted the urge to pick them up and find space for them on one of the other display tables or bookshelves.

There was no point anyway. The shop was a mess. Books, tools, and papers were everywhere. Drawers lay open and emptied, the contents scattered. Shelves were bare, and furniture was broken.

The space housed Mr. Littleproud's workshop at the back. A door led through to a tiny room with a bed in it but little else. For an industry that was mostly done on a large scale with machinery nowadays, this one-man business operated with traditional equipment. From where I stood, I could see uncut pages on the floor near one of the two tables alongside binder's boards, rulers and cutters. The splintered half of a sewing frame sat on one of the tables, the other half in the shadows somewhere. A press with heavy cast iron legs was the only thing that looked to be in its rightful place, in front of the second work table.

From what I could make out from the mess, Mr. Littleproud was very skilled. Lady Stanhope had claimed the paper in her purchases were magician-made, but I wondered if the bookbinder was a magician himself. He was a master craftsman, after all, although he didn't create the source materials he worked with. I suspected a magician bookbinder worked the same way as a magician watchmaker. He could assemble artless-made parts that held no magic, and put them together quickly, easily and flawlessly by hand without using a spell. The use of a spell would enhance their superior quality further, perhaps make the books unbreakable, until the spell wore off.

I breathed deeply to draw the scent of paper and leather into my lungs, only to gag and cough. Either the smell of death clogged my throat or the idea of it did. I quickly swallowed the rising bile before anyone saw. Unfortunately, it wasn't quick enough. Willie scowled at me, daring me to embarrass her after she'd stood up for me outside.

Gabe placed a hand on my lower back. "Do you need fresh air?"

"I'm fine." I moved to inspect the books on the floor near the overturned display table.

"Don't touch anything yet," Cyclops said. "The scene has been processed, but Gabe and Alex need to have a good look around before things are put to rights."

"And me," Willie snapped. "I've got eyes too."

"But you're not on the police force in any official capacity."

"And whose fault is that? If women were allowed to join, I'd be a great detective."

Cyclops snorted. "Detective work requires patience and focused observation. You've got the patience and focus of a five-year-old."

She tossed him a rude hand gesture that had him chuckling into his chest.

I inspected the crime scene, starting with the books that had been on display. They were lovely examples of Mr. Littleproud's skill, with cloth or leather covers decorated with patterns, floral borders or images, all in gold or done with colored stamps. Most sported corner protectors, some in worked silver, others of plain brass. I was relieved to see the books weren't damaged.

I was about to inspect the workshop area when one fallen book caught my eye. Two drops of blood marked the beautiful leather cover decorated with a design of gold strapwork in interlocking inlays of green, gold and red leather. There was no other blood in the immediate vicinity.

Gabe came up alongside me. "You can pick them up soon," he said gently.

I pointed to the book with the blood droplets. "There's more blood here."

He crouched to get a better look then stood again. He returned to the front door, inspecting the floor as he went.

"You say he was tortured," Alex said to his father. "What evidence led to that conclusion?"

"There were signs of strangulation." Cyclops tugged on his stiff shirt collar. "There was blood under his fingernails, but it could have been his own as he tried to remove whatever was around his neck. One arm was broken, as if it had been wrenched behind his back. His legs and torso were badly beaten, his face less so, but he had been hit in the jaw. He'd lost a tooth. We found it near the counter."

I winced and tried to focus on the books, something familiar and comforting.

"The autopsy will reveal how he died," Cyclops went on. "It wasn't obvious which particular injury killed him."

"He didn't bleed to death." Gabe indicated the blood splatters. "There's not enough."

"He may have bled internally."

I moved to the workshop near the back where Alex was looking over the contents on and near one of the tables. The tools of a bookbinder's trade were strewn about. Two needles protruded from a pincushion shaped like an open book, and another two had rolled into a ruler. A set of bone tools used for folding paper littered the floor, and unwound spools of thread lay in a tangled pile nearby.

Alex opened a long box he found and pulled out lengths of woven fabric strips. "What are these?"

"Endbands," I said. "They go at the top and bottom of the spine."

He found more boxes containing lengths of ribbons. The boxes had probably been arranged in color order in a drawer, but the killer had tossed the boxes out. Luckily the lids had remained in place and the ribbons inside were untouched and untangled.

"Bookmarks," I told Alex.

We found square boxes full of corner protectors made from various metals. Like the ribbons, they'd stayed in their boxes, but each box had been pulled out of its drawer and thrown aside. I dug my fingers through the most intricately worked silver corner protectors, letting them cascade through my fingers like water. If they held magic, I couldn't feel it.

Would I feel magic if it existed anywhere in this shop? I wasn't entirely convinced yet that I was a magician of any description.

Alex turned to the wall of empty shelves behind us then looked down. He indicated the lengths of colored cloths that lay unrolled on the floor near our feet. "For book covers?"

I nodded. "The bookbinder cuts whichever one his customer wants to size then starches it to stiffen it."

Gabe joined us and we all looked upon the uncut endpapers that covered the floor like a patchwork blanket. There must have been hundreds of them. They were in an array of colors, many of them marbled with others patterned like wallpaper. I crouched and fingered one of the thicker papers edged in gold. It was smooth to touch.

"Lovely," I said on a breath.

Behind me, Willie clicked her tongue. "The killer turned it over real good. Nothing's where it should be."

"They were looking for something," Cyclops agreed.

"A book, do you reckon? Or the books sold to Lady Stanhope, maybe."

Cyclops made his way through the wreckage to the front counter and found the sales ledger. He flipped the pages as he returned to us then handed it to Gabe. "The sale to Lady Stanhope isn't recorded."

Gabe ran his finger down the date column of the last page before handing the ledger back to Cyclops. "We don't know if the killer wanted those particular books. He might have been looking for something else. The murder could be unrelated." From his tone, it was clear he didn't think so.

"What else could a bookbinder have worth taking?" Willie asked, looking around. "Worth murdering for?"

"Do you know if anything is missing?" Alex asked his father.

"It's hard to say, given the state of the shop. But there was money in the cash register so it wasn't a theft gone wrong." Cyclops tucked the ledger under his arm as he also surveyed the mess. "I think the intruder came here looking for something specific, most likely the magician-made untitled books. He killed Littleproud when the bookbinder tried to stop him then searched the shop. When he didn't find what he wanted, he realized the books could have been sold so checked the ledger. That's why it was lying open on the counter to the last page when everything else has been tossed onto the floor."

Gabe walked over to the blood splatters near the door. "I think you're partially right. But why murder Littleproud *before* finding the books? It's not logical. I think the intruder tried to ask him, but he refused to answer. The intruder then beat up Littleproud in an attempt to force the answer from him, but he went too far and Littleproud died."

I shuddered. It was so macabre, it almost didn't seem real.

We stood about in silence as we considered the horror of Gabe's theory. It certainly made sense and explained why the shop was shambolic. The killer couldn't find what he was looking for, most likely because the books had already been sold. It also explained the terrible injuries inflicted on Adolphus Littleproud.

Alex indicated the sales ledger under his father's arm. "I agree with your theory, simply because Lady Stanhope isn't dead, nor has her house been broken into." He raised his brows at Cyclops who nodded. "If whoever did this knew she'd purchased the books, she'd be in danger too."

"*If* the killer was after her books," Willie pointed out.

We all gave her arched looks.

She put up her hands. "All right, all right. You don't believe in coincidences, so it's likely her books are the ones the killer wants."

"We'll call on her and warn her," Gabe said. "After we speak to the widow."

Alex picked up pieces of a broken chair. "Not me. I'll stay and tidy up if you've finished processing the crime scene."

Cyclops squeezed his son's shoulder and gave him a sad smile. "Mrs. Littleproud will appreciate that. I'll ask the constable to assist you." He checked his notebook for the widow's address and wrote it down for Gabe. "She's staying with her sister for the timebeing."

Outside, Willie cranked the engine of the Hudson, while Gabe sat behind the steering wheel. As he pulled the ignition switch, he half-turned to me, seated in the back.

"Are you all right, Sylvia? That was probably too overwhelming for your first murder. Sorry. I should have been more considerate. For me, death has become normal. Too normal."

My fingers twitched with the urge to touch him, caress his cheek to soothe and reassure him. I balled my hand into a tight fist and forced a smile instead. "While it was awful, it wasn't...affecting, if that makes sense. I never met Mr. Littleproud so I suppose his death feels unreal. It's like watching a moving picture on screen, except in color."

Willie swore loudly as the engine kicked back. She shook out her hand and swore again at the motor. Cyclops offered to crank the engine for her but she gave him such a cold glare that he stepped back onto the pavement, hands in the air. She tried again and this time the engine rumbled to life.

She climbed into the front passenger seat and stored the crank handle on the floor near the door. She rubbed her hand. "Why didn't you bring the Vauxhall?"

"This is more comfortable with four," Gabe said.

"I hate this old thing. It's time to get something newer."

Gabe steered the motorcar away from the curb. "I do have something newer. The Vauxhall Prince Henry. Anyway, this one's not very old and until it completely gives up, my parents will keep her." He patted the steering wheel. "There's nothing stopping you from buying a motorcar of your own, Willie."

"There is. It's called money. I ain't got none."

"You would if you worked."

"Who'd employ me?"

Gabe didn't have an answer for that.

We drove to Mrs. Littleproud's sister's home, located in a nice middle-class suburb some distance from the shop. Gabe parked the motorcar outside the semi-detached house. None of us immediately got out.

I voiced something that had been on my mind during the drive. "What I don't understand is, a bookbinder binds books for his customers. He's not a bookseller. So why did he sell those particular books, the ones Lady Stanhope bought? Where did they come from and why did he have them in his possession? And how did the killer know about them?"

Gabe rested his arm on the seat and turned to me. "Something led him to Mr. Littleproud's shop the night before last, mere hours after she purchased them. Whatever it was, he wanted the books so desperately he tortured Littleproud to get them." He heaved out a breath and indicated the house. "Ready?"

"I'll stay here," Willie said. "I hate talking to widows. Unless they're the merry kind."

Mrs. Littleproud's sister led us through to the parlor after we introduced ourselves and stayed for the interview. Both sisters were in their early fifties, their gray hair swept up in a pompadour style common among ladies their age. Mrs. Littleproud was a stout woman with broad hands that clutched her handkerchief tightly. Her face showed signs of distress, in her red eyes and deeply furrowed brow, but she bravely welcomed us and thanked us for investigating her husband's murder.

"Do Scotland Yard employ women now?" she asked politely.

"Not yet," I said. "I'm a librarian at the Glass Library."

"India Glass's magic library?"

I smiled. Many people thought of it as magical, even though the books in the collection were about magic, and few actually contained it. "Given the possibility this crime involves magic, Mr. Glass has asked me to assist him in his investigation. He's India Glass's—Lady Rycroft's—son."

"I see. And what do you mean, the crime involves magic?" Mrs. Littleproud asked.

"We think the murderer was looking for some books in your husband's possession that were made with magic paper."

She clutched her throat and swallowed hard.

"You know which books I'm referring to?"

"Yes. Although he'd had them in his shop for years, he only told me about them a few weeks ago."

"Years?" Gabe prompted. "Do you know how many?"

"About thirty. He couldn't recall precisely when they were brought in, but it was around then. When he finally decided to retire, he told me about them. He assured me we'd be well off because he was going to sell them. He said the books had magic in the pages and were handwritten by a well-known author. He hoped they'd sell for a small fortune at auction. We were going to use the money to buy a cottage in the country." Her chin wobbled as tears welled in her eyes.

Her sister clasped Mrs. Littleproud's hands. "Take your time, dear."

When she was ready, Gabe asked another question. "Do you know how they came into your husband's possession?"

"A customer brought them in for binding but never returned to collect them. Adolphus held onto them in case he did, but..." She shrugged. "Apparently the customer was a collector of magical objects and knew the manuscripts were written on magic paper."

"Was your husband a magician? Is that why the collector came to him?"

She smiled wistfully as she tapped the handkerchief against her breast. "Adolphus was a bookbinder magician, but he didn't know any spells. His work was exceptional, though, even without them. His customers came from all over the country after your mother made it possible for magicians to live openly alongside artless craftsmen." She offered Gabe a small smile before tears welled in her eyes again.

"Did Mr. Littleproud tell you the name of the collector who brought the manuscripts to him?" Gabe asked.

She touched the handkerchief to the corner of her eye and shook her head.

"Does the name Honoria Moffat-Jones mean anything to you?"

"Was she the author of the books?"

"They're her unpublished manuscripts."

"I wonder if she was aware the collector possessed them."

It was something we needed to establish. Honoria Moffat-

Jones may have nothing to do with her stories finding their way to Mr. Littleproud's shop, but if there was a link, we needed to uncover it. It could lead us to the killer.

Mrs. Littleproud teased the damp handkerchief between her fingers. "Adolphus should have made a greater effort to contact the customer after he failed to collect the bound books."

"I'm sure he tried everything within his power," her sister said.

Mrs. Littleproud shook her head. "When he told me about them, I asked if he'd tried contacting the customer over the years. He was evasive, claiming it wasn't his responsibility. I think as time passed, he became more and more confident they wouldn't be collected."

"Did your husband keep records going back that far?" Gabe asked.

"If he did, they'll be in the shop."

"What about the silver corner protectors?" I asked. "Is it possible the collector who brought in the pages for binding also provided the corner protectors for your husband to use on the covers?"

"I doubt it. Adolphus had a variety of metals and styles on hand, some of them finely engraved. He bought them in bulk from suppliers. If they were magic ones, I suppose the customer *could* have brought them in and requested he use them. If he was a collector of magical objects and the protectors contain magic, it even makes sense. *Do* they contain magic, Miss Ashe?"

"We're not sure. The new owner of the books told me Mr. Littleproud mentioned only the magical paper."

"Oh? You know who purchased them?"

I glanced at Gabe, worried I'd revealed too much.

"Yes," he said.

Mrs. Littleproud's eyes darkened. "Adolphus said he had

a potential buyer coming to the shop." Her chin wobbled. "That conversation was the last I had with him." She sobbed into her handkerchief.

Gabe waited until she regained her composure before asking his next question. "His death occurred around midnight. Does he usually work that late?"

"Sometimes. When he does, he stays overnight so as not to disturb me. There's a bed in the back room at the shop, and he keeps a few personal items there. When he doesn't come home, I visit him first thing in the morning and take him a sandwich and a Thermos full of tea. That's why I was the first to come across his body." Her pitch rose, bursting into a sob at the end. She buried her face in her handkerchief.

Her sister wrapped her arm around Mrs. Littleproud and indicated with a jerk of her head that we should leave.

Gabe and I rose, but Mrs. Littleproud gathered herself and asked us to sit again. "There's something I need to tell you. In the days leading up to his death, my husband was worried. I tried to find out why, but he wouldn't say. Looking back, I'm quite sure it had something to do with the auction catalog."

"What auction catalog?" Gabe asked.

"He was going to sell the books at auction. He hoped that would bring a higher price. But after the auction house's catalog came out last week, he became nervous. He pretended everything was fine when I asked what troubled him, but I know Adolphus. He was wary when he came home from the shop the day after the catalog was issued."

Gabe frowned. "I don't understand. The books *were* sold privately. Are you saying he was going to auction them but changed his mind?"

"He must have, yes. The auction was scheduled for next month."

Lady Stanhope had told me the bookbinder contacted her and asked if she wanted to purchase them. She was becoming known amongst magician circles as a collector, and a wealthy one at that. If Mr. Littleproud wanted a quick sale, it made sense to negotiate with her instead of waiting for the auction. He would have had to accept less, however.

"I don't have the catalog here, but there's a copy at home. I can give it to you after I return tomorrow."

Her sister patted her hand. "You're welcome to remain here for as long as you need."

"I can't stay forever."

"We don't recommend you return home just yet," Gabe said. "The killer hasn't found those books. It's possible he'll search your house next."

Mrs. Littleproud clutched her throat.

"But he doesn't know where she lives," her sister pointed out.

"It won't be too difficult to find the address."

The murder was two days ago. It was likely the killer had already been through the house searching for the books while Mrs. Littleproud was here. "We can check for you," I offered.

"Would you? That would be a relief. I'll fetch my key."

While she went to get the key, Gabe asked her sister for the telephone number. A few minutes later, she saw us out.

Willie was asleep on the front seat of the motorcar, her hat pulled low over her eyes. She awoke with a start when Gabe opened the door. She yawned and sat up. "How'd it go?"

He picked up the crank handle. "About as well as can be expected. We learned a few things."

"Like what?"

"Sylvia will tell you while I crank the engine."

She turned to me. "What did you learn?"

She interrupted my account so often that I hadn't finished by the time Gabe took his place behind the wheel. "If you'd joined us, you wouldn't need to ask so many questions," he said as he pulled the motorcar away from the curb.

"I was making sure no kidnappers followed us and lurked in the vicinity."

"With your eyes closed?"

Willie grunted. "Don't get smart with your elders, young man."

He drove the short distance to the Littleprouds' house. Being so far from the Paternoster Row shop in the city, Mr. Littleproud would have to catch a train to work. It was no wonder he stayed at the shop overnight if he decided to work late.

The house was a small semi-detached similar to Mrs. Littleproud's sister's home. A path led from the front gate to the porch, carving through stands of purple foxglove swaying in the breeze on their long stems. The path and porch were neat and clean, and there wasn't a weed in sight.

Gabe inserted the key into the front door but didn't turn it. The door opened. It wasn't locked. He pushed it open further.

Willie clicked her tongue as she peered past him. "Looks like the killer's already been."

The carpet runner was bunched up on one side of the narrow hall where someone had shoved it aside to inspect what lay underneath. But it was the kitchen at the end of the hall that made my heart sink. From what little of it I could see from the front door, it had been turned over, just like the shop on Paternoster Row.

# CHAPTER 4

e righted as much of Mrs. Littleproud's house as we could. Like the shop, nothing was left untouched by the intruder. Every cupboard and drawer had been emptied, every container and bag rifled through. Potted plants had been uprooted and floorboards lifted. Glassware and crockery lay in pieces on the kitchen's tiled floor. The search had been thorough. Desperate almost.

After an hour of solid work, Willie dusted her hands as she surveyed our attempt to tidy up the parlor. "At least we know for certain the killer didn't find what they wanted in the shop the night they killed Littleproud. If he had, he wouldn't have come here."

"Which further points to them wanting the books Lady Stanhope bought," I said.

Gabe telephoned Mrs. Littleproud at her sister's house to tell her about the break-in and advise her not to come home. He suggested she take a holiday out of London until the killer was caught. He then telephoned Scotland Yard and informed Cyclops of everything we'd learned and our theory that every clue pointed to the killer wanting the untitled books with the magician-made paper. He studied the collection's entry in the auction house's catalog as he spoke. The books were described in detail, with the fact that they contained magic pages typed in bold. The accompanying photographs clearly showed the covers, the title pages, and a close-up of a finely worked silver corner protector.

"Did you come across any old ledgers in the shop dating back thirty years?" Gabe asked Cyclops. He listened to the response then shook his head at us. "Let me know if you do. And one more thing. Find out everything you can about Honoria Moffat-Jones, the author of the manuscripts."

After Gabe hung up, we questioned the neighbors, but none had seen or heard anything suspicious at the Littleproud house in the previous two days.

"Now what?" Willie asked as we returned to the motorcar.

"Now we question Lady Stanhope."

Willie screwed up her face. "I'll keep an eye out for kidnappers again."

"Try keeping your eyes open this time."

\* \* \*

LADY STANHOPE LIVED with her husband in a grand five story Mayfair townhouse not far from Gabe's home in Park Street. Huggins, the snooty butler, greeted us at the front door. He lifted his chin, pointing his nose in the air, and left us standing there while he inquired if his mistress was at home for callers.

A few minutes later, she swanned down the stairs dressed in a black silk gown embroidered with pink blossoms on the bodice. "Darling man, you've caught me before I leave for cocktails at the Savoy. What a lovely surprise it is to see you. You too, Miss Ashe."

At least she remembered my name this time.

"I'm afraid we come with sad news," Gabe said. "Mr. Littleproud is dead."

"The bookbinder? How unfortunate. It was good of you to come and tell me in person, but I hardly knew the fellow. Our only interaction was that one transaction. Do you want to see the books, Mr. Glass? They're quite special." As she talked, she led the way up the stairs.

"You've had the books verified by a magician?" Gabe asked.

"I have, and all contain magic." She paused on the landing. "I must say, I am pleased that Mr. Littleproud didn't sell me fakes, considering he's dead. It would have been unpleasant getting a refund now."

She continued up the stairs to the drawing room where she indicated a glass display cabinet. The untitled books were stacked up on the middle shelf with the top book opened at the title page.

"Are they not lovely?" she cooed. "I was going to ask Mr. Hobson or Ivy to verify they contained magic, but decided against seeing them. I don't want them thinking I am on their side." She touched Gabe's arm. "You did the right thing ending it with her, Mr. Glass. It's best if you stay far away from the Hobsons while they're embroiled in controversy. You don't want to be tainted by their scandal."

"Hardly a scandal," Gabe growled. "One batch of their army-issue boots missed receiving their magic spell. It was a terrible mistake, but a mistake nevertheless. I'm not avoiding Ivy to avoid being associated with her family, and that's the last word I'll give on the matter of the Hobsons."

It may have been his last word, but it wasn't hers. "They've denied it. Did you know that? Mr. Hobson put out a statement saying none of the boots were missed. They all received the same spells. They won't claim responsibility for the trench foot cases that resulted from their inferior quality."

Gabe didn't take the bait. Instead, he indicated the books in the cabinet. "What sort of magician verified them for you?"

"My husband's tailor is a wool magician."

"Could he be specific about which part or parts contain magic?"

"He didn't say. Perhaps he isn't a strong enough magician to identify precisely. Anyway, I know the books contain paper magic. Mr. Littleproud told me so."

"He couldn't be entirely certain either, and was simply repeating what the former owner of the books told him. May we borrow one of the books to show other magicians? We want to make sure the magic is in the paper, and not the cover or ink, for example."

She gazed upon the books in the cabinet. "I don't want to let them out of my sight."

"Lady Stanhope, we haven't quite told you everything." He hesitated. "Perhaps you should sit down."

She sat, her brow furrowed. "What is it, Mr. Glass? Is something wrong?"

"I told you that Mr. Littleproud died. What I didn't tell is that he was murdered."

"How extraordinary. Are you investigating?" While I wasn't expecting her to care overmuch, I thought she'd follow social norms and at least *feign* shock or horror. It seemed she was more concerned about how his murder affected her than the fact it had occurred at all.

"Where were you on the night before last, after you took the books to the Glass Library?"

She gasped. "Are you implying I killed him?"

He arched his brows, waiting for an answer.

"It's the social season," she said, sounding miffed. "I was at a private dinner party. There were over a dozen witnesses. Any more questions, Mr. Glass?"

"That's all for now. If we can take the books away with us to have the magic verified, that would be helpful."

She bristled, and I thought she might refuse. Instead, she opened the cabinet door. Perhaps it was Gabe's intensity that caused her to back down. He certainly possessed a compelling air about him as he focused his stare on her. It was the sort of stare that conveyed more than words ever could. She probably thought it best not to refuse or she might find herself hauled into Scotland Yard for formal questioning.

She retrieved one book and handed it to him. "Don't let it out of your sight."

"I'll return it as soon possible." He opened the book to the first page. It was the manuscript titled *The Nymphs of Bridlemarch Forrest*.

"Do you feel it, Mr. Glass?"

He frowned at her. "Feel what?"

"The magic?"

"You know I'm not a magician."

She simply gave him a smile as if they shared a secret. There was no way she could know about Gabe's ability to manipulate time to save his own life, but she'd always suspected he'd inherited magic from his mother. In Lady Stanhope's view, no child of such a powerful magician could be born artless.

Even though Gabe possessed a supernatural skill, he couldn't feel magic in an object that had a spell placed on it, as magicians could.

He closed the book. His thumb caressed the silver protector on the front cover's top corner. "Can you tell us how you came to know about the books?"

"As I told Miss Ashe and the librarian, Mr. Littleproud contacted me and asked if I'd like to purchase them. He was going to take them to auction, but changed his mind. I assumed he needed a fast sale, but I didn't ask."

"How did he contact you? Telephone? Letter?"

"Telephone. He found me through my connection to the Royal Academy."

"How did he seem?"

"What do you mean?"

"Did he seem eager when you spoke to him? Concerned?"

"He did seem nervous, now that you mention it. His shop door was locked when I arrived, which I thought was odd. It's certainly not very good for business."

"Did he say anything about the provenance of the books?"

"Just that he'd had them in his possession for many years and wished to sell them now as he was planning to retire. He couldn't recall who gave them to him, but he assured me a paper magician had made the paper. Even so, I wanted to have the magic verified and told him so. I would have demanded a refund if they'd proved to be artless. Happily for everyone, they do contain magic. It would have been quite a process to get my money back from a dead man's heirs." She sat forward and regarded Gabe. "You ought to look at who inherits. Money is usually the reason someone is murdered."

"Mr. Littleproud's shop was searched on the night of his death. It's likely the two incidents are connected, and the killer was looking for something. It's too much of a coincidence for it not to be these books."

She blinked at the book in his hand. "Are you quite sure?"

"We haven't ruled any theories in or out at this stage. Why? Don't you think it's possible someone would kill for these?"

"Quite frankly, no. While they are special and quite valuable, they're not extraordinary. Paper magic isn't common, but I don't think it's very rare, either. Nor is Honoria Moffat-Jones a highly sought-after author. She is reasonably famous, but that's all. It seems somewhat excessive to kill for them."

The validity of her point quite took my breath away for a moment. She was right—it was unlikely the killer wanted the books simply because they contained magic paper. So why did he want them? Was it because they contained another kind of magic, something rare, like silver? Or for another reason entirely? Something that had nothing to do with magic?

Whatever the reason, the timing of the murder, coming so soon after the books appeared in the auction house's catalog, was too coincidental to be ignored. The killer wanted these books, I was sure of it.

Lady Stanhope didn't agree. When Gabe told her she needed to be careful, she dismissed him with a wave of her hand. "Pish posh. There's no need for concern. We have excellent security here."

Gabe's gaze wandered to the open door where the butler was probably listening on the other side.

"You are very sweet to be worried about me, Mr. Glass. Very sweet indeed. Now, I must continue to get ready. Do you have the time?" She looked pointedly at the gold chain of his pocket watch, the gift from his parents.

Gabe glanced at the clock on the mantelpiece. "It's five minutes past five o'clock." He rose. "Thank you for your help, Lady Stanhope. Please ask your staff to keep the doors and windows locked and not to let anyone into the house they don't know."

She clasped his arm. "Do return again soon, Mr. Glass. There's a woman I'd like you to meet. Her sweetheart died in the war so she's available again. She's a cotton magician, and quite pretty, too. Isn't it interesting how these girls used to have their pick of beaus, but now the tables are turned after so many young men died. Now it's the men who survived who can afford to be selective in their choice."

"Interesting?" Gabe bit off.

Lady Stanhope barreled on, either ignoring the icy steel in his tone or unaware of it.

"Don't leave it too late. Her family's magic is strong and their manufacturing business is doing very well. She won't remain on the market for long."

Gabe stared at her with all the incredulity her comments deserved.

She must have realized how callous she sounded because she quickly added, "I know you think me insensitive, but I'm a practical person. I never dwell on the past. It can't be changed. The future, however, is in our hands to make of it what we will."

I thought Gabe might challenge her response to the unthinkable death toll from the war, but he simply placed his hat on his head and walked off.

Willie leaned against the motorcar, her arms crossed. She frowned as we approached. "Why the angry faces? Looks to me like you got what you came for." She nodded at the book in Gabe's hand.

Gabe tucked it under his arm and opened the door for me. "That woman's obsession makes her say the most insensitive things."

"Obsession with what?"

"Magic."

I could have said "You," but held my tongue. I didn't think he wanted to hear it.

* * *

WILLIE DIDN'T WANT to remain with the motorcar for our next visit. She wanted to come in and see Huon Barratt, the ink magician, who should be able to tell us if the book held ink magic. "He reminds me of Davide," she said as Gabe drove to the Marylebone townhouse. "My second husband," she added for my sake.

Gabe tapped his temple. "Mad."

She thumped him lightly on the arm. "Eccentric. Davide was one of the happiest, most uninhibited people I know."

Then he wasn't similar to Huon. The ink magician might have all the outward appearance of uninhibited happiness, but scratch the surface and he was as full of shadows as the rest of the men returned from the war. Unlike Gabe and Alex, he attempted to drown his shadows in alcohol and goodness knows what else. Gabe and Alex were learning to live with theirs.

Willie didn't mention her late husbands often. From what I could gather, she'd married a police detective first in what was a love match, going by the way her gaze turned soft when she spoke about him. It was a relationship I found difficult to imagine. I'd found it even harder to picture her with an earl, her second husband. In my experience, countesses were dainty ladies who drank tea and attended charity balls. The bourbon swilling, buckskin wearing, crude woman with a gun tucked into her waistband was not countess material.

But hearing that Lord Farnsworth was an eccentric helped me make sense of the relationship. I'd wager they caused all sorts of havoc when they were together. I still wasn't sure how he'd died, but the constant teasing from the others about her murdering both husbands had me intrigued. One day, I would get the stories out of her. I suspected I'd have to get her quite drunk first.

On the occasions I had seen her drunk, the music had been too loud for talking. She also always found a companion to keep her company. A female companion. I wasn't sure if her romantic interest in women was a new development or whether it had always coexisted alongside her interest in men. Perhaps it was the former journalist in me, but Willie was a mystery I wanted to unravel. I suspected I might never fully understand her, however.

Huon wasn't at home. We left a message with the house-keeper for him to telephone Gabe later and returned to the library. He escorted me to the front door while Willie escorted him, her hand resting at her waist where her gun was tucked into the top of her buckskins.

Gabe and Willie didn't come inside, leaving me to inform Professor Nash of all we'd learned about the murder. I was about to head home at six o'clock when the telephone on the front desk rang. It was Gabe.

"I'm glad I caught you before you left. I've just heard from Barratt. He invited us to return to his house tonight with the book. I'll pick you up at nine...unless you have plans? Are you seeing anyone? Tonight, I mean. Are you seeing anyone? Like Daisy...or someone?"

I smiled. "I'll be ready at nine, Gabe."

\* \* \*

ALEX AND WILLIE joined us for the visit to Huon Barratt's house. We weren't the only visitors, going by the noise that spilled out when the front door opened. A blonde woman wearing a green and silver figure-hugging dress answered it. She beckoned us inside with a wave of her cigarette that extended from the end of a slender silver holder.

"Where's Barratt?" Gabe asked her over the noise.

She took his hand and led him upstairs, tossing a seduc-tive smile at him over her bare shoulder. On the landing, he removed his hand but continued to follow. Willie eyed the chic blonde as she sauntered off.

The furniture in the drawing room had been pushed back to allow space for the partygoers to dance. The gramophone blared jaunty music that had the girls kicking up their heels and the men tapping their toes. A miasma of cigarette smoke hung in the air.

Huon spotted us and made his way through the crowd. The host of the party looked like he'd just crawled out of bed. Dark circles under his eyes were stark against his pale skin, and he wore no shoes, tie, waistcoat or jacket. "Glad you could make it!"

Willie embraced Huon as if they were old friends, kissing him on both cheeks like the French. It caught him by surprise.

"Sorry," she said brightly. "Old habit you bring out in me. Are you having a party?"

He looked around as if surprised to see his drawing room had become a dance club. "Just a gathering of my nearest and dearest. Didn't I mention it over the telephone?"

Gabe accepted a glass of Champagne from a passing maid and handed it to me. "No."

"Ah well, never mind. You're all very welcome to stay. In fact, Sylvia, your friend is here, somewhere."

"Daisy?" I stood on my toes and tried to find her.

At the mention of her name, Alex looked around too.

"Or perhaps she's coming later." Huon took my hand and led me to some vacant chairs. "Let's conduct business first then we can all enjoy ourselves." He collapsed onto the sofa as if he were exhausted. He stretched out his legs and rested one bare foot on the other. He yawned. "Sorry. I'm still recovering from last night. It was wild." He plucked a smoldering cigarette from the ashtray on the table beside the sofa. I wasn't even sure it was his. Any number of people crowding around, chatting in groups and moving to the music, could have left it there. "Do you want to hear about it?"

"I do if it involves that tattoo," I said.

He frowned as he followed my gaze to his bare chest. He pulled back his white shirt, unbuttoned to the waist, and touched the tattoo of an *aquila*, the Imperial Roman eagle symbol used by the legions. The skin surrounding the ink was still red and swollen. "Well. Look at that."

Willie inspected it, squinting to read the word tattooed below the eagle. "Does that represent your battalion?"

Huon blew out a puff of smoke above her head and nodded. "I went out with them last night. What's left of them," he added with a mutter. "I wonder if we all got one or it was just me."

"How could you not know it was there?" I asked. "Doesn't it hurt?"

He lifted a shoulder in a lazy shrug. "I no longer feel pain."

I suspected that was because he was drunk or under the influence of a pain suppressant like morphine. Some of the soldiers came back from the war addicted to it after being given it in hospital while they recovered from their injuries.

Gabe cleared his throat to gain our attention. "If you've both finished inspecting Barratt's chest, perhaps he can take a look at this book."

Huon tossed his head as he held out his hand for the book. "It amuses me that I, a humble fellow, have to continuously help the son of the greatest magician in the world with matters of magic."

Gabe got up to pass him the book. "There's not a humble bone in your body, Barratt."

Huon didn't appear to be listening anymore. The moment his fingers touched the book, he turned serious. "It does contain magic." He flipped it open and caressed the title page. "Strong magic." He turned more pages, stroking each one with his fingertips as if they could read the words. "But it's not in the ink. It is good quality ink, but there's no spell in it."

"We've been told the magic is in the paper," I said. "Can

you tell if that's the case, and it's not in the cover or silver protectors?"

Huon's lips twisted to one side. "The magic is strong, that I do know. And I do feel it particularly when I touch the pages. Given that it's not in the ink, my guess is that it *is* in the paper. But I wouldn't take my word for it." He turned back to the title page. "Honoria Moffat-Jones...didn't she write a children's book years ago?"

"She did," Gabe said.

"'*The Nymphs of Bridlemarch Forest*.' Nymphs, eh?" He smirked. "Is she trying her hand at naughty novels?"

"It's a book for children."

"Whose is it and why do you want to know if it contains magic?"

Gabe accepted the book from him. "The former owner was murdered the night after he sold it."

"Murdered? For that book?"

"That's what we're trying to find out."

Huon stroked his jaw, roughened with stubble. "It's not an overly remarkable tome but I suppose the strong magic makes it valuable among collectors, particularly if the magic turns out to be rare. You ought to look among them for your suspects."

"We are," Willie said.

Gabe shot her a censorial glare.

She ignored him and barreled on. "Lady Stanhope purchased it from the victim. He told her it contained paper magic."

"If she already had it in her possession, why is she a suspect?"

"Everyone is a suspect until they can be ruled out," Gabe said.

Huon rolled his eyes. "You are a walking cliché, Glass."

"I'm not the only one." Gabe pointed to the tattoo on

Huon's chest. "You might want to put something on that before it gets infected."

Huon looked down at the tattoo. "Do you think sherry will do?"

"It'll do for me." Willie waved a maid over and asked for a glass of sherry.

Huon pushed himself to his feet. "Now, if you'll excuse me, I must mingle. Do take advantage of my generous hospitality. Gentlemen, you'll find some very agreeable young ladies here." He gave Alex an exaggerated wink. Then, remembering Willie's fluid preferences, he gave her a wink too before disappearing into the throng of dancers in the center of the room.

Alex got up to look around, but I settled back into the chair to watch the partygoers.

Gabe stayed seated too. "We need to verify how rare the magic is. We may not be able to locate any silver magicians, but I'll check my parents' records for paper and leather ones."

Willie had got up to follow Alex but sat down again. "You know leather magicians, Gabe. Two of 'em. Three, if you count Ivy's brother."

"I won't go to the Hobsons. It's not right to ask them for help after what I did to them."

"You did nothing wrong. You ended your engagement respectfully so Ivy could keep her dignity and reputation. Many wouldn't. Not after her family used your name to defend themselves in the newspapers without your permission. You owe them nothing. So you go to them with your head high and ask if they feel leather magic in that book. If they don't want to help Scotland Yard find a killer, then they're worse folk than we thought, and you'll know for certain you're better off without them."

It was quite the speech coming from someone who'd once been eager for Gabe to stay with Ivy Hobson. Willie had been upset with me when he ended it, blaming me for Gabe's change of heart. In the end, she realized Gabe had been reconsidering for some time before we even met. Even so, she still hadn't quite warmed to me, although she was no longer openly hostile.

I held my hand out for the book. "I agree with Willie. There's no point searching for another leather magician if we already know an entire family of them. Anyway, I'm not convinced the reason for the murder is the magic contained within the books coupled with Honoria's name. I tend to agree with Lady Stanhope and Huon—even if they contain magic, is that worth killing for?"

"People kill for less." Gabe handed over the book. "I want to pursue this avenue until we find clues that lead us in a different direction."

I hardly heard his response. The moment my hand touched the book, I felt a throb deep within me. It was as if something inside me had come to life, something that had been previously dormant, waiting. My blood warmed as it rushed through my veins and my skin tingled with awareness, responding to the book.

Responding to the magic in it.

# CHAPTER 5

"**S**ylvia?" Gabe clasped my shoulders. "Sylvia, are you all right? You look flushed."

"I...I don't know."

"Willie, fetch a glass of water." Gabe crouched before me. His cool fingers touched my cheek and his concerned eyes peered into mine. "Sylvia? Do you feel faint?"

I shook my head. "I'm fine. I've just had a...a shock, I suppose."

His frown deepened. "What do you mean?" He followed my gaze to the book. He drew in a breath and let it out slowly. "You felt the magic in it, didn't you?"

"I think so. This is the first time I've held it, or any of the five books, and the moment my fingers touched it I felt something within me respond."

"A warm sensation?"

I nodded. "It was as if the magic resonated within me. As if it awoke my..." I swallowed. I couldn't say the word. It seemed so alien to associate it with myself.

Gabe said it for me. "Magic." Those cool, confident fingers of his were back again, this time touching my chin, encouraging me to raise my gaze to his. His eyes were bright with his smile. "I thought you were a magician. Ever since you found the Medici Manuscript faster than anyone else, I've suspected. All we need to do now is find out what sort—leather, silver or paper. It has to be one of those if it responded so strongly to the book."

"I think we can rule out silver magic once and for all. I didn't feel this way for the silver clasps on the Medici Manuscript. Oscar Barratt was convinced *they* held magic, not the paper or cover."

"True, but it was your response to that silver magic that helped you find the book quickly. That means your magic— whether it's leather or paper—is stronger than most." He looked around to see Willie approaching, carrying a glass of water, followed by Huon. "It's stronger than his. Neither of you are silver magicians, yet it was *you* who found the Medici Manuscript first in that little experiment we conducted in the library."

I clutched the book to my chest and blinked back at him. He smiled again. It was warm, encouraging. It helped clear my head although it didn't quite banish my confusion. How could I go my entire life and not know I was a magician? What did it mean? Was it even relevant to me, or to anything? Did it even matter?

It was Willie who brought me the rest of the way back to earth. "Want me to throw the water in her face?"

Gabe took the glass from her and passed it to me. "It's for drinking."

"I reckon my way's better at stopping fainting spells."

"I'm not going to faint," I told her.

"We should make sure."

Huon muscled forward and leaned down, hands on his knees. He peered at my face as I sipped. "Do you want something stronger than water? Champagne? A cigarette? Opium?"

Willie punched his arm. "That won't help. You can see she ain't in pain. She just had an attack of the vapors, or whatever it is the delicate ladies suffer from these days."

"I'm not delicate," I said. "And it wasn't an attack of any sort. I was...overwhelmed." I glanced at Gabe, not sure how to explain it, or whether I should even tell Willie and Huon yet. I wanted to take my time to digest it myself first.

Huon mistook the meaning of my gaze. He smiled a smug little smile. "Well, well. I see how it is here."

"No! That's not... We weren't..."

"You misunderstand," Gabe said quickly. "It's not what you're thinking."

Huon's meaning suddenly dawned on Willie. Her jaw firmed. She jabbed her finger at Gabe then me. "It better not be that. He doesn't need another girl fawning over him, trying to trap him into marriage before he's ready. The next woman he's with is going to love him for who he is, not for his mother's magic."

I tried not to laugh. I really did. But I couldn't help myself, and I burst into giggles. Perhaps it was the sheer relief of finally discovering something about myself, or perhaps it was the absurdity of her suggestion that I wanted to trap Gabe because his mother was a magician, but I found her warning ridiculously amusing.

Gabe grinned, too.

Willie stamped her hands on her hips. "What's so funny?"

Daisy suddenly appeared as if from nowhere, Alex behind her. "What's the joke? What did I miss?"

"I don't know, but I need another drink." Willie stormed off to find the maid.

"I didn't know you were invited to Huon's party, Sylv," Daisy said.

"We came for work." I held up the book. "We didn't know he was having a party."

"I'm glad you're all here. It'll be fun!"

"You're glad *all* of us are here?" I flicked my gaze to Alex, standing behind her. He hadn't taken his eyes off her so far. Considering she wore a shimmering gold dress that clung to her curves, it was no wonder.

Daisy's smile proved she was very aware of the effect her figure had on him.

The music ended and someone put Selvin's Novelty Orchestra on the gramophone. Daisy's eyes widened. "I love *Dardanella*. Come and dance with me, Sylv."

"I don't feel like dancing at the moment. Perhaps later."

She turned around, coming face to chest with Alex. They stared at one another for a long moment before they walked off together to join the dancers. They hadn't exchanged a word.

Gabe leaned closer to me. "Do you think this could be the start of something?"

"Possibly. Although I suspect tomorrow they'll pretend they dislike each other again."

"I don't know why they're not together already. They clearly want to be."

We watched as Daisy was bumped by another dancer, losing her balance. Alex caught her by the shoulders and pulled her a little closer than necessary. They exchanged awkward smiles before he let her go. They continued to dance together.

"Daisy thinks she's not good enough for him," I said. "She thinks herself too silly for someone with Alex's intelligence and seriousness."

"He's not always serious."

"I do think she needs to grow up a little more before they

can be equals. She lived a sheltered life until she came to London, and it shows."

"It's good of her parents to let her come. Many of the gentry wouldn't allow their daughters off the leash, and certainly wouldn't let them live independently in the city."

"I'm not sure they had a choice. Once she inherited a little money from her grandparents, they could no longer control what she did." I turned to look at him properly. "I suppose you know many young women like Daisy."

"I knew a few, before the war, mostly sisters of friends from school or university. Like Daisy, they lived sheltered lives. They were from privileged backgrounds and didn't need to work, and they weren't given a higher education. I thought of most of them as annoying little sisters."

They would have loathed that. No doubt the handsome, charming Gabriel Glass was a popular house guest during summer holidays. "Most?" I echoed.

His lips tilted. "Nothing gets past you."

"That's why I noticed you avoided answering me just now."

He laughed softly. "And I will continue to avoid that question." His smiled vanished. "Anyway, that was before the war. I've changed. They probably have too, but I haven't seen those girls in years."

"You don't bump into them at dance halls and clubs?"

"I rarely go out. In fact, the girls I know the best are Alex's sisters. I thought I knew Ivy, but..." He shook his head. "I realize now that our conversations were superficial. We rarely discussed anything that revealed ourselves to the other." He huffed out a breath. "That seems such an odd thing to admit...we were engaged for three years yet I hardly knew her."

"The war changed you. The man you were when you met her is different from the one sitting beside me." Something

Cyclops had once told me came to mind. "Perhaps not different. Perhaps you've become the man you were always meant to be."

"You mean I've grown up. I'm no longer the rogue the mothers warned their daughters about."

I could well imagine my mother warning me not to go near a man who could charm a girl at a party with a few smiles and easy conversation. Rogues, even the charming ones, were to be avoided. Even the more mature post-war Gabe would worry her. She'd be horrified to see me sitting so close to him that our arms touched.

It would seem my proximity to Gabe was a concern for another, too. Willie strode up, sherry glass in hand, and ordered us to move apart. When the gap was wide enough, she wedged herself between us.

"So what are you two talking about?"

"Nothing," I said quickly.

She narrowed her gaze at me. "It didn't look like nothing, the way you had your heads together. Looked to me like you were sharing a secret."

Perhaps we ought to tell her about my magic to divert her attention from our real conversation.

Gabe had another idea. "We were discussing family. Mothers and daughters, specifically."

She screwed up her nose. "What about them?"

Gabe's gaze connected with mine over the top of her head. "Uh...how different they can be. Take Alex's mother Catherine, for example. She's a wonderful mother to all three of her daughters, even though they're all very different."

"True." Willie sipped thoughtfully. "Your Aunt Beatrice has three daughters and she was a terrible mother to all of 'em. They're grown now," she added for my benefit. "The eldest hates her mother and her other two sisters, and with good reason. They treated her like she was worthless. The second daughter is either mad or manipulative, I ain't sure which. Prob'ly both. And the third...well, Hope's a downright bi—"

"Willie," Gabe warned. "That's my father's cousin you're referring to."

"The Glass side of the family are living reminders of why the English upper classes need to breed outside their immediate circle. Fortunately the middle daughter never married and the other two didn't have children with their husbands."

Gabe rolled his eyes. "Not this again." To me, he added, "Willie thinks Hope's child isn't her husband's."

"Let's hear what an impartial party thinks." Willie pointed the sherry glass at me. "Her son was born *ten* months after her husband died."

"It could have been a longer than average pregnancy," I said.

"And he looks like her driver who's been with her for years."

"How much like him?"

"Red hair, tall and skinny. Hope's blonde and not overly tall, and her late husband, Lord Coyle, was fat. Also, the thought of him and Hope doing what's necessary..." She pulled a face. "It's enough to turn me to drink." She downed the contents of her glass in a single gulp.

Huon danced his way over to us and crooked his finger at me. "Don't be dull and sit in the corner all night. Come and dance with me, you pretty little thing."

I hugged the book to my chest. "I think I'll stay here and look after this."

"Bring it with you if you don't want to let it go." He grabbed my free hand and managed to haul me half-way off the sofa.

Willie pushed me from behind the rest of the way. "Go and dance with him. I'll take care of the book."

I hesitated, holding the book tightly. It wasn't that I didn't want to let it go as much as I didn't want to dance with Huon and give him the wrong idea.

Whether Gabe could read my mind or whether he wanted to dance, too, I wasn't sure, but he got up and plucked the book out of my grasp. "Willie will take good care of it while we dance."

Huon didn't seem to mind that Gabe invited himself to join us, but Willie did. "Three's a crowd, Gabe."

He indicated the dancers gyrating to the ragtime music. "There are a lot more than three out there."

She scowled at his deliberate misunderstanding of her meaning.

He smiled back at her. "If you would try and dance once in a while, you could join us."

"Then who'd look after the book?"

"Why won't she dance?" I asked Gabe as we followed Huon into the middle of the room. The carpet had been rolled up to allow the dancers' shoes to spin and glide frictionlessly across the floor when one of the dances called for such moves.

"She thinks she looks ridiculous."

"And does she?"

"Like a newborn calf still getting used to her legs."

I threw my head back and laughed.

\* \* \*

WE DIDN'T STAY LATE at Huon's party. Gabe and I had to work the following day. Willie insisted on leaving with us, but I suspected that was more to ensure we had a chaperone in the motorcar since Alex had decided to remain at the party. He claimed he wasn't ready to leave yet, but I secretly suspected he wanted to keep an eye on Daisy. The other men were circling.

The following morning Gabe was cheerful and bright-eyed when he arrived at the library carrying the book we'd borrowed from Lady Stanhope. His two companions, on the other hand, looked like they needed more sleep. They pounced on the professor's offer of coffee.

"You both just had coffee at breakfast," Gabe told them.

Willie pushed past him, stifling a yawn, while Alex followed, his shoulders stooped. "It's not enough," he muttered.

I watched them retreat to the reading nook where both slumped into the sofa. "Why is Willie tired? We didn't leave late."

"She returned to the party. They both left around dawn."

"Did Daisy stay the entire time?"

"That's apparently why they left around dawn, even though Alex would have preferred to come home at a decent hour, considering he's working today. Daisy didn't want to go and he didn't want to leave her on her own."

"She would have been fine. Besides, Huon might be casu-ally eccentric but I don't think he'd let anything happen to her under his own roof. Was Daisy drunk?"

"Apparently not, despite Willie's best efforts. She spent most of the night dancing and flirting."

"With Alex?"

"Going by the morose look on his face, I don't think so."

I moved off, but he caught my hand. "How are you, Sylvia? After the revelation yesterday...I've been wondering what's going through your mind."

It felt good to be asked. To know I was in his thoughts...it was a heady feeling. "I couldn't sleep last night. I kept turning it over in my mind, wondering whether I inherited magic from my father or mother. And wondering why she never told me."

He squeezed my hand. "Perhaps she didn't know. You didn't."

He could be right. My mother may have been many things, but she loved me. She wanted what was best for James and me. She wouldn't keep such an important thing a secret.

And yet she did keep secrets from us. Important ones. The name of our father, for one thing, and the reason for our frequent moves.

"What are you two talking about?" Willie called out from the sofa. "Don't exclude us."

Gabe sighed and indicated I should walk with him into the library. "I wonder if she knows she's turning into the spinster relative from a Jane Austen novel."

"You read Jane Austen?"

"My mother encouraged me. I like most of them." An impish smile touched his lips. "*Pride and Prejudice* should be required reading for all young men before they set out into the world to find their mate."

"To teach them that being haughty and rude doesn't matter as long as they're handsome and rich?"

"Darcy wasn't haughty and rude, he was reserved and misunderstood."

I laughed. "You would take his side."

"What are you two talking about?" Willie demanded.

"I think Sylvia is comparing me to Mr. Darcy."

"Who?"

Alex grunted but kept his eyes shut and his head tipped back. "He's more of a cross between Captain Wentworth and Darcy."

"Who are these people?" Willie pushed herself to her feet. "Don't bother telling me, I don't care. I'm going to see how the coffee's coming along." She yawned again. "I'm getting too old for this."

We all stared at her.

"It was a joke. I feel better than I did when I was twenty." She turned away as she smothered another yawn.

"How old *are* you?" Alex asked.

She bent down and crooked her finger. He straightened and leaned closer to hear her whisper but received a smack to the side of the head instead. "Ask me that again, and next time it'll be harder."

He rubbed his head. "I'll just ask my parents," he called after her as she walked off.

"They don't know," she called back over her shoulder.

Alex closed his eyes again and relaxed into the sofa.

Gabe perched on the edge of the desk and crossed his arms and ankles. "I checked my parents' catalog of magicians this morning. They listed several paper magicians around the country, but they knew of only two currently living in London. They're a brother and sister, co-owners of a paper manufacturing business in Bethnal Green. Even if the paper in the untitled books didn't come from their factory, they should be able to identify whether the magic in the books is paper magic or not."

"Shall we call at the factory after coffee?"

He nodded. "Since Huon thinks the magic is most likely in the paper, not the leather or silver, we'll start there."

* * *

WE INFORMED Willie of our plans as we walked along Crooked Lane. At the mention of paper magic, she stopped. "What's the name of the brother and sister?"

"Peterson," Gabe said. "Walter and Evaline Peterson, both aged in their mid-forties according to my parents' file. Evaline never married, but Walter has two children."

Willie grunted and continued on.

Gabe and Alex exchanged frowns. "Do you know them?" Gabe asked.

"No."

"Then why the interest in them?"

"I ain't interested in them. Did India and Matt's files mention other paper magicians?"

"It listed several, but they're the only ones with a London address."

She grunted again and walked through the covered exit to the adjoining street.

Alex moved around her and blocked her path to the parked motorcar. Despite her glare, he remained unmoving. "Why the interest in paper magicians?"

She sighed. "One of them tried to kill me. Tried to kill your parents, too, Gabe."

"I read that in their files. Do you know why?"

She tapped her temple. "He was mad."

"The file mentioned he disappeared, presumed dead."

She shrugged. "This Walter Peterson fellow is too young for it to be him, so you'll be fine. But if you do happen to get into an argument with a paper magician, just be sure to do it in a room where there ain't much paper lying about."

"Why?"

"I invented the saying 'death by a thousand paper cuts' after an encounter with him."

"That phrase has been around longer than you've been alive," I said. "And it's 'death by a thousand cuts', not paper cuts."

"I *am* talking about the paper cuts version, and I *did* invent it. You might have all the book learning, Sylvia, but that don't teach you creative thinking." She tapped her temple again as she had done when mentioning the mad paper magician. I doubted she meant to equate creativity with madness by repeating the gesture, but that's how it appeared.

Gabe, Alex and I wanted to hear more about the paper cuts, but Willie refused to discuss it further, saying she didn't want to think about the incident that had happened so long ago. "Anyway, I hardly remember it."

I got the impression she remembered it rather well. Perhaps a little too well. I suspected she didn't want to bring it to the forefront of her mind again after so much time had passed. It must have been a traumatic experience.

The Petersons were not in the factory and their assistant would not give out their home address. He recommended we return another day.

Disappointment weighed heavily as we headed back to the motorcar. I wanted to meet the Petersons very much. They could be my relatives.

I hadn't realized my hopes had risen. Given that I wasn't even sure I was a paper magician, it seemed foolish to entertain the hope that the Petersons were my relations, yet I couldn't help entertain it.

I folded the book against my chest. My head might not be ready to believe that I was a paper magician, but my flesh and blood seemed sure as my body warmed in response to the book's magic.

Gabe opened the back door of the motor for me while Willie retrieved the crank handle. He slid onto the seat beside me in thoughtful silence.

Once the engine was rumbling and Willie was seated, Alex asked where we wanted to go next.

"Hobson and Son," Gabe said. "If we can rule out leather magic, that leaves us with only silver or paper."

"There are other leather magicians in London," Alex pointed out. "We can call on one of them instead."

"Mr. Hobson's magic is strong. It's why his company won the contract from the military to provide the army with boots.

He'll know for certain whether the cover of that book contains magic."

Willie clicked her tongue and shook her head. "I don't know. I don't reckon it's wise for you to see the Hobsons after the way they treated you."

"I've spoken to Mr. Hobson since my name appeared in the newspapers defending the company."

"But it was a tense meeting."

"The newspapers have printed a retraction after I informed them of the mistake. It's all behind us now."

"Is it? And it weren't a mistake, Gabe. It was deliberate on Hobson's part to use the Glass name. You're too forgiving."

"I need to do this, Willie. If I don't, things could remain awkward between Ivy and me, and I don't want that. We're going to see each other from time to time and it's best if there's no tension between us."

She *humphed* as she turned back to face the road ahead. "You gotta stop trying to please everyone."

Gabe stared out of the side window in silence the entire way to the Bermondsey factory of Hobson and Son. The company had taken over the premises from another boot manufacturer that had gone out of business in the 1890s. When parliament pushed through laws that allowed magicians to trade without fear of persecution, the artless either had to join them or change their business practices to compete. Those that didn't failed as magician-made goods became highly sought after. The former bootmaker of the Bermondsey site was one of them. It must have galled him to sell the factory to a company that had directly contributed to his downfall.

Before its rise, when the company was known only as Hobson's Boots, Ivy's father's one-man business had operated out of the same Jermyn Street workshop as his father and grandfather had done, keeping their magic secret for fear the Cordwainer Guild would revoke their license. Mr. Hobson took advantage of the law change and subsequent wave of interest in magician-made goods in the Nineties and quickly increased production. He outgrew his West End workshop and bought the Bermondsey factory, changing the name of the company to Hobson and Son when Ivy's brother, Bertie, was born.

By the time war was declared, their large-scale operation meant they were well placed to manufacture the quantity of boots required by the military. The excellent reputation and proven longevity of the magic-infused leather meant no other bootmaker could compete for the contract. The Hobson family's fortunes grew further throughout the war, and they were now one of the wealthiest families in England.

Tanning of the leather hides wasn't done on site, so we weren't confronted with offensive odors. However, we were confronted by a small group of protestors marching up and down the pavement outside the factory's main entrance. Two of them carried signs calling for a government inquiry into the company's army-issued boots. Another six were using crutches to help them get around on one foot. One man was in a wheelchair, his trouser legs pinned up so they didn't flap in the breeze. He was missing both feet. The sign he held called for compensation for the men who lost limbs due to Hobson and Son's negligence.

We entered the building via a door marked OFFICE. The large reception area was comfortably furnished with a rich brown leather sofa and armchairs. I breathed deeply, drawing the pleasant smell of new leather into my lungs.

A smiling young woman at the front desk greeted Gabe by name. "It's lovely to see you again."

"You look well, Miss Fisher."

"I am, thank you. Are you here to see Mr. Hobson?"

"Is he in?"

She gave the closed door leading from the reception area a pained look.

"I know I don't have an appointment, but my visit is professional, not private. There's a matter that requires his expertise."

She leaned forward and lowered her voice. "It's not that he isn't available. There's a little time before his next appointment." She glanced at the door again. "Mrs. Hobson is in there, too, you see. I wasn't sure you'd want to see both of them given...your recent change of circumstances."

Gabe thanked her and eyed the door as if it were a portal to a battleground.

"Let's leave," Willie said with uncharacteristic gentleness. "There ain't no need to go through this again."

Gabe shook his head. "We're here, now. Besides, it's water under the bridge." He asked Miss Fisher to announce us.

She rose and lifted a hand to knock on the office door but suddenly withdrew it when Mr. Hobson bellowed. "Enough, woman! Go home and leave me in peace!"

Miss Fisher bit her lip and glanced at Gabe. He nodded at her to continue.

She knocked.

The four of us drew in a collective breath, steeling ourselves for a meeting none of us wanted and all of us dreaded.

# CHAPTER 6

The last time I'd seen Mr. Hobson, he'd accused
Gabe of hurting Ivy, not just because Gabe ended
their relationship, but also because he refused to let Mr.
Hobson use the Glass name to pacify the protestors and
media. The accusation had rattled Gabe. He felt guilty for
abandoning his former fiancée when she needed him the
most. The situation with her family's business wasn't her
fault, yet she would suffer too if there was a fallout.

Mr. Hobson was as hostile this time as the last. "What are
you doing here?" It would seem he wasn't going to bother
with pleasantries.

To his credit, Gabe tried. "Mr. Hobson, Mrs. Hobson. It's
good to see you both again."

"Is it?"

Mrs. Hobson was a little less rude but still somewhat
frosty. "And you, Gabriel. I see you've brought the cavalry."
Her cool gaze took us all in but it ultimately settled on me,
turning positively icy.

My mother taught me to always be polite. I'd come to
realize over the years that it was good advice. Not simply to

keep the peace, but also to get what you wanted. Today, we wanted Mr. Hobson's help. "You both look well."

My attempt to be pleasant was met with silence.

Mr. Hobson picked up a newspaper from his desk and threw it in the waste basket, but not before I saw the headline accusing his company of negligence. "Unless you've come to apologize, Glass, we have nothing to say to one another."

"He's got nothing to apologize for," Alex said through a clenched jaw.

Mr. and Mrs. Hobson ignored him. It seemed he and I were both beneath their notice.

Willie surged forward like a tidal wave and slammed both hands down on the desk.

Mr. Hobson stepped back while Mrs. Hobson jumped in fright. It was impossible to ignore Willie.

"You should be the one apologizing, Hobson. If you hadn't lied to the papers, there wouldn't be a problem. All Gabe did was tell them the truth. India didn't verify every batch of your boots. How could she? Admit that one batch missed receiving your spell and this'll all be over."

Mr. Hobson's nostrils flared but he had enough sense not to disagree with her. Perhaps his silence stemmed from the fact he could see her gun from where he stood.

Mrs. Hobson, however, took it upon herself to fight back. She plucked the newspaper out of the waste basket and showed it to Gabe. "Do you see that article?" She shook it in front of his face. "Do you see what you've done?"

He took it from her and read.

"They claim we have something to hide," she said stiffly. "There's speculation that my husband and son are criminally negligent and should be taken to court." Her voice shook as her pitch rose. "All because you wouldn't vouch for the magic!"

"I can't vouch for the magic," Gabe growled. "I'm not a magician. They would have reported that, sooner or later."

She snatched the newspaper from him and shook it again. "Do you not care for Ivy even a little? It's humiliating enough that you moved on so quickly." The glare she shot me was as sharp as cut glass. "Do you have to ruin her family's business, and therefore her future, as well?"

Alex and Willie's protests were loud, but Gabe's drowned them both out. "Enough!"

The seething man in front of me couldn't have been more starkly different from the gentle version I was familiar with. It was a reminder that there was more to him than met the eye. He would put up with a lot, but if pushed too far, he would push back.

Gabe indicated the newspaper. "I've said it before, but I will say it again. You brought this attention upon yourselves. If you'd admitted a batch was mistakenly missed and offered compensation to those affected, you could have avoided this publicity disaster. Secondly, I *do* care for Ivy. I'll always care for her. But I don't love her, and I won't be made to feel guilty for that. In time, she'll come to see that she doesn't love me, either."

"I doubt that," came a soft but determined voice from the doorway.

I spun around to see Ivy standing there, as tall and slender as an oak and just as unyielding. Where many women would be in tears after admitting she'd always love the man who ended their relationship, she stood proud and defiant. She was as beautiful and regal as ever with her dark hair and big eyes. She gave Gabe a sad smile as she entered her father's office.

It wasn't until she was in the room that I realized her brother, Bertie, was with her. The brother and sister shared a similar look. Both were tall and slim with dark hair and high cheekbones, but Bertie's features were more feline than Ivy's. Some would say he looked more feminine.

They both had better manners than their parents and greeted us all individually. Bertie even shook Gabe and Alex's hands, although when he spotted his father scowling at him, he quickly lowered his gaze to the floor.

"To what do we owe this pleasure?" Ivy asked Gabe. "And yes, it is a pleasure to see you again. I'm not ashamed to admit that I've missed you."

"It's good to see you too, Ivy." Gabe indicated the book in my hands. "We came to ask your father—or Bertie—to verify whether there is any leather magic in this book's cover."

"Oh? Why?"

"It's a clue in a murder we're investigating."

"A murder? How dreadful." She gave me a worried frown. "I do hope it's not someone you know, Miss Ashe."

"No," I said. "I'm simply helping."

"Another investigation in which Gabe requires your assistance? Scotland Yard will stop hiring him and simply go straight to you, soon." She smiled. It was thin and brittle, disappearing as quickly as it appeared. "I can take a look at the cover for you, if you like. My magic is as strong as my father's."

"No," Mr. Hobson snapped. "Don't help them."

"Come now, Father. It's important."

"It's nothing to do with us."

She regarded her parents with the same cool regard she gave us. "It's time to let bygones be bygones."

Mrs. Hobson shook the newspaper at her daughter. "This is not a bygone! The situation is very current, and it's dire."

Ivy drew in a deep breath and let it out slowly. "Sorry," she muttered to Gabe.

Mr. Hobson flicked his wrist at the door. "If you don't mind, I have work to do."

Outside, the protestors suddenly became louder. "Make Hobson pay! Make Hobson pay!"

Mr. Hobson bared his teeth and stormed past us and out the door. Mrs. Hobson clicked her tongue and watched him go. "Do something, Bertie, before your father makes it even worse."

Bertie was torn. He wasn't the confident sort, not like his sister. I'd wager he preferred pleasing his parents to confronting them.

He looked relieved when Ivy suggested she go. "But first, let me quickly touch the book's cover."

I handed her the book. She held it for barely a second before handing it back.

"There's no leather magic in it."

"Are you sure?" I asked.

"Of course." She touched Gabe's arm and gave him a sad smile that softened her features. It wasn't until that moment that I realized how tightly wound she was. "If you have any more questions about leather magic or...anything, let me know. We can meet for lunch. Now, if you'll excuse me." She eyed the door, blew out an exasperated breath, and walked quickly from the office.

We exited the building behind her and were greeted with the angry shouts of the protestors. They circled Mr. Hobson, drowning him out, chanting over the top of his retorts. I could just make out his face, blisteringly red, his hands balled into fists. He was close to lashing out.

Ivy clutched Gabe's arm. "Do something! Help him, please!"

Willie settled her feet apart, hands on hips. "Don't play the damsel in distress card. Gabe ain't falling for it. He ain't responsible for you no more, Ivy, and he doesn't want to get involved in your family's mess. Come on, Gabe, let's go."

Gabe extricated himself from Ivy's grip and stepped

around Willie. He and Alex trotted down the steps to the pavement side by side, calling for calm. Willie cursed under her breath.

Ivy followed Gabe, albeit at a safe distance.

Gabe put up his hands to placate the group. "This won't achieve the outcome you want! Let's talk and we can determine the best way to move forward."

"The time for talking has passed!" one shouted. "He's had every opportunity to speak with us, and he refused. He'll send for the police who'll make us disperse. It's the same every time."

"Then you need to think of a smarter way to get what you want. Tell me your grievances."

"Their grievances are irrelevant." Mr. Hobson sneered.

Gabe's jaw firmed. "I want to hear them."

"Who're you?" asked one of the men on crutches.

"Their lawyer?" asked another. "Do you work for this greedy pig?"

"I'm a consultant for Scotland Yard, here on a matter of business that required Mr. Hobson's expertise."

"You should investigate him for criminal negligence!" cried the woman wheeling the man in the chair. "Look at my husband! Look at what Hobson and Son did to him!"

The other protestors chimed in with their individual grievances, all speaking over each other. Mr. Hobson shouted back at them, making everything worse. A small crowd had gathered at a distance to watch proceedings. It wouldn't be long until a journalist arrived. Mr. Hobson couldn't see that he was fanning the flames. He was letting his anger master him and not thinking clearly.

Again, Gabe put up his hands and called for calm. "A batch of boots must have been missed and unfortunately you were the recipients. It was a mistake, not criminal negligence."

"Then why not just admit it? Why not compensate—"

"There was no mistake!" Mr. Hobson shouted. "We personally ensured *every* batch received a spell."

"Can you state that categorically, sir? Would you swear to it in a court of law?"

Mr. Hobson's nostrils flared, his chest heaving with his snorted breaths. He was a bull preparing to attack.

The woman pushing the wheelchair sneered. "Why are you so vehement in your denials, Mr. Hobson? What are you hiding?"

Mr. Hobson charged. Ivy gasped. "Father! Don't!"

Thankfully Gabe and Alex blocked him and held him back. There was no telling what he might have done. He was fuming.

"Go away," Mr. Hobson snarled at the protestors, "or I will summon the police again, and this time I'll make sure you're charged. I know the commissioner! He won't turn a blind eye. He won't let misguided sympathy stop him from doing what's right."

"What's *right*?" more than one protestor spluttered in disbelief.

"You're pathetic! All of you!"

"Father, please." Ivy's desperate cry somehow got through to him amidst the rising voices of the protestors.

He turned and stormed back to the office. Bertie hurried after him. Mrs. Hobson watched them go with pursed lips, her spine rigid. She did not comfort her daughter nor go after her husband and son. She was a rock amid a tumultuous sea, very different from the woman we'd witnessed in the office.

Ivy pressed her hand to her stomach. "Thank you, Gabe. I know this must be difficult for you, but it is appreciated."

"Is it?" Willie snapped. "You do remember there's a kidnapper after him. It's dangerous for him to be out here where anyone could snatch him."

Gabe drew in a deep breath, as if drawing in a measure of patience. I wasn't sure how he remained so calm. "Ivy, you should try to convince your father to pay compensation. It's the right thing to do."

"He's stubborn. He won't listen to me." She clutched his sleeve and opened her mouth to say something before turning to me. "May we have some privacy, please?"

"We have nothing to say to one another in private," he told her.

She let him go and her hand dropped to her side like a stone. She blinked rapidly before regaining her composure. "I'm glad I could help with your investigation. Good luck."

"And to you."

Mrs. Hobson strode up to her daughter. "Ivy. Come. The chauffeur is waiting."

Before she followed her daughter into the back seat of the motorcar, Mrs. Hobson turned to us. Even from the distance, the glare was unmistakable. It began with Gabe, but it settled on me.

Gabe wasn't watching them. He watched the protestors marching up and down the pavement on crutches and in wheelchairs. They didn't chant anymore—they didn't want to create a scene that would get them arrested. But their spirits remained defiant.

I shivered from the remnants of Mrs. Hobson's glare as their motorcar drove away.

* * *

ALEX and the constable who'd helped him put Mr. Littleproud's shop to rights hadn't found any more clues to the killer's identity. He'd found the name of the current supplier of Mr. Littleproud's silver corner protectors, but the records stated he'd only been the supplier for the last fifteen years, not at the time the manuscripts were bound.

It was a place to start, however. Silversmithing was a relatively small industry, and he might know who supplied the victim with the corner protectors around the time the books were handed to Mr. Littleproud.

Gabe watched me closely as we waited for Mr. Rinehold to finish serving a customer. Surrounded by shiny silver objects in locked display cabinets, from jewelry to cigarette cases and hand mirrors, I ought to feel *something* if I were a silver magician. Even if they held no magic, I should want to caress them. But I felt no compulsion to do so. I was content to admire them through the glass.

The customer left and Mr. Rinehold greeted us from behind the counter with a smile. "Are you looking for something in particular?"

"We're consultants for Scotland Yard," Gabe said. "We're investigating the death of Mr. Littleproud."

Mr. Rinehold's smile vanished. "I read about the murder in the newspapers, but the article said very little. What happened?"

"I'm not at liberty to divulge that information at this point. You supplied him with silver corner protectors, is that correct?"

"Yes, for many years."

"Do you know who supplied them to Littleproud before you?"

"I'm afraid not."

I showed him the book I'd been carrying and pointed to one of the corner protectors with the JF engraving. "Do you recognize these?"

Mr. Rinehold pushed his spectacles up his nose in a way that reminded me of Professor Nash. He squinted through them as he studied the protectors. "That's the signature of a silversmith named John Folgate."

A tingle rippled down my spine. Although we'd suspected the F referred to Folgate, we now had confirmation.

"Apparently he placed his signature on some of his pieces, but not often. It is an odd thing to do, and I wouldn't recommend it unless it's discreet. It's quite dominant on those corners." Mr. Rinehold removed his spectacles and folded the arms. "I'm glad you came in. I was hoping you'd contact me again so I could tell you what I'd learned about him."

Gabe frowned. "Again? You're mistaken. This is the first time I've been here."

"It wasn't you who telephoned two days ago?"

"No. Mr. Rinehold, are you saying someone telephoned two days ago and asked about John Folgate? Who?"

"Another detective. I didn't catch his name. Or perhaps he didn't give it. Anyway he told me he works for Scotland Yard and wanted to know about the supply of silver corner protectors to bookbinders. He wanted to know how long I'd been supplying Littleproud. I hadn't read about Littleproud's death at the time. I suppose this detective found my name amongst his paperwork, like you did."

"What did you tell him?"

"That I've been Littleproud's supplier of silver corner protectors for fifteen years. He asked who the previous supplier was, but I didn't know. He then asked if I knew a silversmith named John Folgate whose corner protectors ended up on a set of manuscripts bound by Littleproud."

Gabe tilted his head to the side. "He told you the name John Folgate? He didn't just ask about the initials?"

"He mentioned the full name, yes. I hadn't heard of Folgate, which means he isn't well known here in London. The detective ended the call, but my curiosity grew. Later that day, I telephoned the archivist at the Silversmiths' Guild and asked him to look into John Folgate. Just yesterday he got back to me with what little he could find. I was going to contact Scotland Yard later today and pass it on, but...here you are. Well, not *him*, but a colleague."

Gabe gave him a reassuring nod. "The case was assigned to Miss Ashe and me only yesterday. Back to John Folgate. Is he any relation to a woman named Marianne Folgate?"

"I don't know."

"You said your archivist friend learned a little more about him. What exactly?"

"Folgate was a silversmith from Ipswich who died in 1890. He doesn't appear to have been very prolific. It's likely he served the local community and never made a name for himself outside of Ipswich. A pity, really."

"Why?" I asked.

Mr. Rinehold pointed his folded glasses at the book I held. "The silver in those corners is good quality and the engraving is very fine. He was an excellent craftsman." He put the glasses back on. "But not all craftsmen make good business-men. Perhaps Folgate lacked the drive necessary to expand his business."

Either that or he knew his talent would come under close scrutiny and bring him to the attention of the powerful Silver-smith Guild in a time when magicians were persecuted.

"What does Folgate's silverware have to do with Littleproud's death?" Mr. Rinehold asked.

"Perhaps nothing," Gabe said. "We're still making inquiries at this stage. Is there anything else you can tell us about Littleproud? Do you know of anyone who'd want to kill him?"

"I didn't know him at all. We met only once, all those years ago when we established our business relationship. Ever since then, we've only communicated by post." Mr. Rinehold walked with us to the door to see us out. "I'm not sure if this is relevant, but he didn't pay me on time. He did at first. Never missed a payment. But the last two or three years, each invoice was paid later and later. The last time, he was almost three months late."

"Did he say why? Was his business in trouble?"

"I don't know."

Gabe opened the door to leave but hesitated. "One last thing. This investigation is confidential. All inquiries *must* go through me. Don't give any information to other detectives." He handed Mr. Rinehold a card. "If you can think of anything else, telephone me on this number."

We thanked him and returned to Willie and Alex in the motorcar. Gabe repeated what we'd learned from Mr. Rinehold. The revelation about John Folgate didn't cause a flicker of an eyelash. We'd all considered the prospect that the F in JF belonged to a Folgate.

The mention of the detective who'd telephoned two days ago with the same inquiry as us caught their attention, however.

"It must be the killer," Alex said. "He got Rinehold's name from Littleproud's list of suppliers the same way I did—by looking through Littleproud's books."

"Which he did after he killed Littleproud," Willie finished. "He must have seen the JF engraving in the auction catalog photograph, recognized the initials as those of John Folgate, and gone to Littleproud to find a current address for him, only to learn someone else now supplied him with silver corners."

Gabe got out to crank the engine. I sat in the back seat and stared at the silversmith's shop. Our investigation had taken a dramatic turn, one that could personally affect me. If my brother suspected he was a silver magician, then we were most likely related to the Folgates—and the killer wanted to find John Folgate desperately. Desperately enough to kill. One thing we knew for sure: whoever had telephoned Mr. Rinehold wasn't interested in the magic paper; he was interested in the silver corner protectors. Specifically, he was interested in the man who made them.

We needed to find the Folgate family before he did. Gabe's lawyer was trying to find out who owned the house Marianne Folgate and her husband, Mr. Cooper, rented in 1891. Now we had an extra lead—John Folgate was from Ipswich.

With the engine rumbling, Gabe returned to the front passenger seat of the motorcar. He'd clearly been thinking the same thing as me. "I'll telephone Cyclops and ask him to contact his Ipswich counterparts. Hopefully there are some Folgates still living there."

Willie indicated the silversmith's shop as we pulled away from the curb. "Good thing the killer never called him back or he'd know where to look next."

Gabe twisted to look at me over his shoulder. "I know this is a lot to take in, Sylvia, and you're probably thinking the family you never knew could be in danger. No doubt the fake detective already checked with the Silversmiths' Guild. You don't have to be a member to speak to the archivist."

I hadn't thought of that, but he was right. The man who posed as the detective must know by now that John Folgate was from Ipswich.

"Don't worry," he went on, speaking with quiet yet convincing reassurance. "Cyclops will see that they're protected."

"Something is bothering me," I said. "Why would the man who pretended to be a detective get rough with Littleproud? Surely the name and address of a supplier he no longer uses isn't worth defending until the death. Why wouldn't Littleproud just give the information up?"

"Maybe the killer wanted the information *and* the books,"

Willie said. "But Littleproud had already sold 'em. The man got angry and killed him."

Gabe shook his head slowly. "I agree with Sylvia. It seems odd."

Willie *humphed*. "She's been a detective for five minutes and you believe her theory over mine."

"You haven't done much investigating over the last twenty years or so, Willie. Perhaps you've grown rusty."

Alex chuckled. "He means you're old."

She *humphed* again. "My mind's as sharp as ever. It's so sharp, I've thought of something none of you have."

"What's that?" Gabe asked.

"Rinehold told you that Littleproud's been paying him late the last couple of years. Sounds to me like he's in financial trouble."

"How does that fit in with the fact the killer wanted Folgate's name and address from Littleproud?"

"I don't know, do I? I can't do *all* the thinking for you."

Her point about Littleproud's financial difficulty was worth following up. According to Alex, however, the bookbinder's accounts were all in order. He'd given them a thorough inspection when he'd tidied up the shop and found it was a stable business that made a modest profit.

We drove to Mrs. Littleproud's sister's house and found the widow in an agitated state. She'd just come from the bank to withdraw funds to pay the undertaker, only to find there was no money.

"Where has it all gone?" she murmured into her handkerchief. "There's nothing left, Mr. Glass. Nothing."

"Did he have another account?" Gabe asked. "Could it be in there?"

"The bank manager said we had a business and personal accounts. Both are empty."

I sat on her other side and touched her arm. "Do you

know if the accounts have always been this low? Or is it something new?"

Mrs. Littleproud shrugged. "Adolphus took care of all our finances. He gave me enough to pay the baker, butcher and grocer each week, plus some pin money. According to the bank's transaction records, when money did come in, my husband took it out straight away." She pressed the handkerchief to her nose as fresh tears spilled. "Our retirement money...gone. How will I live?"

Her sister placed her arm around Mrs. Littleproud's shoulders. "You'll live here with me. We'll take care of each other."

"But...where has it gone? That's what I'd like to know. What did Adolphus spend it on?"

It was a question that needed answering. If Mr. Littleproud took the money out as soon as it came in, either he was paying something off in instalments or the money went to paying bills. But Mrs. Littleproud claimed *she* settled the household accounts.

So where had the money gone? To whom? Had Littleproud fallen behind on repayments? Was that the reason he was killed?

The sobering thought occupied my mind all the way back to the library, where we parted ways. Gabe, Alex and Willie went to Scotland Yard to report to Cyclops, while I thought it best to put in an appearance at work. Although the professor was happy for me to assist Gabe with his investigations, I didn't want to take advantage of his good nature. I ought to spend some time doing the job I was employed to do.

I placed my bag in the bottom drawer at the front desk and went in search of the professor. I followed the sound of voices and found him talking to a patron in the section on magical inheritance.

"The study of inheritance is relatively new in the magical

sense," the professor was saying when he looked up from the book and saw me. "Ah, Sylvia, you've returned." He invited me to join them. "Come and meet a new member."

The handsome middle-aged man with red-brown hair held out his hand to me. In his other, he held a straw boater. His light blue eyes crinkled with his smile as the professor introduced us.

"Sylvia, this is Mr. Jakes. Mr. Jakes, my assistant, Miss Sylvia Ashe."

I shook his hand, smiling. I said something welcoming and cheerful, yet all the while, the name repeated over and over in my head like a small pick chipping away at a rock. Jakes, Jakes, Jakes. Where had I heard it before?

"Mr. Jakes wants to understand how magic is passed down through families." Professor Nash showed me the book they were studying. It was a general introduction to the relatively new science of genetics and how that related to magical inheritance. "I was about to tell Mr. Jakes we don't have any books on his particular interest—mutations—but there have been a number of works about magical inheritance published in the last two decades. The rising interest in the topic coincided with both the freedom magicians experienced in the Nineties and the breakthroughs in the study of genetics in general. Fascinating topic, don't you agree, Sylvia?"

I nodded and said something I hoped was appropriate and didn't give away to Mr. Jakes that I'd finally remembered where I'd heard his name. He'd been a commanding officer for Military Intelligence in the war. He'd recently called upon a friend of Gabe's, Francis Stray, a brilliant codebreaker who'd worked for Jakes. In that visit, Jakes had asked Francis what he knew about Gabe's magical abilities and his so-called luck at surviving the war unscathed as well as other incidents that had defied logic.

His interest in Gabe was troubling. The recent kidnapping

attempts only added to my concern. And now here he was, learning about the study of genetics and how that related to magical inheritance.

Yet he didn't appear to be listening to the professor. His entire attention focused on me. The smile I'd found warm upon meeting him now chilled me to the bone.

# CHAPTER 7

M r. Jakes had the easy countenance of someone comfortable with his lot in life. Given he was handsome, intelligent and most likely from a well-to-do family that had cleared his path into a position of authority, he had a lot to be comfortable about. In some ways, his self-assurance reminded me of Gabe.

Yet I couldn't shake the feeling that it was all for show, that he wanted something and knew the best way to get it was to charm. Unlike Gabe, who was charming by nature.

Mr. Jakes thanked the professor for his time and assistance. "You've been very helpful. It's a shame there aren't more books written on the topic of genetic mutations within magician lineages."

The professor slotted the book back into place on the shelf. "Perhaps you can write one."

Mr. Jakes chuckled. "I'm afraid I'm no scholar." He indicated I should walk ahead of him out of the narrow aisle.

"What is your interest in aid of?" I asked.

"It's just something I picked up during the war."

"You served?" the professor asked.

"I worked at the War Office." It was a vague enough response that encompassed many aspects of the army, including Military Intelligence.

He paused as he exited the aisle and gazed around the library, taking in the cozy reading nook, the full stacks, and the display cabinets housing magical objects collected by the professor and Oscar Barratt. "What a glorious place. How fortunate you are to work here, Miss Ashe."

"It's a wonderful library," I agreed.

He indicated the large clock with the brass hands and numbers above the fireplace. "Does it contain Lady Rycroft's magic?"

"Oh yes," the professor said with enthusiasm. "It never loses so much as a second."

"In that case..." Mr. Jakes adjusted his wristwatch to match the clock. "What an incredible magician. Have you met her, Miss Ashe?"

"She and Lord Rycroft went on holidays before I came to work here."

"You've met their son, though. Professor Nash tells me he comes in here from time to time."

I glanced at the professor, wondering how much he'd told Mr. Jakes. How much could he tell him? He wasn't aware of Gabe's magical ability to manipulate time. It was an ability Gabe was born with, that he'd only become aware of during the war when his life was in constant danger. Mr. Jakes clearly suspected Gabe's luck was due to magic of some kind, and he seemed to be fishing for more information from those who knew him.

The question was, *why*?

"How well do you know Mr. Glass?" Mr. Jakes prompted.

"A little," I said, as I led the way to the front desk to see him out. The sooner he left, the better. I didn't want to say something I shouldn't. I didn't want the professor to, either.

"He was in the newspapers recently." Mr. Jakes made it sound conversational, as if he were just passing the time in idle chatter. "That must have rattled him."

"To be written up as a hero for saving that boy's life at sea?" Professor Nash shrugged. "Why would it rattle him?"

"I meant the subsequent speculation about his knack for survival."

"Poppycock, all of it. The journalists have nothing to write about now the war is over. They're looking for sensational pieces. Don't believe a word of it." The professor handed Mr. Jakes his hat. "Do come again soon if you think our collection can help with your research. Sylvia and I would be happy to assist you." He opened the door.

Mr. Jakes put on his hat, touched the brim in farewell, and left.

The professor waited for him to exit the lane before he closed the door. "Do you want to tell Gabe about that or shall I?"

It seemed the professor wasn't as oblivious to the interest surrounding Gabe as I thought. It was a relief to know he wouldn't accidentally blurt out something Gabe didn't want strangers to know.

I reached for the telephone on the desk. "I'll do it."

"Why not go in person? I suspect Willie and Alex would want to know about Mr. Jakes's visit too, and I'm not entirely sure Gabe would tell them. He doesn't like a fuss made about him."

Since they were probably still at Scotland Yard, I continued to work and headed to the Mayfair townhouse after the Glass Library closed for the day. Bristow, the butler, invited me into the library where Gabe sat at the table, a notepad in front of him. I'd been in his library before, but I took a moment to take it all in again. The room was furnished in the darker, more lush style of the last century, with deep leather armchairs, velvet cushions, and a central table polished to a sheen. The wall-to-wall bookshelves were packed with books on all manner of topics, including those Gabe's grandfather had collected on his travels.

I drew the scent of leather covers and old paper into my lungs and finally turned to Gabe. He watched, calmly waiting for me to be ready, the hint of a smile playing on his lips.

He invited me to sit at one of the armchairs by the fireplace while he sat on the other. There was no fire in the grate, given the fine weather, but it was more comfortable than the hardback chairs at the table. "I was hoping you'd come."

"Oh?"

He didn't elaborate. Perhaps there was no specific reason for his hope.

My heart quickened. I turned away, suddenly shy, and focused on the familiar comfort of the books.

He followed my gaze. "You've already read that one, but you can borrow it again if you like."

I frowned.

He got up and removed a book from the shelves. I hadn't realized I'd been staring at it. He handed it to me and I clutched it to my chest without looking at the title, grateful for something to hold onto. My nerves were suddenly dancing a tango.

He opened his mouth to say something but didn't get the opportunity. Willie entered, only to stop upon seeing me.

"You again." Her gaze slid to Gabe. "You didn't tell us you invited her, too. When will everyone arrive?"

I hurriedly rose. "I'm sorry. I won't stay. I don't want to intrude if you have guests coming. I just wanted to warn you of a strange encounter at the library."

Gabe stood and took my elbows, gently steering me back into the armchair. "This sounds like a story that requires cocktails."

Willie strode further into the room and intercepted him before he reached the bell pull to summon Bristow. "She said she can't stay."

"She said she *won't* stay. It's not the same thing. Besides, she was being polite in the face of your rudeness. Sylvia, you're more than welcome to stay and have a drink with my friends. You know them, and I'm sure they'd be pleased to see you again."

"Then I accept. Thank you." I studiously kept my gaze averted from Willie's as she leaned back against the table edge.

Gabe instructed Bristow to make martinis and fetch Alex before resuming his seat. "Tell me about the strange encounter."

"Do you remember a man named Jakes?" I asked.

"Francis Stray's commanding officer? He was at the library?"

I told him what Mr. Jakes wanted, and how he'd asked the professor and me about Gabe. Gabe fell silent, but Willie muttered expletives under her breath when she realized what it meant.

Alex arrived and greeted me with a smile. It quickly vanished, however, when I repeated everything for his benefit.

"Do you think Jakes is behind the kidnapping attempts?" he asked.

"Who else could it be?" Willie said. "Seems to me he wants to know more about Gabe and what better way to know him than study him up close."

"Then why not invite him to his office and do it officially? Why go to the extreme of kidnap?"

"Maybe he doesn't want to study him by asking questions and observing. Maybe he wants to cut him open and see how he works."

"Gabe's not a machine."

"And Jakes is no engineer. He's Military Intelligence, and their orders come from high up. So high up they're accountable to no one."

We fell into silence, contemplating her macabre suggestion and the implications for Gabe, until Bristow arrived carrying a mirrored tray with cocktail glasses.

Gabe plucked off two and handed one to me. "I think it's time I met Jakes."

"Are you mad?" Willie cried. "You can't just walk into his lair. What if he doesn't let you walk out again? If you go, I'm coming with you and I'm bringing my Colt."

"I don't expect anything less from you, Willie."

She picked up a glass from the tray and saluted him with it.

Alex collected the last martini and went to take a sip but paused with the glass at his lips when he noticed us staring. "I'm not going to try to stop you, Gabe, because nothing will happen to you. All you'll succeed in doing is reveal that you suspect him. He'll deny it, but if he *is* behind the kidnapping attempts, then it might force him to stop. That's a good thing in my opinion."

Willie thumped him on the shoulder. "You're smarter than you look."

"Are you saying I look dumb because I'm so handsome?"

She winked and they both laughed.

Gabe pointed out that there hadn't been another kidnapping attempt since the two thugs were arrested outside the library after the last failed attempt. None of us were entirely convinced that meant whoever was behind them wouldn't try again.

I asked them if Cyclops had any new information about Mr. Littleproud's murder, but there was nothing to report. Gabe showed me the notes he'd been making when I arrived, and the four of us went over what we'd already learned in the hope it would shed new light on the investigation.

It didn't.

That all changed when the telephone rang. Bristow announced that Cyclops wished to speak to Gabe. A few minutes later, Gabe returned to the library.

"Cyclops just received the autopsy report. Littleproud died of heart failure."

"Not from his injuries?" I asked.

"Indirectly, yes. It's likely the heart attack was brought on by his beatings. It explains why there was some blood at the scene, but not a lot. The injuries he sustained weren't enough to kill him."

"It plays into the theory that the murderer didn't intend for him to die," Alex said. "He wanted to rough him up a little, probably get him to reveal the location of the books."

"Or the supplier of the silver corner protectors," Willie added. "Littleproud died before he could divulge anything."

Gabe retrieved his glass from where he'd set it down on the table. "Cyclops had more news. He located the author of the manuscripts, Honoria Moffat-Jones."

"So quickly?" Alex said.

"Her details were in an old file. Actually, it was her husband's details, she was simply noted as his spouse. Mr. Moffat-Jones worked for a bank that was embroiled in a fraud case. He was a witness, along with several other employees." Gabe pulled out a piece of paper from his pocket. "I have their address here."

We decided to call on the Moffat-Joneses in the morning. Hopefully Honoria could tell us how her manuscripts ended up at Mr. Littleproud's workshop.

Gabe's guests began to arrive and the staff were kept busy making drinks and handing them out along with delicious little canapes made by Gabe's cook, Mrs. Ling.

I overheard Gabe ask his friend from school, Francis Stray, whether he'd heard from his commanding officer, Jakes, recently. Francis had not.

The other guests were from Gabe's regiment, the Grenadier Guards. I knew Stanley Greville and Juan Martinez from our investigation into the Medici Manuscript. Juan's familiarity with the Catalonian region had been helpful in deciphering the book's codes. Stanley had provided some breakthroughs, too. Pouring over the pages seemed to provide a welcome distraction for him, soothing nerves that had been shredded in the war. In those hours, I'd seen a glimpse of the man he used to be before constant bloody battle shattered his confidence.

I made a point of speaking to him, but conversation proved difficult. He didn't want to talk about himself. I tried talking about my life instead, or the parts of it I didn't mind discussing with a man I hardly knew, but he seemed more interested in Gabe than me. He often looked Gabe's way, and whenever Gabe moved around the drawing room, Stanley's gaze tracked him.

"You like him, don't you?" I hadn't meant to imply anything other than friendship, but Stanley seemed to think I referred to something more.

"No! No. Certainly not." With a martini glass in one hand and a cigarette in the other, he couldn't perform his usual nervous habit where he brushed his cheek or chin. Instead, trembling fingers placed the cigarette between his lips. He drew deeply, blew out the smoke above my head, then drained his glass. He placed it on Murray's tray as the footman passed and plucked off a full one. "He saved my life in France." His voice was steady but quiet as his gaze once again sought out Gabe. "More than once. I find when we're together that I look for him. It's an old habit."

A habit borne from the knowledge that Gabe made him

feel safe. Gabe's power to manipulate time switched on when his life was in danger, but it probably also gave him the opportunity to save those in his immediate vicinity. He'd slowed time to save my life once, after hearing my scream. The same thing must have happened in France with these men.

Juan joined us, and the charming, cheerful Spaniard regaled us with tales of his homeland while getting in a dig or two at the English weather. He made me laugh, and even Stanley chuckled once or twice.

Gabe noticed and smiled. I hadn't realized I'd sought him out, just as Stanley did. My reason wasn't for security, however. It was utterly and completely because I liked to admire his handsome features, his graceful physique, and the way he interacted with his friends.

Unfortunately, I was a little too obvious. Willie moved to stand in front of me, obscuring my line of sight. She handed me a fresh martini, accompanied by a scowl. "You shouldn't have accepted his invitation to stay."

I lowered my glass. "Oh." What does one say to such a comment?

"It ain't personal."

"Isn't it?"

"No."

I waited for her to elaborate, but she didn't. Perhaps the martinis gave me some Dutch courage, but I wasn't prepared to let it slide. "I thought we were getting along now, Willie."

"What makes you think that?"

"You don't scowl at me as much as you used to."

She gave my comments thoughtful consideration. "I suppose I don't *dislike* you."

"Goodness, we're practically best friends now." I tapped my glass against hers then sipped.

She huffed. "You're drunk. And the reason you shouldn't

have accepted Gabe's invitation to stay is because he just ended one relationship. Don't push him into another. He ain't ready."

I bristled. I wasn't used to such brutal honesty. "I'm not pushing him. Friendship is perfectly fine with me. The situation between us is comfortable, and I don't want to jeopardize that. Besides, it's not just his company I enjoy, but the company of all of you. I like undertaking these investigations, too."

"Ha! So you admit you prefer investigating to cataloging. I knew being around books all day was boring for a young woman."

"That's not what I meant. I love being around books. It's not just the way they smell and feel, but it's the expression—"

"Stop before I fall asleep." She pressed two fingers to her mouth and seemed surprised to find them empty. She clicked her tongue and glanced around the room. "I need a cigarette. There's an emergency stash in that empty vase by the window. Cover me. Don't let Gabe see. Do this for me and we can be friends again."

"Willie," I hissed as she walked off.

She ignored me.

I jumped at the sound of Alex's voice behind me. "Daisy should be here."

I blinked stupidly, wishing I hadn't drunk so much in a short period of time. I was finding it difficult to concentrate. I put my glass down and focused on Alex. "Should she?"

"She's missing out. She wouldn't like that."

"I see. Would you like me to telephone her and invite her?"

He shrugged one shoulder. "It doesn't matter to me what you do. Invite her or don't invite her. I don't care. The telephone's in the hallway."

He walked off, passing Gabe who made his way to where

Willie was peering behind a large blue and white vase on the table in front of the window. As I headed out of the drawing room to use the telephone, I overheard him tell her he'd moved the cigarettes the day before and given them to Murray.

"If I'd known they were yours—"

"They weren't," she said, feigning nonchalance. "I saw them earlier. A visitor must have left them behind. I was going to give them to Murray, too, that's why I'm looking. They weren't mine. Why would you think that? I haven't wanted to smoke in weeks."

"Good. Me either."

Gabe's thumb tapped rapidly against his thigh while Willie's fingers touched her lips again to smoke a phantom cigarette. I left to telephone Daisy. Alex was right. She would very much enjoy this party.

* * *

WE DIDN'T WANT to call on Mrs. Moffat-Jones too early, so waited until eleven. That suited Willie. According to Alex, she'd rolled out of bed minutes before they left and just had time to consume one cup of coffee.

"Expect her to be irritable," he said with a wink before he pulled the motorcar away from the curb.

Willie rose to the bait. "And with good reason. This ain't no hangover. Something was added to those martinis. Gabe, you should question Murray. It's the sort of thing he'd do to liven things up."

"Murray did not add anything to your drinks," he said.

She rubbed her temples. "Then why's my head splitting in two?"

"Perhaps you just drank too much."

"I've had more than that on plenty of occasions."

From where I sat, I could make out Alex's grin, but Willie couldn't. "I already told you. It's different when you're old."

Willie must truly have been suffering because she merely groaned.

She and Alex stayed with the Hudson while Gabe and I went to speak to Honoria Moffat-Jones. The Moffat-Joneses lived in a modest house with cheerful yellow curtains that fluttered in the breeze. The windows were open to air out the rooms, so it must be cleaning day.

The maid who answered the door screwed her hands in her apron and smiled a greeting at Gabe. I might as well have not existed. She didn't take her gaze off him. The smile slipped when Gabe explained we worked for Scotland Yard.

"Is Mrs. Honoria Moffat-Jones in?" he asked.

"You mean Mrs. *Eleanor* Moffat-Jones."

"Honoria and Angus Moffat-Jones don't live here?"

"That's the master's name, but Eleanor's his wife. Honoria was his first wife. She died years ago, before my time."

Gabe asked if either of the Moffat-Joneses were home and the maid said they both were. She went to see if they were receiving callers then returned a few minutes later and led us into a neat sitting room that smelled of bees wax polish. A plump middle-aged woman with loosely swept up hair and tired eyes sat with her hands folded in her lap. She rose upon our entry and introduced herself as Eleanor.

She looked to the maid who was biting the inside of her lower lip as she studied Gabe quite openly. Mrs. Moffat-Jones cleared her throat and the maid sniffed then left to fetch her master.

Mrs. Moffat-Jones invited us to sit, but when Gabe selected a wingback chair upholstered in burgundy velvet, she gasped. "Not there. That's my husband's chair." It must be his favorite, going by the faded seat and backrest.

Gabe sat on the sofa beside me. "You're the second Mrs. Angus Moffat-Jones?"

"His first wife died a long time ago. She left behind a one-year-old daughter who I've raised as my own. She's a fine young woman now, and a mother herself. Angus and I married almost two years after Honoria's death. We had two boys." She indicated a family portrait hanging on the wall. It must have been taken during the war as one of the men wore a uniform. I wondered if he was the reason she looked drawn, sad. My own mother had gone from being a strong woman to a defeated one after James died.

She stood again as Mr. Moffat-Jones arrived. He paused in the doorway, filling it with his large frame. He leaned on a walking stick that was too short for his height, making his gait awkward. He smiled in greeting and extended his hand to Gabe but not me.

"I must say, when Martha said you were inquiring after Honoria, I became intrigued." Mr. Moffat-Jones eased himself into the wingback chair with a wince. "She's been gone for years."

"Miss Ashe and I are collaborating on an investigation into the murder of a bookbinder on Paternoster Row."

Mrs. Moffat-Jones gasped and clutched her throat.

"Good lord," her husband said. "Poor fellow. But what does his murder have to do with Honoria?"

I showed him the manuscript. "We've borrowed this from its owner for the duration of our investigation. Do you recognize it?"

He opened the cover and read the title page. "It appears to be one of Honoria's stories. Where did you get it?"

"The murdered bookbinder sold it before his death. We believe the killer is looking for it, or information about it. The bookbinder claimed the paper contains magic, and the silver corners may, too."

Mr. Moffat-Jones removed a magnifying glass from a small drawer in the table beside his chair and squinted through it at the silver corners. "JF. I'm afraid that means nothing to me. None of this does." He tapped the magnifying glass on the book's cover. "I don't understand, Mr. Glass. The bookbinder was killed over this? Why?"

"That's what we're trying to find out. Can you tell us how your first wife's handwritten manuscripts came to be in a bookbinder's possession?"

"I have no idea. I can't imagine she'd want them presented in this form. She wasn't sentimental enough about her stories to bind them. Indeed, the allowance I gave her wouldn't have covered the expense. Honoria enjoyed the process of writing, you see, so having them bound wouldn't matter to her. The maid we had back then reported that Honoria would tap away at that infernal typewriter all day, writing her little stories. She only wrote during the day, never in the evening after I came home from work. I used to tell her she needed to get out of the house more, make friends, but she claimed she was happy writing. Odd little thing, was Honoria, but a good wife and mother. I can't fault her there." He handed the book back to me. "Have you read them?"

Since he addressed Gabe, not me, Gabe answered with a shake of his head.

"I read a few pages once," Mr. Moffat-Jones went on. "Not that one, a different one. Rather childish and simple, they were."

"I believe they're for children," I pointed out.

"Quite right, Miss Ashe. Although not even her publisher thought they had merit."

"She sent them off to the publisher of her first novel?" Gabe asked.

"Woodhouse and Collins, yes. They didn't want them."

"What about other publishing houses? Did she try them?"

"I can't be entirely sure, but I imagine she did. No point letting them sit around in a drawer."

Gabe removed his notepad and pencil from his inside jacket pocket. "Do you know the names of the publishers she sent them to?"

"I'm afraid not. I suppose that's how they ended up with a bookbinder. Either someone from Woodhouse and Collins took them in, or one of the other publishers. Illegally, mind you. The unpublished manuscripts belonged to my wife and then me after her death. But why did the bookbinder still have them after all these years? Why didn't the publisher collect them when the bookbinder completed the job?" Mr. Moffat-Jones didn't seem to expect an answer. Like us, he was musing out loud, trying to solve the puzzle. "You say the bookbinder sold them recently?"

"To a collector of magical objects," Gabe said.

"I don't suppose you can give me his details after your investigation is complete. I'd like to make him an offer. I think Lucille, my eldest and Honoria's daughter, would like them as a memento of her mother."

"Of course," Gabe said. "What do you know about the magic paper?"

Mr. Moffat-Jones shook his head. "This is the first I've heard about magic paper. I suppose back then the magician papermaker kept his skill a secret out of fear of expulsion from his guild. Those days were not so long ago and yet we've come so far since then, fortunately."

"Can you recall where you purchased it?"

"Honoria took care of the household expenses, including purchasing paper. I never got involved in things like that."

Gabe and I rose and thanked him for his time.

"No, thank *you*." He heaved himself to his feet with the aid of his walking stick.

His wife rushed to his side and took his elbow to assist

him, but he shook her off. She stepped back, bowed her head, and clasped her hands in front of her.

"I'm rather pleased you've located some of Honoria's manuscripts," Mr. Moffat-Jones said as he showed us to the front door. "My daughter will be thrilled when she hears. She has so little to remember her mother by, and something as personal as her stories will be very special indeed."

We returned to the motorcar and reported back to Alex and Willie. Well, we reported to Alex. Willie was asleep in the back seat, her mouth open, a dribble of drool on her lower lip.

"What was she like?" Alex asked.

"Dead," Gabe said. "We spoke to Mr. Moffat-Jones. He claimed Honoria sent her manuscripts to publishers of children's' books. One of them must have realized they were written on magic paper and decided to get them bound."

"But why?" I asked. "If they didn't want to publish them, just send them back to Honoria."

Willie *humphed*, proving she was awake, although her eyes remained closed. "You're so naïve, Sylvia. Whoever took them to Littleproud to get them bound never intended to give them back to her. They planned to keep 'em, maybe sell them to a magic collector." She opened her eyes and sat up. "Paper with magic in it isn't so rare nowadays, but back then, when magicians were persecuted, it was."

"Whoever took them to Littleproud failed to collect them," Gabe said. "I doubt they simply forgot. There's only one other explanation I can think of as to why they never picked up the bound manuscripts."

I could only think of one other reason too. "Because they died."

# CHAPTER 8

The walls of the reception area in the office of Woodhouse and Collins were decorated with framed illustrations copied from the pages of their bestsellers. They didn't only publish children's books but had a stable of adult books, too. None of the photographs came from Honoria's one and only published work.

We waited in the comfortable room for Mr. Woodhouse to be free to meet with us. His assistant, Miss McCain, informed us rather curtly that he was very busy and could spare only a few minutes. "May I ask what this is regarding?"

Gabe explained the reason for our visit, including the theory that the murder was related to the untitled manuscripts written by Honoria Moffat-Jones which were sold by the victim shortly before his death. The assistant had a no-nonsense manner about her that seemed to appreciate his candor.

The wrinkles on her face did settle into a pattern of surprise, however. "Is Mr. Woodhouse a suspect?"

"No, nothing like that," Gabe assured her. "We simply

need to ask him a question about Honoria Moffat-Jones. Did you meet her?"

Her lips thinned. "How old do you think I am, young man?"

I bit my lip to contain my smile.

"It's a standard question," Gabe said smoothly.

"I've worked here twenty-two years, so no, I never knew her. Her book was published before my time at Woodhouse and Collins. Not that Mrs. Moffat-Jones would have come into the office. We published only the one book of hers and it was a low seller at the time. It wasn't until she died that the public became interested in it."

"Your knowledge is astounding considering you didn't work here then."

"I've made it my duty to learn everything about the business. Mr. Woodhouse appreciated my efforts. The former Mr. Woodhouse, I mean, not his son." She cast a disdainful glance at the closed door to the publisher's office.

Gabe frowned. "The current Mr. Woodhouse isn't the same one who published Honoria's book?"

"No. He handed over the reins to his son eighteen months ago. Sadly, he died last week after a long battle with illness."

I approached the desk. "What day did he die?"

She stiffened. "What an odd question."

"You don't remember?"

"Of course I do. It was six days ago. The funeral was on Tuesday. It was very well attended." Her gaze turned distant. "He would have liked that." She plucked out a handkerchief tucked into her sleeve and dabbed at her nose.

The murder also occurred six days ago. I wasn't sure if the death of the man who published Honoria Moffat-Jones's book on the same day as Mr. Littleproud's murder was significant, but it was certainly a striking coincidence.

"Did he ever mention Honoria Moffat-Jones to you?" Gabe asked.

She frowned. "Once, in passing. He said her book was a classic example of a sleeper."

"Sleeper?"

"A title that garners little attention or sales upon release but gathers momentum over time as people read it and talk about it. Her book was a case in point, although I'd argue that her death played a significant role in its later success. It was reported in all the newspapers at the time. The fact she was an author of a children's book gave the journalists an angle, as they call it."

"Did Mr. Woodhouse express regret that he never published any more of her stories?"

"Not to me. Indeed, he gave no indication that he was aware she'd written more manuscripts. It's likely he didn't have any idea."

"Does the company keep records of manuscript submissions?" I asked.

"Not unsolicited ones by unpublished authors. We get an inordinate number from every Arthur and Martha who think they have a novel in them." She rolled her eyes. "We can't possibly make a note of them all, let alone read them from start to finish."

"You don't even read them?"

"Our editors are far too busy reading manuscripts by authors we already publish, Miss Ashe. If an unsolicited work doesn't engage them by the end of the first page, there's no point reading further. It's unlikely to improve on page two or two hundred."

"What about submissions from authors already published by Woodhouse and Collins?" Gabe asked. "Are they recorded anywhere?"

"Each of our authors has a file." Her voice trailed off and her frown returned.

"Do you keep author files going back as far as Honoria Moffat-Jones's time?"

The office door suddenly opened and an elderly man with ink-stained fingers shuffled out, his head bowed. As he passed, I thought I saw a tear glisten on his cheek.

Miss McCain went after him, but he shook off her hand when she went to pat his shoulder. She returned to her desk, her lips pursed so tightly they were white. "Another good editor gone," she bit off.

"Why is that?" Gabe asked.

"Many of our long-term staff have been told to pack their things and not return. Mr. Woodhouse is undertaking some house cleaning now that his father has gone. Apparently the company needs to make some changes." She clicked her tongue. "This never would have happened in Mr. Woodhouse Senior's day. Profit over integrity, that's Mr. Woodhouse Junior's motto."

She invited us to follow her into her employer's office where a middle-aged man with long wisps of thin hair combed over the bald patch on his head sat behind an expansive desk. "Mr. Woodhouse, this is Mr. Glass and Miss Ashe. They work for Scotland Yard and are investigating the murder of a bookbinder. You may have read about—"

"Thank you, Miss McCain, that will be all." Mr. Woodhouse signaled for us to sit as Miss McCain closed the door. He screwed the lid onto his pen and set it down beside a folder. "How may I help you both?"

Gabe told him the same things he'd told Miss McCain, explaining why we needed to find out how Honoria Moffat-Jones's manuscripts ended up in Mr. Littleproud's possession. "Her husband informed us that she sent them here, but they were rejected by Woodhouse and Collins. Do you know anything about the stories?"

"No, nothing. Her book was published before my time. I didn't start working here until after university, in '97. How extraordinary that unpublished manuscripts from one of our authors wound up in a murder investigation decades later. Will Scotland Yard reveal that detail to the newspapers?"

I could practically see the pound signs in his eyes. Renewed attention could stimulate sales of her published book, just as it had done when she died.

"You clearly know of her," Gabe went on.

"Yes, of course. Her book did quite well for us after her death. If we'd known she'd written more stories, we would have snapped them up."

"According to Mr. Moffat-Jones your company did have that opportunity, but her manuscripts were rejected."

Mr. Woodhouse leaned back and clasped his hands over his stomach. "That would be because they were submitted when she was still alive." When neither of us responded, he added, "Before her published book became popular."

"Your assistant says your company keeps records of submissions from authors already in your stable."

He parted his thumbs before drawing them together again. "That's true."

"May we see Mrs. Moffat-Jones's file?"

"Of course." He rose and opened the door. "Miss McCain? Oh. She's not here. I'm sure she'll return in a moment." He turned back to us. "You say the manuscripts were printed on magic paper and bound by the murdered bookbinder, but you don't know who commissioned him. Have you considered that Mrs. Moffat-Jones took them herself? Perhaps her husband is wrong and she never did submit them to us. Perhaps she planned to bring them in after she bound them but died before she could collect them."

"Why would she bind them?"

"Perhaps she knew they'd be valuable one day. That would also explain why she wrote them on magic paper, to make them extra special after they became bestsellers. A collector's item, if you will."

"That might be a possibility, except Mrs. Moffat-Jones wasn't a bestseller before her death, as you pointed out."

Mr. Woodhouse sighed. "I suppose you're right. It doesn't make sense. Ah, Miss McCain, you've returned. Where did you go?"

She closed the file she'd been reading and handed it to him. "In the archives, looking for Honoria Moffat-Jones's file."

"I didn't ask you to retrieve it."

"I'm good at anticipating the needs of my employer." She gave him a tight smile, spun on her heel, and strode to her desk.

Mr. Woodhouse's nostrils flared as he opened the file. Inside were several pieces of paper, yellowed with age. He flipped through them. "The contract for her book...some correspondence between her and her editor..." He shook his head when he reached the end. "No notes about further submissions. Usually the editorial assistants write the details of submissions and file them with the author's other documents." He passed the file to Gabe to look through. "Nothing, I'm afraid. This proves she never submitted the manuscripts to us."

Gabe and I looked over the pages, but also found nothing of relevance. Gabe handed the file back to Mr. Woodhouse and thanked him.

"I hope I helped." Mr. Woodhouse smiled. "I do have one question of my own. Where are the bound manuscripts now?"

"I'm not at liberty to say." Gabe gave him a business card and asked him to telephone if he thought of anything. He also gave Miss McCain one.

She stared at it for some time before tucking it up her sleeve, along with her handkerchief.

\* \* \*

I RETURNED to the library to work while the others left to research London-based children's book publishers. The day passed quickly and I didn't realize how late it was when Daisy arrived. We took advantage of the longer, warmer days of late spring and went for a stroll after saying goodnight to Professor Nash.

London was busy at this time of day, with gentlemen who worked in the city heading home in motorcars or on buses, and shop assistants lowering shutters and locking doors. It was at such times that I wished I lived in the country. Although I'd only ever resided in cities and large towns, I'd never enjoyed the hustle and bustle of urban life. I'd heard things were different in the country, that life was slower, and part of me craved a sedate pace.

After my brother died, my mother wanted to move again. I'd broached the idea of living in a village but she wouldn't consider it. When she saw my disappointment, she took me in her arms and reminded me that the grass wasn't always greener on the other side. I'd snapped back that it would be greener in the country than the city.

Daisy would have agreed with my mother. Raised in the country, she found the city more to her liking. The energy of it appealed to her, the constant amusements around every corner, and the anonymity. She could get away with a lot more in London without it reaching her parents' ears.

She walked beside me, chatting away about everything and nothing. She didn't stop talking even when a telegraph messenger in a pillbox hat almost ran us over on his bicycle. The only time she paused was to intercept a costermonger's cart pulled by a tired nag, heading back to the stables at the end of a long day. She purchased two carrots from the bunch he'd not managed to sell to the cooks in his patch of the West End. It soon became evident why he couldn't sell them. They were as flexible as rubber hose.

Daisy fell silent again when we passed a soldier with his cap out on the edge of St. James's Park. The empty sleeve of his right arm was pinned to his jacket, and a scar ran from his right cheek to his chin. I dropped a few coins in his cap. He thanked me, keeping his scarred side averted, embarrassed. He reminded me of the men outside the Hobsons' factory, asking for compensation for the poorly made boots. Injured service men received a pension from the government, but everyone knew it wouldn't last, and some of these men might never find full employment again. They had a hard road ahead.

As did men who'd come home physically able but damaged in other ways. Former soldiers suffering severe shell shock were cared for in asylums, while those who could still function in society tried to rebuild their lives as best they could in a world that wasn't equipped to interact with them. There were men like Stanley Greville, too anxious to continue with his university education, and Huon Barratt, drowning his nightmares in alcohol and painkillers. Good men that could be lost forever.

As much as she liked talking, Daisy made a good listener too. I told her about the incident outside the Hobson and Son factory, as well as my concern for men like Stanley and Huon. "I wish I could help them, but I don't know what to say."

"Perhaps you don't have to say anything. Perhaps you just need to be prepared to listen when they're ready to talk. If they ever will be ready." She sighed heavily. "You and I are in unchartered territory, Sylvia."

"The whole nation is."

We strolled along the footpath in St. James's Park in silence. My mind drifted off to the investigation, and I thought Daisy had moved on from our conversation, too, but her next words proved she hadn't.

"Hope is important for those men. I do believe Huon still holds hope that he'll one day forget the horrors of war. I don't know Stanley Greville very well, but I think he must have some hope left too. Otherwise, why get out of bed in the morning? He hasn't given up, and nor has Huon."

I looped my arm through hers. "You're right. Hope is important to keeping mankind moving forward."

"Hopes and dreams," she said. "We all need dreams, don't you think? Something to strive for?"

"You're very wise today, Daisy."

"Yes, I know."

"Talking about dreams makes me think of Honoria Moffat-Jones, the author of the manuscripts at the center of our investigation. She held a dream of becoming a published children's book author and, while she did achieve that dream on a modest scale before she died, I feel a sense of disappointment that she didn't become famous until after her death. She never got to enjoy her popularity."

Daisy wasn't listening to me, however. She suddenly gasped and rounded on me. "I should become an author!'

I frowned. "I thought you were going to be an actress."

"I've decided it's not for me."

"Why not?"

"There's no point in being an actress unless you become a

star, and the only way to become a star in the moving pictures is to be cast in the good roles. The good roles go to the girls who are *very* friendly with the producers and directors, if you understand my meaning."

"Loud and clear."

"I don't mind flirting with them, but I draw the line there. I know a lot of girls are prepared to go the extra mile, but I'm not. I may be old fashioned, but I want to be in love with the fellow. And everyone knows I only fall in love with handsome men. The producers and directors I've met are all old and dreadfully superficial. I couldn't possibly fall in love with a man over thirty-five, let alone one who thinks I need to be blonder." She self-consciously touched the strawberry blonde hair at the nape of her neck.

I hugged her arm. "You'll find someone who loves you and your hair just as it is one day."

"I hope you're right."

"Perhaps you've already met him."

"Perhaps I have. Do you think I should chase after the costermonger and ask him to meet me for coffee?"

We both burst out laughing.

\* \* \*

CYCLOPS TELEPHONED Gabe and Alex the following morning and suggested they call on a chemist in Paternoster Row. The chemist thought he might have seen something relevant in the days leading up to Mr. Littleproud's murder. Gabe telephoned me and asked if I wanted to join them. I jumped at the opportunity.

"Cyclops also told us he's still looking into the publishing houses," Gabe said over the rumble of the Vauxhall Prince Henry's engine. He and Alex had come without Willie. She hadn't returned home after meeting an old friend at a dance hall the night before.

"Some of the publishing companies have closed down," Alex added. "He's having trouble locating employees who might remember Honoria Moffat-Jones's manuscripts."

So much time had passed, it seemed like an insurmountable task. We couldn't rely on that angle to give us a new lead. Hopefully the witness had something interesting to report.

Boots chemist shop occupied the corner opposite Mr. Littleproud's workshop. The busy pharmacy smelled delightfully floral thanks to the perfumery department situated near the entrance. The smell became more medicinal the further we moved inside.

The manager asked us to join him on the pavement outside where we could see Mr. Littleproud's workshop. He apologized, in case what he had to say was irrelevant. "I may be taking up your time for nothing."

"Sometimes what we think is irrelevant turns out to be the most helpful clue," Gabe assured him.

The manager took encouragement from the words. "Boots is open twenty-four hours, so staff come and go. I left early on the night the bookbinder was murdered, so didn't think I had anything to offer the police when they questioned us. However, yesterday I was discussing the murder with a customer and mentioned that I worked late on the nights leading up to the murder, but not on the night of the murder itself. She asked if I'd noticed anything unusual on those nights, and that got me thinking. I *had* seen someone in the vicinity watching the bookbinder's shop. Twice, in fact." He pointed at a lamppost a few doors down from where we stood. "He leaned against that."

"When would that have been?" Gabe asked.

"The two nights before the murder, at ten. That's when my

shift ended. I noticed him because there are very few people around at that time, and he was the size of a mountain. I avoided going near him. I thought he was just lounging about, waiting for someone. It's not until yesterday that I realized he might have been watching the bookbinder's shop."

"Can you describe him?"

"I only saw his face in profile. He was not as tall as either of you gentlemen, but he was thickset. He wore a cap and a woolen coat although it wasn't a cold night. The collar was up, but I could just make out a scar on his cheek." He tapped his left cheek. "When he lit a cigarette, I noticed he only wore one glove, which I thought odd."

A flicker of recognition passed across Alex's face. "Do you know how long he was there?"

"No, sorry. I avoided him and went on my way."

We thanked him then returned to the Vauxhall parked down the street.

"I think I know who it is from my days at the Bow Street station," Alex said. "It sounds like a thug named Billy Burgess."

He used to be in the police force before the war, but hadn't returned to that profession afterwards. Like Gabe, war had changed him. According to Gabe, Alex used to laugh a lot. He'd been carefree, happy, and not very keen to settle down. But the month he'd spent in hospital convalescing after having shrapnel removed from his back changed him. He'd become serious, broody. War turned him into a very different version of himself. The former version was more like Daisy, flirtatious and sunny. Even though I'd only come to know him recently, I suspected both versions of Alexander Bailey would have liked her.

"Billy Burgess always wore just one glove. His left hand got burned as a child so he covered it," he went on. "The facial scar is new."

"Perhaps he got it in the war," Gabe said.

"I doubt he served. Not because he was a conscientious objector—Burgess has no conscience. He would have used his hand as an excuse not to get involved in a conflict that held no personal gain for himself. He was a selfish, mindless brute. We arrested him three or four times, at least. He was convicted just the once. He got off the other charges thanks to a good lawyer."

"What were his crimes?" Gabe asked.

"Assault. He was the thug of choice for a local money lender by the name of Thurlow."

"That explains the good lawyer."

"Thurlow could never be definitively tied to any crime, but he was well known at Bow Street, and probably Scotland Yard, too. My father will want to know about this development."

I looked across the road at Mr. Littleproud's workshop. It was locked, the shutters drawn, but no constable stood at the door anymore. "Do you think Billy Burgess was watching the shop because Littleproud owed Thurlow money?"

Both men nodded.

"But why simply watch it? Why not just confront him and make him pay up?"

"Perhaps Thurlow posted Burgess there merely as a warning," Gabe said. "Burgess made himself visible to Littleproud, making Littleproud nervous enough to pay Thurlow back what he owed."

"Except he didn't pay," Alex said. "Perhaps Burgess did confront him. He roughed Littleproud up, hoping to shake the money out of him. It fits with Burgess's modus operandi."

"But this time, Littleproud's heart gave out and he died," Gabe added darkly.

It made sense. It also meant the murder had nothing to do

with Honoria's manuscripts and their magic paper. He'd been killed because he owed Thurlow money.

Gabe fished a key out of his pocket. "I want to take another look inside the workshop."

I wasn't sure what we'd find now. Alex and the constable hadn't come across anything relevant while they put the shop back to rights. On the other hand, they hadn't known about the money lender's thug.

Given the illegal nature of Thurlow's operation, it was unlikely Littleproud kept details of their transactions in his official accounts. We searched in the more unlikely places instead. Taped to the underside of tables, inside false drawer bottoms, between book pages, and under loose floorboards. After two hours, we gave up. If there was evidence he owed money to Thurlow, it wasn't here.

The search hadn't been a complete waste, however. It had given me time to think. We'd assumed the untitled books weren't linked to Thurlow, but it was possible the money lender had seen them listed in the auction house's catalog and wanted them as collateral against Littleproud's loan.

I told Gabe and Alex my theory as we crossed the road to the motorcar. "Perhaps he planned to hold the books until Littleproud repaid him. Except he found out about the books too late, and Littleproud had already sold them to Lady Stanhope. Before he could reveal the buyer's name, he died, so Burgess searched the premises for the books, coming up empty handed."

Gabe held the Vauxhall's rear door open for me. "It explains the timing." He took his place behind the wheel and pulled the ignition switch. As Alex cranked the engine, Gabe turned to face me. "You're an excellent detective."

"I don't like interviewing witnesses."

"That'll become more natural with experience."

It sounded like he intended to continue this arrangement

for future investigations. I wasn't sure how that would be possible. Not every case would have a connection to me.

Receiving praise from a man like Gabe led to the inevitable blush creeping across my face. I dipped my head and brushed dust off my skirt that I hadn't noticed was there after our search of the workshop.

"Sylvia—" Gabe cleared his throat as Alex slipped into the passenger seat.

Alex arched his brows at his friend. "Go on."

"Nothing. We were just...never mind." Gabe glanced over his shoulder to check for a gap in the traffic.

Alex smiled at his friend, even though he couldn't see it. "Where are we going?"

Gabe faced the front again. "Nowhere. I don't know. Have you got a plan?"

"I do. I remember where Billy Burgess lives. We should pay him a visit."

Gabe glanced at me.

"I'll stay in the motorcar," I assured him.

Alex directed Gabe to a street in the East End that was surprisingly wide for the rundown slum. Featureless tenement houses on both sides rose three stories high, blocking out all but a narrow strip of sunlight down the middle. Children played on cobblestones grooved by centuries of carriage wheels, and washing flapped on lines strung between the buildings high above their heads.

They came running upon seeing the flashy Vauxhall pull up, their dirt or chalk-stained fingers touching the clotted cream paintwork. Gabe and Alex flipped them coins and asked where they could find Billy Burgess. Some of the children pointed to two boys aged about seven and five. The younger one clutched a wooden toy lorry to his chest as if worried the bigger boys would try to take it from him. Its bright red paintwork gleamed even in the shadows.

"Is Billy Burgess your father?" Gabe asked the elder of the two boys.

The boy folded his arms over his chest. "I ain't telling you. You're pigs."

A dark-haired girl who'd been playing hopscotch with other girls stamped her hands on her hips. "You're an idiot, Wally. Girls don't work for the police." She thrust her chin at me. I wasn't sure if her petulance was directed at me or the police for their narrow employment policy.

Wally accepted her opinion with a shrug and pointed to a nearby door. "We live in there. Mum's working. She takes in sewing for toffs."

"And your father?"

The boy shrugged while his younger brother stared up at the men as if he'd never seen anyone like them.

Gabe approached the building, but Alex hung back. "Shouldn't you older children be in school?" he asked.

"It's mid-term holidays," the dark-haired girl said with a roll of her eyes.

Gabe knocked on the door and a few minutes later, a woman opened it. She glanced past them to the children, still inspecting the motorcar. Satisfied they were all right, she folded her arms in a mirror image of her eldest son, as she listened to Gabe. It soon became clear from where I sat that she wasn't going to answer his questions.

Billy Burgess's eldest son opened the front driver's door and slid behind the wheel. Several other boys, awed by his audacity, crowded around. I opened my door and invited the younger brother to sit beside me. Without letting go of the lorry, he climbed inside.

"That's a nice toy," I said. "Is it new?"

The boy clutched the lorry to his chest and nodded.

"Did your father buy it for you?"

Another nod. The boys in front weren't listening. They

were too intent on fighting over who should sit in the driver's seat next, while the eldest Burgess boy pushed them back with one hand and pretended to steer the motor with the other. I kept one eye on the brake lever to ensure they didn't push it into the off position.

"Did he buy something for your brother, too?" I asked.

The younger boy nodded again. "He got a train set. A real good one. Wally doesn't play with it out here in case it gets wrecked. And Pa gave Mum a gold ring!'

"Gold? How lovely. Your father is a very generous man."

"And he said he'll give her more. And he said he'd give us more, too. Wally's getting a new ball when Pa gets back. I want a puppy, but Mum said no, so Pa will bring me a toy dog instead."

"How exciting. And when will your Pa come home with your new toy dog?"

The boy shrugged. "Mum said we're lucky to have Pa as our Pa. The others don't have a Pa who brings them toys. Some don't have a Pa at all."

"Do you know where he is now?"

"Gone, but Mum said he'll come back when the pigs stop looking for him. He has to come back because I want my toy dog."

I smiled. "I'm sure he'll be home soon."

"Oi!" The boys' mother strode up to the Vauxhall and stabbed her finger at each of her sons. "Get out! Both of you, inside now!"

The younger boy scrambled out of the motorcar and raced home, the red lorry safe in his tight grip. Wally took a little longer, reluctantly vacating the driver's seat as one of the other boys took a turn. His mother grabbed his arm and marched him to the front door, shooting a glare at Gabe and Alex as she passed.

They supervised the future generation of British motor

racing for a few minutes before ordering them out and taking their places. The boys and girls chased us to the end of the street where Gabe accelerated to join the traffic.

"Any other ideas?" he asked Alex.

"We could make inquiries at the local pubs."

"I'll ask Murray to do it."

The task was right up the footman's alley. As a trained policeman, he had all the necessary skills. He would also enjoy it. Murray didn't have the right attitude for service, but the Metropolitan Police wouldn't re-employ him after he lost his foot and lower leg in the war. He needed work and Gabe's household had a vacancy, so he'd grudgingly taken the position as footman. Helping investigate from time to time kept his policing skills from going rusty, and as a former colleague of Alex's, Gabe knew he could trust him.

"Not that it'll do much good." Alex's mutter was barely audible over the engine. "Billy Burgess must have suspected we'd be looking for him in connection to the murder and disappeared."

Both men assumed the lead had come to an end. I was a little more positive, however. "Burgess will be back. Perhaps not in a day or two, but he'll return to his family shortly."

Alex swiveled in his seat to look at me. "What makes you say that?"

"His son. Despite being a thug, Billy Burgess is a good father who seems to have come into money recently. He promised his sons toys upon his return. A good father doesn't do that if he's leaving forever."

"That's true *if* he disappeared voluntarily. If Thurlow thought he was a liability he could have *made* him disappear—fatally."

"Oh. I hadn't thought of that."

The notion of those boys growing up without a father silenced me for the rest of the journey. Burgess may be a local rough, but he wasn't all bad. I found myself hoping he was still alive, and merely in temporary hiding until this all blew over.

The problem was, if he had something to do with Littleproud's murder, it wouldn't blow over until he was caught by the police or, as Alex put it, Thurlow made him disappear. It wasn't looking good for Billy Burgess.

# CHAPTER 9

We returned to the library to reassess the investigation and plan our next moves. Gabe telephoned his house to give instructions to Murray and invite Willie to join us. We were going to need her help. Gabe and Alex had decided to observe Thurlow the money lender.

When we heard the front door open we thought it was her. Unfortunately, it was Lady Stanhope. There was a collective groan when Professor Nash escorted her upstairs to the first floor reading nook where we sat.

"I'll fetch the tea," Professor Nash said.

She waved a hand in his general direction, dismissing him.

I rose and offered to assist him, but he declined. "I'm sure Lady Stanhope would like to speak to you about her books," he said.

I wasn't so sure she even knew I was in the room.

She gazed up at the mezzanine walkway hugging the bookshelves above our heads, and the arched window spanning the full height of the room. Light streamed through and shone on the golden accents of the ornate ceiling. "This space reminds me of our library at the country house." She inspected the globe on the desk before sitting on one of the chocolate brown armchairs. "It's my husband's domain, of course. I never venture into it. The decoration is not to my taste but he refuses to change it." She indicated the globe. "Was that made by a mapmaker magician?"

"I don't know," Gabe said. "Are you here about the murder? I'm afraid we can't divulge details about an ongoing investigation."

"I don't care about that. Although I do care about my untitled book." She nodded at Honoria's bound manuscript in my lap. It was the closest she'd come to acknowledging my presence. "May I have it back?"

"We'd like to keep it for the duration of the investigation."

"How long will that be?"

"I'm afraid I can't answer that."

"Mr. Glass, as much as I would like to help the police find the bookbinder's murderer, I would like even more to have my book back. It belongs with me, in my collection, along with the other books I purchased. Need I remind you I paid a lot of money for them?"

"The books are evidence. We need to hold onto at least one for the time being. We'll take good care of it."

"I see." Lady Stanhope didn't look as irritated as I thought she might. Her hands, gloved in black lace, smoothed her black silk and lace skirt. "Do you have the time, Mr. Glass?"

He glanced at a clock on one of the bookshelves. She was perfectly capable of seeing it herself from where she sat. "You always ask me the time. Is there a reason?"

Her hands stilled. She laughed softly. "Am I that obvious? I hoped to see you look at your watch again, but instead you chose the clock. Is it one of your mother's?"

"Probably."

"Is it for sale?"

"Lady Stanhope, we've been through this." His tone was politely chiding, but the edge of steel was there if one was tuned into his voice. "My mother's timepieces are not for sale."

"What if I offer you that book in exchange for one? I don't mean for a few more days, I mean forever. You can keep it here in the library, if you like, or sell it. I don't mind. I have four others at home."

"Very generous of you," Alex said with a sardonic smile.

"Mr. Glass?"

"My mother's things are not for sale or exchange." Gabe indicated the book in my lap. "You can have it back after the investigation is finished. It's evidence and should remain in police custody for the duration. You're lucky we're holding onto just one. My superiors wanted us to hold all five, but I talked them down to one."

Whether she believed him or not, it was hard to tell. She simply continued to smile that false smile of hers. "If not one of Lady Rycroft's watches, what about one of yours?"

Gabe had been matching her smile with his own, but it now slipped off. "Pardon?"

"Not your pocket watch you wear all the time, of course. I know it has sentimental value. But what about another? You would have worn a wristwatch when you served. Will you exchange that for the book?"

"No."

"Another, then? Something with fewer memories, that you can live without? It must be something you've worked on, though. Something you've pulled apart and put back together with your own hands."

Gabe frowned. "I don't understand. I'm not a watchmaker magician. Why do you want something of mine? It won't contain magic."

Her lips curved with a knowing smile.

A sense of dread echoed within me. Did she know? She couldn't possibly. So few people knew about Gabe's ability, all of them trustworthy. She must suspect, however, just like the journalists and Mr. Jakes...and the kidnapper.

Gabe shook his head. "I'm not a magician, Lady Stanhope. I assure you."

"Then why not exchange one of your old timepieces for the book? A magical item for a non-magical one...it's more than fair."

Her insistence didn't make sense, until I remembered that she liked to purchase items from magicians before they were even aware of their skill. It allowed her to buy them cheaply. I suspected the real value to her was in being the one to boast about discovering a new magician. It's what she'd done with the artist magician during the Royal Academy's exhibition. That fellow now felt indebted to her for informing him of his magical abilities and thereby increasing the value of his paintings. By all accounts, Lady Stanhope made sure everyone knew she'd discovered him and insisted he accompany her to parties to talk about her influence on his career.

I thrust the book at her. "Take it. We no longer need it."

"Sylvia," Gabe said. "Not yet."

I placed it on her lap. Disappointment weighed heavily as I stepped back. It might be the last time I saw it.

Lady Stanhope opened the book to the first page then flipped to the end. "Perhaps we can make an exchange another time, Mr. Glass. When you're alone." She rose. "Did you discover who made the paper?"

"Why?" Alex asked. "So you can find out if he knows he's a magician, and if he doesn't, you can buy up all his stock before informing him?"

She sniffed. I thought she wouldn't deign to answer him, but she proved me wrong. "Of course not. The man who made this paper has probably passed away. The bookbinder told me the books came into his possession years ago." She inspected the cover, caressing the green leather with the palm of her hand. "I wonder if he had children."

No one responded. From our own research, we'd discovered a manufacturer of paper in London operated by the Peterson siblings, both paper magicians. I'd forgotten about them. We'd been too busy to return to their factory after not finding them there on our first visit. Without the book, we could no longer ask them to touch the pages and feel if they held paper magic.

Oh dear. No wonder Gabe hadn't wanted to give it back to Lady Stanhope. By doing so, I'd just hindered the investigation.

I eyed the book in Lady Stanhope's hand. Perhaps if I begged...

"Anyone home?" came Willie's shout from downstairs. A moment later she appeared at the top of the staircase with Daisy. She took one look at Lady Stanhope, screwed up her nose, and said, "What are you doing here?"

"Put away your pistols, Lady Farnsworth, I was just leaving."

Willie indicated the way to the stairs with an exaggerated sweep of her hand. As Lady Stanhope passed, she frowned. "Why did you give her back the book? We might need it."

I didn't admit that it was my fault. I felt guilty enough; I didn't need one of Willie's lectures as well.

Daisy glided up to me with the elegance of a swan and planted a kiss on my cheek. "All this fuss over magician made paper. Perhaps I should buy a few pages for my novel. It might make the writing process easier."

"I don't think that's how writing novels works," I said wryly.

"Paper infused with a spell is expensive," Gabe said with

a nod in the direction Lady Stanhope had gone with the book. "Magician made without a spell is more affordable."

Alex grunted. "She can afford it." He frowned at Daisy. "What novel?"

Willie threw herself onto the empty sofa, stretching out her legs across the seat. "She's writing a romantic story about a couple lost in the Arabian desert. They start out hating each other and end up falling in love."

Alex laughed. "Have you ever been to the Arabian desert, Daisy?"

She bristled. "No. I haven't been in love either, but that won't stop me using my imagination to write the story. That's what writers do." She tapped her forehead. "They make it up."

She went to help Professor Nash as he arrived carrying a tray with tea things. He seemed unsurprised that Lady Stanhope had already left, and he greeted the new arrivals with enthusiasm. He passed the tray to Daisy and went to fetch more teacups from his kitchen.

Gabe sliced up the cake while Daisy poured. "I thought you were going to be an actress."

"Didn't Sylvia tell you I've changed my mind? I thought you two were inseparable these days."

"That doesn't mean they talk about *you*," Alex said.

She deliberately spilled tea over the side of the teacup, filling the saucer. She handed it to him with a tight smile. "Don't drop any on the carpet."

"Inseparable?" Willie glared at Gabe as he tried to pass her a plate.

"Because of the investigation," he assured her with a pointed nod at the plate he still held.

She shifted her glare to me then back again before accepting the plate. "You left without me this morning."

"You weren't there. The investigation can't be delayed because you had a liaison with an old flame."

"It wasn't an old flame," she mumbled into the teacup. "It was his son."

Alex choked on his tea. "How old is he?"

"Old enough."

"But—"

"Leave her alone," Daisy snapped. She turned to Willie and saluted her with her teacup. "Good for you. I hope I have as much fun when I'm your age."

Alex looked from one to the other. "If I mentioned your age, you'd scold me, but when she does it, you accept it with a smile."

"It's all in the tone and intention," Daisy said with a haughty jut of her chin. "Isn't that right, Willie?"

"You bet it is, Daisy. You boys should take a leaf out of her book. You too, Sylvia."

I bristled. "I've never mentioned your age."

Willie merely *humphed*. "So how're you going to get the Petersons to verify if the paper in those books contains magic if you don't have a book to show them?"

I nibbled my slice of lemon cake, regretting my hasty act. If I'd not said anything, Gabe might have been able to convince Lady Stanhope to leave it with us without any conditions attached. He was a master at the art of persuasion.

"We're fairly certain the book contains paper that has had a spell cast on it," he said. "We know it's definitely not the leather cover, and considering silver is rare, it's unlikely to be that."

"Fairly certain?" Willie shook her head. "That ain't good enough and you know it, Gabe. Besides, if John Folgate made the silver then it's likely the corner protectors contain magic."

I leaned back with a sigh. She was right. We needed to get the book back from Lady Stanhope. I just wish I knew how.

Willie had an idea. Explaining it required setting down her teacup and saucer and putting up her hands in defense. "Before you say no, hear me out."

"No," both Alex and Gabe said together.

Professor Nash returned with the extra cups. He peered over his spectacles at us as he set them on the table. "What have I missed?"

Daisy picked up the teapot and poured. "Lady Stanhope won't loan her new books to anyone, and they need to show one to a paper magician to find out if it holds magic. Willie has thought of a way to get one back, but the men think her plan won't work without even listening to it." She passed a cup to Gabe but addressed Alex. "I think it's sexist to automatically assume a woman can't come up with a good plan."

Alex put his cup in the saucer with a loud *clank*. "Let me ask you a moral question, Daisy. What do you think about theft?"

"It's illegal." She gasped. "Willie? You were going to suggest *stealing* one of the books?"

Willie lifted a shoulder in a shrug as she sipped.

"How?"

"The usual way," Alex said. "Breaking and entering."

"Willie?"

Willie nodded. "He's right."

Gabe showed no surprise. "Let's make one thing clear, Willie. You are *not* breaking into Lady Stanhope's house."

"Why not? I'm good at it."

Daisy gasped again. "You've done it before?"

"'Course. I'm an expert. Never once been caught."

Alex snorted. "You have, you've just never been charged. It was convenient having a husband who was a detective inspector. Sometimes I think you just married him so he could keep you out of prison."

"That ain't true. I loved Jasper. My first husband," Willie

C.J. ARCHER

told Daisy and me. "He was a fine man. Real smart, and kind too. Don't know what he saw in me."

Alex chuckled into his teacup.

Gabe didn't find anything about the conversation amusing. "You are not breaking into anyone's house, Willie. Just because you did it a couple of times years ago does not mean it was a good idea then, and it's definitely not a good idea now." He put up his finger to ward off her protests. "That has nothing to do with your ability or age, and everything to do with it being illegal."

"First of all, I wouldn't get caught. Second, if I did, Lady Stanhope wouldn't call the police. She wants you to like her, and having your favorite cousin arrested ain't no way to go about making friends. Third, if she did press charges, Cyclops would get me off."

"You can't ask him to jeopardize his career for you."

"I wouldn't jeopardize it. They love him at Scotland Yard. He's got the commissioner eating out of his hand."

I listened to their banter but took no part in it. The cogs in my mind started to turn, and by the time Willie had finished explaining the reasons why we should steal back the book, I'd made up my mind.

I'd go with her. It was my fault the book was back in Lady Stanhope's possession, after all.

"You can't tell me what to do," Willie said. "I'm older than both of you so you got to respect me."

"Ha!" Alex scoffed. "So you mention your age when it's convenient for you."

Before she could dig herself into a hole that resulted in Gabe and Alex keeping a close eye on her overnight, I winked at her. She closed her mouth and blinked rapidly at me.

Time to change the subject. "Thurlow the money lender," I said. "We need to find him. Alex, you say you don't know where he lives."

He dusted cake crumbs off his fingers onto the plate and set it down on the table. "I telephoned my father before, and he says they don't have an address for him. He also said that Thurlow is trying to become legitimate. Or at least *appear* as though he's turning legitimate. He's a licensed bookmaker."

Willie snorted. "A legitimate bookie? Is your father becoming stupid as well as fat?"

"Why can't a bookmaker be legitimate?" Daisy asked. "I saw them all the time when I went to the country races with my family. Surely if they were operating illegally, they wouldn't be allowed on the premises."

"Many have illegal side operations," Gabe told her. "They run a legitimate book at the race meeting and either have an illegitimate one off-site or a money lending service, like Thurlow. Without catching them in the act, the police can do nothing about it. It's been a problem for years."

Daisy looked a little dumbstruck by the news. "I laid my own bets when I was old enough to go to the races with my parents. My father used to give me a little money to place on a horse. The bookies were always nice to me. One even gave me a sweet."

"Your naivety is charming," Willie said with a heavy dose of sarcasm. "Don't you agree, Alex?"

Alex gave her an unreadable glare.

"The Epsom Derby is tomorrow," she went on. "Real big occasion it is, and it's popular with toffs. There'll be plenty of money for the bookies."

Gabe nodded. "We'll go and watch Thurlow. Just the three of us. Sorry, Sylvia, but Thurlow might be dangerous. He'll certainly be unpredictable and clever. He has to be to have gone this long without being arrested." He gave me an apologetic smile.

I smiled back and told him it was all right. And it was. I was already planning to do one thing he wouldn't approve of in the next twenty-four hours. I had no intention of doing two.

They discussed how to go about observing Thurlow unobtrusively. Given the race meeting was a key one on the social calendar, they decided the best way to blend in was to dress in formal attire.

Willie refused to wear a dress, however. "The last time I wore one, it almost killed me." Not even Gabe or Alex knew the story behind that statement, but she wouldn't elaborate. "I'll wear a tailcoat and trousers."

It remained to be seen if they'd let her in.

I needed to get Willie on her own before they left, but it was she who sought me out after I emerged from the privy in Professor Nash's flat. She caught my arm and pulled me into one of the aisles between the bookshelves.

"Why'd you wink at me?" she hissed.

I glanced along the aisle to make sure no one was nearby. "I want to come with you tonight."

"Where?"

"To Lady Stanhope's. You are still planning to break in and steal back the book, aren't you?"

"I don't need help. I can do it alone."

"Don't you need someone to keep watch? I could alert you to anyone approaching."

It must have been on her mind, because she didn't immediately dismiss the idea. "Gabe won't like it."

"Don't tell him."

Her gaze narrowed. "I don't like lying to him."

"I don't like it either. But it's my fault the book is in her possession. I want to make amends for my mistake."

She ran her thumb over her lower lip as she considered my proposal. "All right, you can come. But you've got to do as I say. Understood?"

I nodded. "How will we get in?"

We both turned as Gabe called our names, looking for us.

Willie lowered her voice. "Leave the details up to me. Meet me outside your boarding house at three. Wear black." She left me between the stacks and cheerfully greeted Gabe.

How could she be so calm? My heart beat with the chaotic rhythm of a drum in a jazz band. I drew in a deep breath and let it out slowly in an attempt to compose myself before joining Gabe and the others. As Willie said, he wouldn't like me breaking into Lady Stanhope's house.

That's why I had no intention of him finding out.

# CHAPTER 10

$\mathcal{J}$'d never known London to be so quiet and empty. The rumble of the Vauxhall Prince Henry's engine was loud in the eerie silence of my street. I was sure it would wake my landlady up and she'd order me back inside. Fortunately, the lights in my building remained off, the door locked. I tucked the front door key into my pocket for later.

The closer we got to Mayfair, the more motorcars we passed. Willie's driving was as erratic late at night as it was during the day, perhaps more so since the lack of traffic meant she could go faster. I had to grab hold of the door as we turned corners or I would have slid all over the seat. The occasional drunken youth staggered along the pavement, returning home to his parents' house after a night out with chums. That would have been Gabe and Alex before the war, by all accounts.

Willie parked around the corner from Lady Stanhope's place and we walked the rest of the way. "That the only black outfit you could find?" she asked as we passed beneath a streetlamp.

I looked down at my plain cotton dress. "I wanted to wear

trousers but didn't know who to borrow them from without giving away too much. What's wrong with this?" I had a sudden image of us scaling drainpipes and climbing through windows. It was so absurd that I giggled.

My laughter quickly vanished as I realized that could be precisely what Willie had in mind.

"Skirts get tangled around your legs when you run," she said.

"I'll lift my skirt if I have to."

"If you fall behind, I ain't waiting for you. Just return home. Got that?"

"I understand. But what if I'm caught?"

"Use your knife to cut them."

"I don't have a knife."

She swore under her breath as she removed a small knife from her pocket. As she flipped back her jacket, I noticed the gun in its holster, strapped around her waist.

I held the knife gingerly between thumb and forefinger. "I don't want to cut anyone."

"Then don't get caught."

"Will you use your gun if you have to?"

I took the glare she gave me to mean I was a fool for thinking she'd allow herself to be caught.

We observed the townhouse for a few minutes from the opposite side of the street. All seemed quiet inside. The lights were off, the curtains drawn.

We crossed the street and Willie handed me the lantern she'd been carrying. Instead of trying the front door or windows, she headed down the steps behind the iron fence to the basement service door. She pulled two slender sticks out of her pocket and bent to the lock. It clicked open moments later.

She put a finger to her lips to silence me and entered the corridor. We passed the kitchen and other service rooms. In two hours, the lowest maid would be beginning her day's work, but now it was as silent as the grave. The servants would all be asleep on the top floor, Lord and Lady Stanhope on the floor below them, still well above our heads.

Willie took back the lantern and led the way up the narrow flight of stairs. We emerged on the first floor and headed towards the front of the house. I knew from a previous visit that Lady Stanhope kept her magical possessions in glass cabinets in the drawing room, and given most Mayfair townhouses had the same layout, the drawing room was easy to find, even though I came from the service stairs this time.

Willie signaled for me to stand by the door and keep watch while she searched the cabinets. After a few minutes, I peeked inside and saw her on her knees, picking the lock on one of the cabinets, the lantern on a table next to her.

A floorboard creaked overhead. Willie stopped. We both looked up.

All fell silent again and Willie returned to her task.

My eyes had adjusted to the darkness so I could just make out the main staircase and the narrow passageway beyond where a panel in the wall led to the hidden service stairs. I thought I heard another floorboard creak, but if I had, it was somewhere distant in the house.

Willie rejoined me and handed me one of Honoria Moffat-Jones's untitled books. I folded it against my chest and breathed a deep sigh. Now all we had to do was get out without being seen.

She opened the wall panel to the service stairs but suddenly stopped. Light footsteps sounded on the stairs above. More than one set. She closed the door and signaled for me to hide. I crouched behind a tall vase, trying to make myself as small as possible. Willie extinguished the lantern and flattened herself against the wall. It didn't seem like a very good hiding place to me, but at least she was making an attempt. It was better than confronting the occupant with her gun drawn.

The footsteps passed us on the other side of the wall then receded. Whoever it was, they'd been heading down. We also needed to go downstairs to get out. I strained to hear if the front door opened and closed, but the house was once again silent.

Willie signaled to me then opened the service door, hidden in the wall paneling. I caught her arm and shook my head. It was too dangerous to continue when one or more people were down there.

"We should wait until they return upstairs," I whispered.

"What if they don't? What if that was a maid starting work early? We've got to take our chance now." She plunged into the darkness before I could stop her.

It was truly dark on the back stairs. I couldn't see a thing in front of me. When Willie's hand reached out and touched me, my heart leapt into my throat.

Her warm breath brushed my ear. "Hold on to my shoulder with one hand so you don't bump into me. I'll hold the rail."

We descended the stairs carefully. I felt for the edge of each step with the toe of my shoe before stepping down. We'd just set foot in the basement service area when we heard laughter. It was a woman and a man, and it came from the kitchen. Light streamed through the doorway into the corridor, making it possible for us to see our way to the front door. But we had to pass the kitchen first.

I caught Willie's hand. If I hadn't, she would have continued on. I shook my head. She nodded and jerked her head towards the front door. She wanted to keep moving.

It was madness. We'd be caught. We had to hide and wait until the couple left. Going by the moans coming from the kitchen, they weren't planning on staying down here the rest of the night. They'd probably just come down for a private liaison and would return to their respective rooms after they finished.

"Best to go now while they're occupied," Willie whispered.

I wasn't so sure, but she crept forward before I could stop her. I followed until she reached the doorway. The amorous sounds of the couple became louder.

I held my breath as Willie peered around the corner. She turned back to me with a smirk. She mouthed 'Lady Stanhope' and gestured a crude signal with her free hand and tongue. Thankfully it was too dark for her to see my blush.

She quietly scampered past the open doorway then waited for me on the other side. But I couldn't move. My feet felt like lead. I wasn't as experienced at this as Willie and could never be as silent. Surely they'd hear my footsteps or see me.

She angrily signaled for me to hurry before moving on without waiting. She would leave me behind if she had to.

I gathered my courage and peered around the corner. Lady Stanhope sat on the edge of the table, a bowl of peaches beside her. Her nightdress was bunched up on her thighs and her head thrown back in ecstasy. A blond man crouched before her. I couldn't see his face, but I knew a youthful head of hair when I saw it. Her husband was neither youthful nor blond.

I raced past the doorway on my toes and followed Willie.

We took the stairs two at a time. My skirt tangled around my ankles and with only one free hand, I couldn't lift it away properly. It slowed me down, but I didn't stop running until I reached the motorcar. I leaned back against it, breathing hard, clutching the book against my chest. A chest that suddenly felt tight, as if a rope had been tied around my heart and someone pulled the ends, squeezing the air out of me.

Willie went to unlock the passenger door but noticed my shallow breathing. She placed a hand on the back of my neck, forcing me to bend forward. "Take deep breaths. It'll pass."

I was relieved to see she was right and my breathing soon returned to normal. She unlocked the door and removed the crank handle from the floor.

"Do you know how to start the motor?" she asked.

I climbed into the driver's seat while she cranked the engine. Once it roared to life, I slid across to the passenger side and she replaced me behind the wheel.

She sped off and let out a *whoop*. "Wait until I tell Alex what we saw in the kitchen!"

"You can't tell him! He'll tell Gabe."

"They're going to find out." She tapped the book on my lap. "Otherwise how do we explain that?"

She had a point. I felt a little stupid for not considering it. I'd left all the planning up to her so I hadn't used my own brain to think through the consequences. To be honest, I wasn't sure I'd been capable of clear fore-thought. Like my feet outside the kitchen door, my mind had been frozen ever since Willie agreed that I could join her tonight.

"Don't worry," she said, grinning. "I'll keep your name out of it." She *whooped* again and thumped her hand on the steering wheel. "That was fun."

"Fun is not the word I'd use. Terrifying is more like it."

"Aw, come on now. Don't be so negative. You did well for your first crime. You didn't get caught. Mind you, that's on account of me. I had it all under control. But you did your part real good."

"Did I?"

"Sure did. Now go home and get some sleep."

"I don't know if I can sleep now. My heart is racing."

She grinned. "See? It was exhilarating, wasn't it?"

It *was* exhilarating, and I felt giddy with it, and more energetic than I'd ever felt at this time of night. "I could run all the way home and still have energy left," I said, smiling.

She laughed. "You should come to Epsom today."

"What?"

"Come to the Derby. It'll be fun."

I'd never been to the races. The Epsom Derby was one of the most famous race days, with royalty often in attendance. I would very much like to see the ladies' outfits and watch the horses.

I absent-mindedly flipped the pages of the book on my lap. Perhaps it was the blood still thrumming in my veins, but I suddenly felt like I *should* go. The investigation was as much mine as it was Gabe's.

"Only if it's all right with Gabe," I told her.

"He ain't your master or your manager, Sylvia." She waved a hand at the book. "Look what you can achieve without his approval."

"This is different. Thurlow is a dangerous character. Gabe is just trying to protect me."

"All right, here's what we'll do. I'll tell him you're coming, but assure him you won't go anywhere near Thurlow. You'll just watch the racing, maybe put on a bet or two. Agreed?"

I hesitated before giving an emphatic nod. "Agreed."

She thumped the steering wheel again. "Excellent! We'll come past the library and get you."

I couldn't wipe the smile off my face for the rest of the journey home. Now all I had to do was find a suitable outfit to wear and try to get some sleep.

\* \* \*

AFTER TOSSING and turning for a few hours, I got up when the other boarders rose for breakfast. I telephoned the professor and asked for the day off then called on Daisy. The early June day promised to be warm, so she outfitted me in a summery dress of royal blue with pale pink chiffon across the décolletage and a sash of the same pink shade tied around my waist. She paired it with a black straw hat trimmed with a blue ribbon and a large pink flower. She sent me on my way with a spray of Guerlain.

Willie collected me from the library in the Hudson Super Six. Thankfully Gabe's chauffeur, Dodson, drove so I didn't arrive at the racecourse with shattered nerves.

"You look very fetching, Willie," I said, admiring her top hat and tails ensemble.

She doffed her hat in thanks. "So do you."

"Why are we going separately to Gabe and Alex?"

"I wasn't ready when they left."

How long did someone dressed in a man's suit need? She hadn't bothered to alter her simple hairstyle and wore no makeup. Getting ready would have taken mere minutes.

We arrived at Epsom Downs Racecourse an hour later, but instead of dropping us off, Dodson parked with the other motorcars on the slopes overlooking the racecourse. He could see the entire racetrack from there.

Entry wasn't as exclusive as I thought it would be, but Willie explained that anyone could enter as long as they purchased a ticket. The owner's pavilion, however, was reserved for "the toffs", as she put it. I refrained from reminding her that she was a dowager countess, and her cousin a baron. They probably wouldn't let her in dressed like that anyway.

I stood on my toes, but couldn't see far ahead. I was too short and the crowd too thick. "Are we meeting Gabe and Alex somewhere?"

"The betting circle."

"Which is where?"

She led me to the stairs of the colonial style owners' pavilion with its wide verandah and British flags flapping in the breeze. The staff dressed in formal gray suits with a yellow rose tucked into their jacket buttonhole looked ready to pounce, but thankfully they remained at their posts by the door when they saw we were going no further than the middle step. Below us, a sea of boater hats and parasols amassed in the public viewing area and stretched into the grandstand. The crowd was at its thickest near a large building.

Willie pointed to it. "That's the bar. It'll get rowdy in there later. See the area to the side of it? That's the betting circle. All the bookmakers in there are independent and need a license to set up on their pitch for the day. Licenses are expensive for a day like the Epsom Derby, but it'll be worth it. Someone like Thurlow has a few bookies working for him. Maybe he loaned them money so they could buy their licenses, or maybe he bankrolls them, or both. Whatever way you look at it, they owe him a percentage of their takings."

"Then how can they be considered independent?"

"Exactly. That's one of the reasons this is the most corrupt business in the country."

A couple dressed in formal attire approached on the stairs. They gave Willie a wide berth and a sneer as they passed. One of the staff asked us to move along.

We headed down the stairs and plunged into the crowd. A brass band playing *It's a Long way to Tipperary* competed with the track announcer over the loudspeaker. Racegoers moved to get a better look at the horses as they were led around the parade ring by grooms. The thinning of the crowd near the racetrack allowed me to catch my first glimpse of it up close. It was here that one of the suffragettes ran into the path of the king's horse in protest. She later died of her injuries but her desperate act made national headlines. It didn't seem that long ago that I'd read about it, yet it was another lifetime. Women now had the vote. Well, as long as she was over thirty and owned property, or married to a man who owned property.

Willie took my hand and we pushed our way towards the betting circle. Dozens of bookmakers stood on portable wooden platforms, shouting out the odds they were offering for the runners of the first race. I couldn't see Gabe or Alex, and I didn't know what Thurlow looked like. He might not even be in the betting ring, but the others had been certain he'd be here today.

"Come on," Willie said, tugging me by the elbow. "Let's place a bet."

"How do we know which ones work for Thurlow? I don't want to give them my money."

"We don't. And you won't be giving them your money if you win. They'll be paying you. Just pick a good horse."

My eye-roll was lost on her as she inspected one of the bookies' blackboards. The odds assigned to each horse were scrawled in chalk beside its number and jockey. I might not know much about horse racing and betting, but I knew enough about odds to work out which horse was this bookie's favorite. "Apparently he thinks Wild Rose will win, but I won't win much if I bet on it at those odds."

"Then pick another."

"I can't just choose from a list of names. Even I know there's more to it. Anyway, I'm not sure I want to place a bet. I can't afford to lose."

She leaned closer and lowered her voice. "A friend of a friend told me that Prince's Lad is a sure thing." This time she did notice my eye-roll. "Suit yourself. I'm going to find who has the best odds for him."

I let her go and continued to search for Gabe and Alex inside the betting circle. I didn't find them, but I noticed the heavy police presence. Considering how much money each bookie had in their suitcase or satchel, security needed to be tight and visible. With so many constables around, surely speaking to Thurlow here would be quite safe.

I spotted Alex and Gabe before they saw me. They were outside the betting ring, in deep conversation with a beautiful blonde woman wearing a pink silk drop waist dress with white trim and a long necklace of pearls. She had the grace of a dancer as she leaned close to Gabe to be heard over the loudspeaker.

He nodded at something she said then followed her gaze to a man wearing a black tailcoat with a silver-gray waistcoat, matching tie and black silk top hat. He looked small and weedy between the two tall, burly fellows flanking him. Neither sported a scar on their cheek so weren't Billy Burgess.

The woman wrapped both her hands around Gabe's arm and clung to it. She blinked her long lashes and touched his cheek, stroking her finger across his jaw. As if her intention wasn't clear enough, she licked her lower lip seductively.

Gabe extricated himself from her grip, but not before the weedy man noticed. He charged up to them, at the same moment that Willie joined the group. She waved a piece of paper in the air before tucking it into her pocket. She beckoned me with a wave.

Gabe turned sharply to face me. His brow plunged into a frown that became more severe the closer I got. He didn't get the opportunity to scold me or Willie because Thurlow demanded an introduction.

The woman transferred her doe-eyed attention from Gabe to Thurlow, a man much older than her. "Darling, this is Mr. Johnson and his associate, Mr. Bailey."

It would seem Gabe thought it necessary to borrow

Willie's name instead of using his own. Considering his famous mother, it was probably wise.

The woman regarded Willie and me from beneath lowered lashes but made no attempt to discover our names. "Gentlemen, may I present Mr. Thurlow. There. Introductions made. Can someone fetch me a glass of champagne now?" Her whiny Cockney accent wasn't what I expected from the polished beauty. I'd assumed she'd be more like Ivy Hobson, all round upper class vowels and clipped consonants.

Thurlow extricated himself from the woman's grasp just as Gabe had done. "A pleasure to meet you, Gents. Now, who is this little lady?" He took my hand and bowed over it.

The woman *humphed* and turned away with a sniff. Gabe continued to scowl.

"That's Miss Ashe and I'm Willie," Willie said.

"American?"

She gave him an exaggerated wink. "Sure am. We hear you're the man to speak to around here to get business done."

Neither Gabe nor Alex showed any surprise or concern that she'd spoken so I assumed they'd discussed their approach beforehand. They wouldn't be here without a plan.

Thurlow pulled out a gold cigarette case from his top jacket pocket. "That depends on the business." He flipped open the lid and offered her a cigarette. "And who you are."

"My family are glass manufacturers in the States." Gabe replaced his English accent with an American one. It sounded quite natural to me. "We specialize in bottles for beer and bourbon. Or we used to."

"Ah. Prohibition has all but wiped you out. You poor sods." Thurlow offered Gabe and Alex a cigarette. One of his men lit them with a gold lighter. "You should have branched out."

"That's what we wanted to speak to you about. We've got

ideas. Import and export between our two great nations, and we heard you were the man in London to speak to."

"Import and export of what?"

"Special items. Rare and of superb quality." Gabe's gaze flicked to one of the constables patrolling the betting circle. "Can we go somewhere private?"

Thurlow stroked his thin moustache with the thumb of the hand that held his cigarette. "I'm throwing a post-races party tonight at the Degraves Hotel. We'll discuss it there, and play a little cards on the side while the ladies dance for us. If you have any friends who like cards, bring them along. And bring Miss Ashe." He turned a slick smile on me. "She can get to know my girl while we talk business."

"Miss Ashe has other plans."

"Cancel them." Thurlow blew smoke into the air then leaned close to me. "If you want me to do business with him, you'll come to my party." It was said quietly enough that only I could hear. "Wear something..." He touched the sleeve at my shoulder, nudging it aside to reveal more skin. "...appropriate."

The woman in the pink dress pursed her lips. "I want some champagne, Darling."

"Of course, Sweetheart." Thurlow placed a hand on her lower back and steered her away without a backward glance. His two thugs trailed behind.

I blew out a steadying breath. I hadn't realized my heart had started to pound until Thurlow was gone.

"What did he say to you?" Gabe asked.

"That I have to go to the party or he won't work with you."

"Then we'll find another way to get close to him."

"Why?" Willie asked with a wrinkle of her nose. "We already have a way."

"Sylvia won't come to any harm," Alex assured him.

An announcement over the loudspeaker called for everyone to be upstanding for the national anthem. The first race was about to start. The public vacated the betting circle to jockey for position at the track's railing. With their superior vantage point on their platforms, bookies could see the turf from their pitch. No one paid us any attention.

"I thought we agreed you weren't coming here," Gabe growled at me.

I wasn't used to him speaking to me so tersely and it took me a moment to collect myself. "Willie told you I was coming."

Gabe turned his icy glare onto her. "No, she did not."

She cleared her throat. "Sylvia never agreed *not* to come. You just told her she wasn't. That ain't fair. She can do what she wants."

"You didn't tell him?" I cried. "Willie, you said you would."

"When did she say that?" Gabe asked, his voice cold.

"Last night. Yesterday. At the library."

His jaw firmed. "Last night? So you went with Willie to Lady Stanhope's and stole the book back. Damn it, Sylvia." He removed his hat and dragged a hand through his hair. "Willie, what were you thinking, taking her along?"

Willie pretended not to hear then disappeared into the throng crowding the railing to watch the race.

"Don't blame her," I said. "I insisted on going last night. It was my fault for returning the book to Lady Stanhope, so I needed to be the one to take it back. Has she contacted you this morning about it going missing?"

He shook his head. "Hopefully she hasn't noticed. She'll be here, somewhere. Most likely in the owner's pavilion."

Alex followed Gabe's gaze to the building where Thurlow was leading his girlfriend up the steps. "We're avoiding going near it."

"Who was she?" I asked. "And how did you know she could introduce you to Thurlow?"

"She's his latest girl." Alex had to raise his voice to be heard over the crowd's cheers and the race caller. "According to my contacts on the force, she was our best option to secure an introduction to Thurlow."

"How?"

"She's a flirt and he's jealous." He smiled. "They conformed to type exactly as we hoped."

"But how did you gain an introduction to *her*?"

Alex and Gabe exchanged glances. Gabe gave a slight, almost imperceptible, shake of his head. Alex's smile widened. "Let's just say, she has a preference for a certain type of man, and Thurlow doesn't measure up. My contact said she's looking for another fellow. Besides, what woman can resist a handsome face?"

Gabe looked at him like he wanted to throttle him which only made Alex chuckle.

The crowd whipped into a frenzy as the horses galloped down the final straight to the finish. Being heard over the noise was impossible, but Gabe's annoyance vibrated off him loud and clear.

When the race was over, he suggested we leave. Alex and I agreed but Willie wanted to stay.

She tore up her ticket and threw it on the ground. "I've got to win back what I lost on Prince's Lad."

"That's a fool's reasoning," Alex told her.

"I was a fool for listening to someone who thought they had a certain winner. Next time I'll pick a horse the old-fashioned way. By studying its form. You three go. I'll return to London with Dodson."

Gabe, Alex and I wove through the crowd in the public area. As we passed the owner's pavilion, I saw Ivy Hobson standing on the porch with friends. One of them nudged her and nodded at Gabe. Ivy's gaze moved from Gabe to Alex then settled on me. Her lips thinned.

I nodded a greeting, but she turned away to listen to her friend who seemed to be encouraging Ivy to go after Gabe. He hadn't noticed her and forged on, his back and shoulders rigid.

It was going to be a long ride home.

# CHAPTER 11

Instead of returning me to the library, we collected the untitled book from my room at the lodging house and drove to the Petersons' paper factory on Bethnal Green Road. By the end of the journey, Gabe's jaw wasn't as firmly set as when we started.

He opened the motorcar door for me. "I'm sorry I was angry earlier. I have no right to tell you what to do."

"It is your investigation, Gabe." I placed a hand on his arm and smiled to show that it didn't upset me.

His anger was nothing compared to my mother's when she discovered I'd disobeyed her order to go directly home after school. On one occasion when she finished work early and didn't find me in our flat, she'd become worried. I'd stopped at the home of an elderly couple I'd come to know. When they discovered I liked books they'd invited me into their private library to read of an afternoon. I loved those visits, and always went home stuffed full of knowledge, cake and tea. But my mother put a stop to them after that day, even though I begged her to meet the couple so she could see they were harmless. She'd harangued me until her voice was hoarse. Gabe's anger was mild by comparison.

"You understand that I was simply worried about you, don't you?" he asked.

I could have reassured him that I was the least likely person to deliberately place myself in a vulnerable situation with a dangerous man. But that would start a discussion that I didn't want to have. "There were a lot of police about," I said instead. "Thurlow wouldn't risk doing something in the open."

"It's not that." He searched the sky for the right words. "It's more that I didn't want him meeting you. I don't want him to use you against me."

"How would he do that?"

He walked off in the direction of the factory's office door. "And another thing, why did you agree to help Willie last night?"

"Don't blame her. I inserted myself into her scheme to steal the book. She needed someone to keep watch while she picked the locks. If I hadn't helped her, she might have got caught and we wouldn't be here now." I patted the cover of the book in my hand.

"She didn't need to steal it. I was going to offer to take apart Lady Stanhope's watch or a clock and put it back together in exchange for a book. I'm not a magician, but she would have been satisfied with that. God knows why."

"Would she?"

He stopped on the bottom step and looked at me. "What do you mean?"

"She would have continued to harass you. She's convinced you're a magician, and if she doesn't leave you alone, she might..." I glanced around to make sure we were alone. "She might find out the truth."

His gaze searched mine in earnest. "Is that why you

volunteered to help Willie steal it back? Because you were worried about me?"

He might not be a magician, but that intense gaze of his put a spell on me. I felt like we were alone, standing in a meadow sprinkled with yellow daisies beneath a blue sky, not on the steps of a factory under a miasma of dirty smoke spewing from its chimneys.

"Sylvia," he purred. "I can take care of myself when it comes to women like Lady Stanhope."

The spell shattered. I gazed past him to the PETERSONS PAPER sign painted in large black letters on the cream brick wall of the factory. "Yes. Of course. I'm sure you're very capable with the Lady Stanhopes of the world." I continued on up the stairs.

He fell into step alongside me. "I was worried about you, you were worried about me...I think we can call ourselves even."

"Agreed."

"So there's no need for you to come tonight."

"Thurlow insisted." When he didn't respond, I added, "If I don't go, he might use that as an excuse not to talk to you." I pushed open the door before he had a chance to disagree.

A woman at the reception desk looked up and smiled. She remembered us from our last visit and asked us to wait while she informed Mr. and Miss Peterson. She returned a few minutes later with their assistant.

He led us through the office area to a rectangular yard where workers pushed trolleys stacked with large parcels up a ramp into the back of a lorry. Another lorry drove by, piled high with wood chips, and parked in front of the building directly opposite. The rapid-fire *stamp stamp stamp* of heavy machinery pounding pulp came from the building on our right, but we headed to the building on the left. It was quiet and at first I thought it was empty until I saw two men near the back. One stood on a high platform overlooking a vat while the other stood below him, holding a clipboard.

The assistant asked us to wait while he entered an adjoining office. I saw two people inside when he opened the door. A woman sat with her back to us at a desk, a stack of papers to one side. A man stood on her right, his attention on a large ledger.

It was he who joined us, his hand extended. "Walter Peterson, at your service." He was short and round with ruddy cheeks and a button nose. The fan of wrinkles radiating from each eye deepened with his smile. The smile turned to surprise when Gabe introduced himself. "Glass? Any relation to Mrs. India Glass, Lady Rycroft?"

"She's my mother."

"Ho, ho!" He rocked back on his heels. "Should I bow before royalty?"

Gabe laughed lightly. "Please don't."

"Wait until I tell my sister." He indicated the office door, now closed, but made no move to go to her.

"I'm a consultant for Scotland Yard, and Miss Ashe is assisting me. We're investigating the murder of a bookbinder."

Mr. Peterson's face darkened. "Littleproud. Yes, I heard about it. Terrible business. Poor chap. I hope you catch the brute. But I don't see how we can help."

"A collection of books sold by Mr. Littleproud just before his murder is at the center of our investigation. We've been led to believe they contain paper magic, and wondered if you could verify if that's the case."

I passed him the book.

He opened the cover and stroked the front page with the flat of his hand. "It does."

"You can tell already?" I asked.

"Of course. A magician immediately senses when a spell

157

has been used on something, especially when that spell is his own discipline, as this is."

I didn't hear his next exchange with Gabe. The blood was rushing between my ears, making me a little giddy. A part of me felt like I was about to float away, and I was grateful when Mr. Peterson closed the book and handed it back to me.

I grasped it with both hands and held onto it tightly.

The two men working at the vat finished what they'd been doing and approached. The older one, dressed in a brown suit, accepted the clipboard from the younger fellow wearing overalls. The younger fellow left while the older one hung back and waited to speak to Mr. Peterson.

The door to the office opened and a woman with the same pug nose as Mr. Peterson emerged. That was where the resemblance ended. Where he was plump, she was wiry and tall.

"Evaline!" Mr. Peterson cried. "Come and meet the son of the great India Glass!"

"Hush, Walter, I'm not deaf." Her smile softened her features. "Forgive my brother. He's a little hard of hearing."

Mr. Peterson made the introductions and told his sister the reason for our visit. She, too, had read about the murder but neither of them knew Mr. Littleproud personally.

She indicated the book in my hands. "May I touch it, Miss Ashe?"

I handed it over. She opened the cover and ran her hand down the first page, just as her brother had done. She repeated the motion on the second page then flipped through the others before giving it back.

"Walter's right, it contains paper magic."

"Do you know who might have put the spell on the paper?" Gabe asked.

"It's impossible to tell, I'm afraid. It could even have been one of us."

"The spells were put in decades ago."

Mr. Peterson chuckled. "Then it probably wasn't us."

"You use traditional methods here to make your paper?" I asked, looking around at the vats. The man in the brown suit had gone and we were the only ones in the building.

"We use all sorts of methods," Mr. Peterson said. "Most of our paper is produced with wood chips that are soaked in a chemical solution to soften the fibers. That paper is for the masses. It's good quality, of course, but contains no magic. A smaller quantity is made in the traditional way of soaking rags until it forms a pulp. That's the stuff that gets the spells, since we're cotton magicians, not wood magicians."

I recalled my research into paper magic when we were investigating the disappearance of a painting from the Royal Academy. Paper magicians were actually descendants of cotton magicians. Cotton magic had branched into many forms over the centuries, each one developing a specialty. Some were canvas magicians, as we'd discovered in our earlier investigation into the painting, others were clothiers, and then there were paper magicians like the Petersons.

*Like me.*

Mr. Peterson rattled on, not noticing that I'd become distracted. "Our spell-infused paper is a very high quality. Indeed, it's perfection, if I may be allowed to boast." His ruddy cheeks grew redder. "Our premium line is highly sought after."

"I was placing a spell into a batch just now." Miss Peterson indicated the office. The door stood open, revealing the stack of papers on one side of the desk. "Miss Ashe, are you all right? You look a little pale all of a sudden."

I swallowed but my mouth remained dry. "May I have the book back, please?"

She hesitated, frowning, then handed it over.

I grasped at the threads of my thoughts, floating aimlessly

through my mind. "Your paper...those with spells in them... will they be used in books?"

"Mostly invitations, calling cards, and personal stationery."

Mr. Peterson leaned in and lowered his voice, although it was still loud. "For royalty, no less, and members of the peerage. But we speak our spell into ordinary paper, too, if it's *important* paper." He looked like he wanted us to ask, so I did ask what he meant by important paper. "During the war, the government had a great need for our paper." He winked then rocked back on his heels, smiling smugly.

Gabe played along. "Did they use your paper for dispatches?"

"Not just dispatches. *Secret* dispatches."

His sister shushed him. "I'm not sure we should discuss it."

"The war is over, Evaline. Besides, these fine folk are from Scotland Yard. Perhaps Mr. Glass can tell his superiors that they should use our paper for *their* secret dispatches. They can verify our claim with the War Office." He tapped the side of his nose. "You see, we discovered quite by accident that when our spell-infused paper is combined with a graphite magician's spell in a pencil, the result is something completely unexpected." He rocked back on his heels again, grinning from ear to ear. "You'll never guess."

"No, they won't," his sister said tightly. "So just tell them."

"Invisible writing. The marks made by the magic pencil can't be seen on the magic paper."

"That is extraordinary," Gabe said. "I can see why the War Office found it useful."

"As will Scotland Yard, I'm sure." Mr. Peterson tapped the side of his nose again.

Gabe thanked them and started to make his way to the

He gave me a gentle smile. "I understand completely."

If anyone did, it would be him.

*   *   *

I TOLD Daisy all about our outing to the races as she helped me dress for Thurlow's party, but nothing about our visit to Petersons Paper factory. I had an investigation that required me to focus, especially tonight. I needed all my wits about me in the company of the money lender.

Gabe's attention had switched quickly from the revelations at the factory to the task at hand. When he and Alex drove me home after leaving the Petersons' factory, he'd continued to tell me I shouldn't go, that my presence wasn't necessary. When Alex told him the same thing I did, that Thurlow might not speak to them if I wasn't there, Gabe turned silent and broody.

Right up until they collected me in the Hudson, I wasn't sure if he'd come. He was still broody, however, as he opened the door for me. The motorcar was full. Alex sat in the driver's seat. I slipped into the back alongside Willie and Francis Stray. The quiet academic's presence surprised me.

He reached across Willie to shake my hand. "Good evening, Miss Ashe. You look very nice. I like your dress and your hair." The words were spoken without emotion or a flicker of desire. I suspected he was merely repeating sentiments he'd practiced for such occasions.

"Thank you. And please call me Sylvia, if I may call you Francis."

"You may."

"I didn't know you were coming tonight."

"Nor did I until an hour ago. The captain telephoned and asked if I could count cards for him."

Willie swore under her breath. In the front, Alex sighed

while Gabe turned to Francis. "Best not to say that at the party. Counting cards is frowned upon."

"I know. But Sylvia is part of our group so I thought it harmless to inform her."

"Don't mention it to anyone else tonight," Willie said sternly. "Now, I ain't going to be in there to keep an eye on things, so do as Gabe and Alex say."

"Of course. You will find I follow instructions to the letter, Lady Farnsworth."

"Don't call me that."

"But it is your correct form of address. I can call you my lady, if you prefer, or simply madam. Willie is too informal given my station is well below yours."

She sighed. "Don't talk to me and we'll get along fine."

"Why aren't you coming in?" I asked her.

"Thurlow wants to play cards and I don't feel like gambling tonight."

It wasn't until we stopped and exited the motorcar that Alex elaborated. "She lost a lot of money at Epsom today and she has no self-control when it comes to gambling. It's best if she stays away from temptation."

"That's commendable of her."

"Don't let on that I told you."

I watched as Willie slipped into the driver's seat and drove the motorcar away from the curb to find somewhere nearby to park it.

I fell into step alongside Alex, just behind Gabe and Francis. Gabe's quiet words drifted back to me. "Remember what I said. Don't make the signals obvious. If he suspects, get up and leave. If I lose, then so be it."

Francis drew in a fortifying breath. "Yes, sir."

"Why do we need Francis to count cards?" I asked. "If it's frowned upon, then shouldn't we simply not do it?"

"Thurlow cheats, according to several sources," Gabe said.

"If he wants to cheat, I need to level the playing field. I want to earn his respect, and I doubt he respects a loser. Don't worry, I won't win all the time. I know how to handle men like him."

We'd arrived in the foyer of the Degraves Hotel on Piccadilly, one of London's most luxurious hotels. Tall palm trees added a lush tropical feel, perfect for the warm evening. One of the hovering staff escorted us beneath the glittering lights of the triple layer crystal chandelier into an anteroom. A sign welcomed Mr. Thurlow's guests to his post-Epsom party and ragtime music promised a lively evening of dancing in the ballroom.

I unwrapped my shawl from around my upper body and let it drape loosely at my lower back. Gabe's sudden intake of breath was soft but, given how near he stood behind me, I heard it. I turned to see him staring, mouth ajar.

"Something wrong?" I asked.

He shut his mouth, blinked innocently, and shook his head. He offered me his arm.

"Excuse me, Sylvia," Francis said. "Are you aware that the back of your dress is missing?"

I tried to suppress my smile, but it escaped, nevertheless. "Only to the middle of my back. Daisy told me it's the latest fashion in Paris."

"Daisy would know," Alex said. "She has a lot of fashion magazines in her flat." It would have sounded like a criticism coming from most, but not from the man who secretly admired her. "She has a good eye," he added.

Her silver and sequin dress was a little long for me but fitted everywhere else. The air on my back felt strange, and the stares of the people we passed even stranger. I wasn't used to having so many eyes on me. Usually Daisy attracted all the attention. In a way, she still did. It was her dress and makeup, after all. I raised my shawl to cover my bare skin, suddenly regretting letting her talk me into wearing the outfit.

Gabe's thumb lightly caressed the knuckles of my hand, resting on his arm. "They're only staring because you're the most beautiful woman in the room." His whisper sent a thrill through me. It didn't matter that he was exaggerating to give my confidence a boost.

I lowered the shawl again and straightened my shoulders. "Thank you. That's kind of you to say."

"It's not a kindness. It's a fact. It's also a fact that my concern has increased."

I followed his gaze to Thurlow, standing with a group of men. His two thick-necked companions from the races flanked him. They looked equally surly and menacing here as they had at Epsom.

"Whatever you do, don't flirt with him," Gabe said.

"But isn't that what we want? Him flirting with me to distract him and lull him into a false sense of security?" I spotted Thurlow's woman, seated at a nearby table with other women.

"I can do that while we play cards. You should dance and enjoy yourself."

"Away from the gambling and Thurlow?"

"Precisely."

"So you'll put Francis in danger, but not me?" I indicated the mathematician standing beside Alex. He looked small and vulnerable beside the towering figure and not at all equipped for the sort of subtle espionage required this evening.

"That's different," Gabe growled.

"Because he's a man?"

"Because he's not being targeted by Thurlow to get back at me for catching his girl's eye."

He was overreacting but saying so would achieve nothing.

He plucked two coupe Champagne glasses off a waiter's

tray and handed one to me. Before he let go, he offered me a flat smile. "I don't want to fight with you. Truce?"

I nodded. "Truce."

He let go of the glass. "I have a bad feeling about this evening."

# CHAPTER 12

*a*lex approached and lifted his coupe glass to his lips. "Don't look now, but he's coming over."

I took a fortifying sip of champagne then put out my hand for Thurlow.

He kissed it, his lips lingering. I felt the heat of his breath through my glove. "Miss Ashe, what a triumph you are in that dress!"

"Thank you, Mr. Thurlow. Did you enjoy your day at Epsom?"

"Unfortunately, my luck ran out when you left." Had he noticed us leave early? If so, did he wonder why we'd gone to the races at all?

I smiled, but a sense of dread weighed heavily in my chest. "Hopefully your luck will change tonight. Are you going to start playing soon?"

He plucked the glass out of my hand and gave it to Alex. "Dance with me, Miss Ashe."

I did as ordered, smiling all the way to the dance floor, despite his cold fingers caressing the bare skin at my back. I wished I hadn't worn this dress.

Other couples joined us on the dance floor, but not Gabe. I caught glimpses of him mingling with other guests. Once, I saw Thurlow's woman approach him, but Gabe spotted her and moved away before she reached him. If Thurlow noticed Gabe distancing himself from her, he gave no indication. He seemed to be enjoying dancing, attempting the new steps Daisy had taught me. He was a dreadful dancer, but what he lacked in skill, he made up for in enthusiasm.

After an hour, he signaled it was time to stop. He took my hand and led me past his two guards who'd been watching proceedings from the edge of the dance floor. He strode up to a waiter and grabbed two champagne glasses. As he handed me one, he glanced around. He was looking for someone. His girl? Gabe?

I couldn't see either of them. I thought we would go in search of Gabe to begin the card game, but Thurlow gave no indication he wanted to start. Indeed, he was smiling again as he wiped his sweaty forehead with his handkerchief.

"What do you think of the party, Miss Ashe?"

"I like it very much. Thank you for inviting me. I'm thoroughly enjoying myself."

He seemed genuinely pleased. He leaned closer to be heard over the loud music. "I like you. You're more...real than the girls I'm used to. They're all polished and sophisticated, as if they were acting a part in the moving pictures."

"Oh?" Being called unsophisticated wasn't the best way to a woman's heart, but I wasn't about to tell him that.

"For instance, you don't seem comfortable in that dress. Is it new?"

"Is it that obvious?"

He grinned, revealing a mouth crammed full of crooked teeth. "Tell me...you and Johnson...is it serious?"

Telling him that Gabe and I weren't together might let him think he could make a play for me. Or it might make him anxious that Gabe was free to chase after his girl. Thurlow may be with me, but I was quite sure he wanted her, given the way he constantly glanced around the room.

Either way, telling the truth didn't work in my favor. I wanted him as relaxed and unsuspicious as possible. "I don't want to talk about him. I want to talk about you." I stroked his jacket lapel to get his attention. It was something I'd seen other girls do when flirting. "Tell me what you do for a living, Mr. Thurlow."

His hand whipped out and grasped mine. His grip was hard, his eyes harder. I instantly regretted my question. It wasn't a flirtatious one. It was the sort of question gentlemen asked one another, or women who were fishing for information. This man was an expert at recognizing when he was being interrogated. It was a weapon in his armory that had kept him out of jail for so many years.

"Didn't Johnson tell you? I have many business interests." He let my hand go.

I resisted the urge to stretch my fingers to release some of the tension.

He gave me a tight smile. "I've answered your question, now you answer mine. What does Johnson want to import and export?"

"I don't know. He hasn't confided in me."

"I think you do know, otherwise he wouldn't have brought up business in your presence today at the races. He said it was something rare and valuable. To an American, liquor is currently in short supply, so I suppose that's rare. But not to an Englishman. So what is it?"

"I'd rather you speak about business matters with him."

He grunted. "I'm not sure I trust him."

"You can trust him. He's keen to work with you, Mr. Thurlow. Just speak with him. He'll answer all your questions."

He lifted his glass in salute. "You're towing the company

line. Good girl. Well then, let's find him. I want to test his mettle. I don't invest in just anyone."

I released a breath as I followed him across the ballroom. Many of the guests wanted to speak to Thurlow, but he simply bestowed smiles on them and didn't stop for conversation. His money lending business must be doing well. Not only did everyone want to be his friend but hiring the ballroom at a luxury hotel merely to amuse them would have cost a small fortune.

We spotted Gabe and headed towards him, but Thurlow stopped suddenly when he saw his woman with him. The icy glare he shot the pair could have frozen a lake in the Bahamas.

Thurlow's woman broke away from Gabe as we approached. Thurlow stopped glaring at Gabe long enough to smile at her. It was unconvincing.

"There you are, Darling." She pressed her body against his and rested a hand on his shoulder. She kissed his cheek. "I've missed you." She narrowed her gaze at me, just as Thurlow had done when eyeing Gabe. "Who is this?"

"You remember Miss Ashe from Epsom today? She was there with Johnson."

"Enchanted." She placed her long cigarette holder between her lips then blew smoke into the air above my head. "When will the card game begin?"

Thurlow checked his gold pocket watch. "Now." He indicated a door ahead of us. "Follow me, Johnson."

Gabe stepped aside to allow them to go first. As she passed him, Thurlow's woman licked her lower lip and bit it seductively. Gabe pretended not to notice.

I laid a hand on the arm he offered me. "Where are Alex and Francis?"

"Francis is there." He nodded at the small man standing

alone near a potted palm. "Alex left. He recognized a fellow from his days on the force."

"Policeman or the other sort?"

"The other."

No wonder he'd left. If Alex was identified, Gabe's disguise would be in jeopardy, too.

One of Thurlow's thugs closed the door behind us and stood in front of it, hands closed into fists at his sides. We found ourselves in a small antechamber. Unlike the ballroom, it contained no decorations or ornamentation, no tall palm trees or framed paintings. It was plain, windowless, and smelled of the smoke billowing out of the fat cigars smoked by the five men already seated at the circular table. Behind each of them stood a woman, as polished as the furniture.

Waiters dressed in black ties and white lap aprons escorted Gabe, Alex and Francis to spare chairs at the table. Thurlow's woman went to stand with Gabe, but Thurlow grabbed her wrist. He whispered something in her ear.

She swallowed heavily. Her gaze lowered, she meekly allowed Thurlow to lead her to the last vacant chair at the table, where he sat. She took up a position behind him, dutiful yet with an air of defiance in her lifted chin, her disdainful pout.

I went to stand between Gabe and Francis. Thurlow's woman watched me from beneath her lashes.

Thurlow clicked his fingers and the waiters stepped forward. They offered cigars and whiskey to the men, and champagne to the women. As everyone was being served, a dealer dealt the cards.

When he came to Francis, Francis put up his hand. "No, no, not me. I'm simply observing."

Gabe's thumb tapped out a rapid beat on his thigh. I laid a hand on his shoulder. He glanced up at me and I looked pointedly at his thumb. He stilled. I kept my hand where it was so as not to catch Thurlow's attention.

Thurlow's woman, however, had seen. She continued to watch us from beneath her long black lashes.

They played a few rounds of *Vingt Et Un*, in which the players tried to get as close to a value of twenty-one across their hand as possible without going over. At first, Gabe lost more than he won as he usually waited until he reached nineteen or more before placing his hand of cards face down on the table. He accepted his losses with good humor and a devil-may-care shrug. Anyone would think he had money to burn.

If Francis Stray was counting the cards that had been discarded already, he was doing a poor job. It wasn't until several rounds had been played that I noticed the slight movement of his fingers on his knee. He looked like he was simply scratching an itch. No one else seemed to notice, but being seated beside him meant Gabe saw.

It was from that moment on that Gabe won more than he lost. From what I could make out, he wasn't following Francis's instructions every round. If he did, he would have won almost everything. The losses were tactical. By losing sporadically, no one would assume he was keeping track of which cards had already been played.

One by one, the other men lost all their money and bowed out, leaving the room altogether. With only Gabe, Thurlow and one other man left, Thurlow called for a break in play. The men stood to stretch their legs. Waiters offered more drinks and cigars, but Gabe refused both, as did Francis. Indeed, Francis hadn't had anything to drink since we entered the room.

The third player excused himself for a few moments and left. As Thurlow's thug opened the door for him, raucous laughter and the bright blare of a trumpet grew louder before being shut out once again when the door closed.

Thurlow spoke quietly to the dealer and waiters, his back to us, so he didn't see his woman sidle up to Gabe. Her tight-fitting low-cut dress was seductive, alluring, something which her smile implied she knew. Dressed in that outfit and with bright red lips and her hair styled into sleek waves, she looked like she should be gracing the covers of a fashion magazine.

Pinching the long cigarette holder between two fingers at shoulder height, she placed a hand on Gabe's arm. "You play well, Mr. Johnson." Champagne slurred her words, broadening her Cockney accent even further.

"I lost as much as I won," Gabe said with a laugh.

"But you can afford to lose. That's the important thing." She smiled around the tip of the cigarette holder and thrust out a hip. "How long are you in London?"

"That depends on how long my business takes." Gabe glanced at Thurlow who still had his back to us.

"I want to hear all about America before you go. Maybe we can meet for coffee tomorrow, and if I like what I hear, I can take the same ship as you."

"I'm a little busy tomorrow."

"Another time," she said. "You telephone me when you're free. I'm available any time. But don't tell anyone. Do you have paper and a pencil on you?"

"I'm afraid not."

Francis patted his jacket pocket then pulled out a small notepad. "I do."

"Johnson!" Thurlow barked. "I like the way you play. You take risks. Calculated ones. That's a good habit for a man in the import export trade." He plugged a fat cigar into his mouth and shooed his woman away. "Let's talk business." He pointed the cigar at Francis, tucking his notepad back into his pocket. "Who is he really?"

"My accountant."

Thurlow laughed loudly. "I should have guessed. He looks like one."

Francis looked pleased with the assessment.

"So what do you plan to import and export?"

"Magic," Gabe said.

Thurlow had been about to put the cigar back in his mouth but paused. "Magic," he said flatly.

"I know collectors in America who'd pay handsomely for objects with spells in them, as long as they're rare."

"What makes you think I know anything about that kind of commodity?"

"I don't expect you to know anything, Thurlow. I just want some seed money to get me up and running. But if you do know somewhere I can source that kind of thing, any lead will be gratefully received. If someone is trying to offload magical objects quickly and quietly, for example, or they knew where some could be found at a bargain price. I'll pay you a finder's fee, of course."

Gabe's plan finally clicked into place. If Thurlow knew about the untitled books, he'd tell Gabe about them and ask for a cut when he sold them. If he didn't know, he'd say nothing.

Thurlow puffed on his cigar, blowing smoke like a chimney.

"I heard a rumor about some unpublished manuscripts written by a famous author on magic paper," Gabe pressed. "Apparently, they belonged to a murdered bookbinder. I thought I could ask his widow if she'd be willing to sell. If she's short of funds and doesn't know their true value, I could snap up a bargain."

Ash dropped from the end of Thurlow's cigar onto his shoe as he regarded Gabe for several moments. His face gave nothing away. "I'll fund your venture, Johnson, at sixty percent interest."

"Sixty!" Francis blurted out.

Thurlow shrugged. "That's my offer. Take it or leave it." He put out his hand to Gabe.

Gabe smiled. "I'll think about it."

Thurlow clapped him on the shoulder. "As you should." The third player returned to the room. "Come on. Let's finish this game. Sweetheart." He clicked his fingers and pointed to the spot beside his chair.

His woman crossed her arms. "I ain't your dog." She went to stand beside Gabe's empty chair.

Thurlow glared at her. She glared back.

"I think I'm done," Gabe said jovially. "Goodnight, all."

Thurlow put his arm around Gabe's shoulders and steered him to his chair. "Not yet, my friend. A couple more rounds won't hurt. What say you, Miss Ashe? You'd like to stay awhile longer, wouldn't you? Why don't you ladies fetch us gents something to eat."

The thug opened the door.

Thurlow tapped his woman's bottom. "Off you go, Sweetheart."

The woman marched outside. I followed her. Once we were away from the band and partygoers, I fell into step beside her.

"I'm sorry, I don't know your name," I said.

"Jenny."

"Nice to meet you, Jenny. My name's Sylvia."

She ignored my extended hand and smoked her cigarette instead. "He's a berk."

"Berk?"

"Berkley Hunt. It's rhyming slang for…you know."

I wasn't entirely sure that I did, but nodded along anyway.

"I hate him." The words spewed out from between her lips along with a cloud of smoke.

"Then why do you stay with him?"

"Why do you think?" At my blank look, she said, "He pays for my flat, my clothes...everything. He expects a lot in return. Too much, sometimes." She drew deeply on the cigarette. "Don't tell him I said anything about going to America."

"I won't."

"I ain't after your man, you understand. Not like that. I just want...I don't know. Someone to help me get away, I suppose."

"From Thurlow?"

"From London. From everything."

"I do understand. You want to be free from everyone who makes decisions about your life without consulting you."

She slowed her pace and nodded. "You've been in a controlling a relationship too."

"In a way."

"How'd you get out?"

"She died."

We found ourselves in the foyer where partygoers who'd had enough of dancing mingled with hotel guests. Jenny approached the manager and told him to bring food into the anteroom then told him she needed another cigarette.

He couldn't offer her one fast enough. He slotted it into the holder for her before lighting it. He bowed as she strode off without thanking him.

"Being Thurlow's woman does have it perks," she said with a sly smile.

I wasn't sure what to make of her. Being with a man like

Thurlow would be difficult. He treated her like a chattel. Her life wasn't her own. But could she leave? Was she trapped? Or had she chosen to close the door of the gilded cage herself?

We were about to re-enter the anteroom when the door suddenly burst open. Francis ran out, eyes wide with panic. He almost barreled me over.

"Sylvia, run!"

I glanced past him to see Gabe slamming his fist into the jaw of one of Thurlow's thugs. The other was on hands and knees on the floor, wheezing. Thurlow watched on, his face contorted with rage. The third gambler was nowhere to be seen.

Thurlow kicked the wheezing man in the stomach. "Get up, you useless pieces of lard!"

Gabe rushed through the door, grabbed my hand and together we raced after Francis, sprinting across the ballroom.

"What happened?" I asked as we ran through the foyer.

"We overstayed our welcome."

The doorman was too slow so Gabe pushed the door open himself. Outside, Francis stood on the pavement, frantically waving his arms above his head.

"I think that's your motor," he said between panting breaths.

Gabe and I ran past him to meet the motorcar, driving along Piccadilly at speed. It screeched to a stop at the curb.

"Get in!" Alex shouted from the front passenger seat.

Gabe pushed Francis inside and I clambered after him. The motorcar pulled away before Gabe had even closed the door. Willie was behind the wheel, both hands gripping it firmly.

Gabe looked through the rear window. "They're following."

Alex swore but Willie *whooped*. "Hold on, folks. This could get interesting."

Not for the first time, I wished I had something keeping me in place when Willie drove. Gabe and Francis held onto the leather straps above the door, but seated in the middle, I had only Gabe's hand. The first corner proved that wasn't a sufficient anchor. He let me go to circle me in his arm instead. I pressed against him, my cheek at his chest. The thump of his heartbeat was steadier than mine.

"What happened?" Alex shouted over the roar of the engine as Willie changed gears.

"Thurlow accused me of cheating," Francis said. "He didn't like me counting cards. I should have been more subtle."

"It's not your fault," Gabe told him. "He would have accused us of cheating whether we were or not."

"Why? Didn't he want to do business with you?"

"He took an instant dislike to me. I should have aborted the scheme at the races."

"Why did he dislike you? Did he suspect who you really were?"

Gabe merely shrugged.

It was left to Alex to explain. "Thurlow was jealous. His woman took an interest in Gabe."

"Her name's Jenny," I said. "She hoped that by attaching herself to Gabe, she could get out, get to America, away from Thurlow."

"Well, anyone can help her do that," Willie said from the driver's seat.

"Watch out!" Alex shouted.

Willie swerved around a motorcar traveling through an intersection. "I saw it."

Alex swore. "You're going to kill us all."

"Thurlow's men are still on my tail. If I don't drive fast, I won't lose them. Everyone, hold on, there's another sharp corner coming up."

Francis grabbed the leather strap with both hands, his face pale in the light of the streetlamps. Tires squealed and the rear of the Hudson fishtailed. Although Gabe tightened his hold on me, I still ended up in his lap.

I apologized as he helped me sit up.

Although her grip on the wheel was firm, Willie showed as much alarm as if we were on a Sunday drive in the countryside. "Did you see Billy Burgess in there?"

"No," Gabe said.

"What about the books? Did Thurlow reveal anything?"

"I dropped enough hints, but he didn't take the bait."

"He doesn't know about them," I said. "Otherwise he would have told you where to get them, for a price."

"Not necessarily. His silence may simply mean he didn't want to help me. Given he doesn't like me, he may not want my business to succeed."

"Then why not just tell you to your face that he won't loan you any money? That's the surest way for you to fail."

"He did say no, without actually saying no."

"Sixty percent interest is outrageous," Francis added. "No one would accept it."

Something hit us from behind, shooting the Hudson and all passengers forward.

"They drove into us!" Willie cried. "Those low down pig swill!"

"Faster!" Alex urged.

"I'm going as fast as this elephant will go."

Those of us in the back seat whipped around to peer through the rear window. The front panel of the motor behind was dented but the vehicle's mechanics were unaffected. It was a smaller motorcar than ours, capable of traveling at speed. It closed the gap in the blink of an eye. In the moment before impact, the driver bared his teeth in a sickening grin.

Francis and I shouted a warning, but Gabe fell silent.

Except for his arm tightening around my waist, he was utterly still. I held onto him, bracing for impact.

The chasing motorcar slammed into us again, harder than before, sending the Hudson careening. It mounted the gutter, narrowly missing a lamp post.

Then suddenly, out of the darkness, the brick wall of a building appeared. We hurtled towards it, out of control.

# CHAPTER 13

$\mathcal{G}$abe wasn't strong enough to hold me in place. The violent force of the impact should have thrown me into the seat in front, or over it and through the windscreen into the brick wall. I should have broken bones at the very least.

But I was unscathed. We all were.

We sat or lay on the pavement far enough from the crash site to be safe if the Hudson caught fire. A trail of debris littered the road and pavement to where the motorcar hissed steam into the night air. The front had caved in and the back was damaged from where the other motor had hit us. Two of the tires were flat. If I'd come across the accident, I would have assumed all occupants died.

But none of us sported so much as a bruise. The only one looking worse for wear was Gabe. He sat on the pavement, leaning against a lamp post, breathing heavily. The overhead light illuminated the red veins on his closed eyelids, the flushed cheeks and beads of perspiration on his forehead.

I knelt beside him and removed my glove. "Gabe?" I

cupped his jaw and angled his face to the light to see him better. "Gabe? Are you all right?"

He opened his eyes and gave me a wan smile. "I'm fine. A little tired. You?"

I nodded as tears spilled down my cheeks. I couldn't stop them.

He opened his arms to me. "Don't cry." His whisper ruffled my hair as he stroked it back from my forehead.

I wanted to stay in his arms with his warmth enveloping me, but Willie strode up, cursing. "Just wait 'til I get my hands on Thurlow or his thugs. I'll make them regret they crossed me." She nudged me with her toe. "Sylvia, get up. There ain't nothing wrong with you."

Francis scratched his head as he stared at the Hudson. "I don't understand...what happened? How did we end up on the pavement without a scratch?"

Alex offered a hand to Gabe and hauled him to his feet. "Luck."

A look passed between the rest of us. We four knew what happened. Gabe had saved each of us. Time slowed for him, and in that window of opportunity before the motorcar hit the wall, he'd dragged each of us out and placed us on the pavement. His magic had saved him, saved all of us.

But it had rendered him exhausted. He leaned on Alex until his breathing returned to normal.

Other motorists had stopped to lend assistance, and a constable took down statements. All expressed surprise that we'd survived the crash. When the constable noted Gabe's name in his notebook, he paused, his pencil touching the paper but not writing.

"Glass?" he asked. "The son of Lady Rycroft?"

Gabe gave him a flat smile and the constable finished writing.

He returned the notebook to his pocket. "You folks go on

home and rest. I'll see this is cleared away before sunrise." He shook his head at the wreckage. "I don't think it can be salvaged, sir."

Willie had been scowling in the direction the other motorcar had gone, but her face suddenly lifted. "I think we should get a Hispano Suiza to replace it."

"Gabe already has a sports car," Alex said. "Besides, the Hudson was Matt's motor. It'll be up to him what he gets next."

"I'll telephone him tomorrow."

"*I'll* telephone him," Gabe said. "You'll speak about the accident with all the subtlety of a hammer. I don't want my mother panicking and insisting on coming home early."

"Fine," she muttered. "But I reckon Matt'll want you to buy a replacement while he's away, and if he does, I want to help."

We sent Francis home in the first cab that arrived and waited for another. As it pulled to the curb, Alex rolled his shoulder.

"Are you all right?" Gabe asked.

"It's a little sore, like it's been wrenched."

"Sorry. You're heavy."

Willie looked pointedly at Alex's stomach, which couldn't have been flatter.

We didn't discuss the events as we drove to my place. We didn't want the driver overhearing. We traveled in silence, each of us occupied with our own thoughts.

I tried to remember the accident, but it was a blur. There'd been the sensation of being hit from behind, the Hudson being pushed off the road, out of control, the sheer dread as the brick wall loomed large. I couldn't recall Gabe picking me up and moving me, although teasing the edges of my mind was the sensation of being carried.

The others waited in the cab outside my lodging house

while Gabe escorted me to the front door. He no longer looked peaky and his breathing was regular again. He looked healthy and fit as he lounged against the doorframe. Very healthy and fit indeed.

"So I'm forgiven?" His voice purred.

"Forgiven for what?"

"My bad temper today."

"It's long forgotten. Anyway, it would seem you were right to be worried. Thurlow is a thoroughly awful person."

"He won't cause us any problems. He doesn't know who we really are or where to find us." He touched my chin, angling my face up to look at him. "Are you worried? If so, you can come and stay with me."

I'd stayed in his Park Street townhouse before, when we weren't as well acquainted as we were now. The notion sent an even bigger thrill through me than it had last time.

"Gabe!" Willie called from the motorcar. "Quit gabbing. I want to go home."

A light in one of the bedrooms on the second floor went on. "Mrs. Parry is awake." My landlady didn't allow male callers in the house. While she accepted that her lodgers went out of an evening, she didn't encourage it and certainly didn't appreciate being woken up in the middle of the night. I would be assigned extra chores in the morning.

"Then I better leave." Gabe leaned down and kissed my cheek. It was nothing more than a feather-light brush of his lips, but it made my insides flip and my heart trip. "Goodnight, Sylvia."

"Goodnight, Gabe."

\* \* \*

DAISY ARRIVED at the library mid-morning to ask how the dress had fared at the party.

"You mean how *I* fared at the party," I corrected her.

"No, I mean the dress. Did it cause a stir? Did it snare a man for you?"

"Daisy! I didn't want to snare a man."

She picked up a book from the trolley and sighed. "You really are the archetypal librarian, Sylvia, hiding behind your books."

"Oh?"

She handed me the book to slot into place on the bookshelf. "You'll be shushing me in a moment."

"Only if you say something I don't like, which you are very nearly doing." I picked up another book and studied the spine. "The dress did cause a stir. I received quite a few compliments."

"I knew it!"

"All from men."

"Considering it was designed by a man for men to appreciate the female form, that's hardly surprising. I'll collect it from you later. I want to wear it tonight and cause a sensation of my own." She threw her arm around my shoulders and hugged me. "I can't be outdone by my pretty little librarian friend."

"No one can outdo you, Daisy. Not when you're in a flirtatious mood."

She released me and grabbed an armful of books from the trolley. She studied the front cover of the top one, but it was upside down so I doubted she was reading it. Her next question proved it. "Speaking of last night, did the others enjoy themselves?"

"It wasn't really an evening for enjoying oneself. It was more a work function. We were there to observe a suspect."

"Yes, but as part of your disguise, you had to dance and drink and flirt, yes?"

"Yes."

"So...did the others dance and drink and flirt?"

"Willie stayed with the motor outside. Gabe and Francis didn't dance or flirt, and drank very little. They needed their wits about them. I spent some time fending off the advances of a London criminal, while trying to get my measure of him."

"And?"

"And what?" I asked innocently. "Oh, you want to know about Alex?"

She lifted a shoulder in a shrug. "Not necessarily."

I took the books from her and turned away to shelve them. After a few moments, she huffed out an exasperated breath. "I know you think you're being amusing by drawing this out, Sylvia, but I can assure you it's not remotely funny."

"So you admit you're interested in Alex. All right, I'll tell you. There isn't much to say, actually. He left the party early and waited in the motorcar with Willie. He recognized someone from his policing days."

She gasped. "A criminal?"

"Yes."

"But what if they saw him?"

"They didn't."

"How can you be sure?" She clicked her tongue. "He shouldn't have gone."

"It was fine. Nothing happened. The fellow must not have seen him, or if he did, he didn't recognize him."

She tilted her head to the side. "Honestly, Sylvia. He's the most recognizable man in London with his height and dark good looks, not to mention the presence he has about him that's hard to ignore."

I smiled. "Is that so?"

She shoved some books at me. "Stop looking at me like I like him. I don't. He's irritating and smug. I'm just stating a few facts about him that everyone would agree upon."

"Are you talking about me?" came Alex's drawl.

We both whipped around to see him and Gabe standing at the end of the aisle. Both sported the sort of smug smile Daisy had just mentioned.

She sniffed as she set down her pile of books on the trolley. "It just shows how arrogant you are, thinking we're talking about you." She marched down the aisle toward them, not stopping.

They parted to let her through before she smacked into them.

Alex watched her go, still smiling to himself.

Gabe approached along the aisle and picked up one of the books Daisy had put down. He read the spine and slotted it into place on the shelf above my head. "How are you this morning?"

"I'm well. And you? Any ill effects from saving us?"

"A little lingering tiredness, but that could be as much from the late night as the magical exertion. I didn't sleep well when I got home."

"Nor did I." My sleepless night had little to do with the party or accident and everything to do with the intimacy of his goodbye at my front door. If Willie hadn't called out...

I shook off the thought. It was possible I was overreacting to a situation that was as innocent as him politely walking me home.

"Where's Willie?" I asked.

"Shopping for a new motorcar."

I laughed. "She didn't waste any time."

"She says there's no time to waste since a motor has to be ordered in. It could take months for an overseas model to get here. Her plan is to have the new one in the garage before my parents return, that way my father can't complain about the one she chose. What she doesn't know is, I won't necessarily agree with her choice, and in my parents' absence, the insurance company will only release money to me."

"She might be in for a rude shock."

"Most likely. As much as I like the Hispano Suiza, it's not all that different from my Prince Henry. A second sports model is unnecessary. I need something larger and more appropriate for longer country drives. Besides, it's my father's motorcar, not mine." He huffed a light laugh. "My parents would be surprised to hear me say that. I didn't always make sensible choices or put their needs first." His smile slipped off. "I was selfish."

"You were young."

"That's no excuse."

"Don't be hard on yourself, Gabe. Not after everything you've been through in the last few years."

He studied the book in his hands before passing it to me. "Speaking of pasts, do you want to talk about what happened at the Petersons' factory yesterday?"

Movement at the end of the aisle stopped me from answering. Not that I was sure how to answer. With everything going on, I'd hardly had time to digest it.

Cyclops greeted us and announced that tea was being served in the reading nook. "I've got a bone to pick with you, Gabe," he said as we walked.

"Is this about the accident?"

"You mean the one you failed to mention when you telephoned this morning?"

"I was going to let you know."

"When?"

"When I could be sure you wouldn't inform my parents before I have the chance to send them a telegram."

"They made a point of asking me to keep an eye on you." Cyclops tapped his eyepatch. "Not this one."

Gabe sighed. "I appreciate that you feel you have to oblige

them, but between you, the professor and Willie, I have enough nannies."

"Willie doesn't count. She's more a hindrance than a help. How much of last night was her fault?"

"None of it. In fact, it was her driving that stopped us from being in an accident earlier."

Cyclops grunted. "There's a first time for everything." Before we reached the others, sitting in the reading nook, he stopped Gabe with a hand to his chest. "Alex says you used your magic to save everyone."

Gabe tilted his head to the side. "And?"

Cyclops's hand dropped to his side. He glanced at his son, who was in a debate with Daisy if their matching scowls were an indication. "Thank you."

"You don't have to thank me for saving my best friend. Besides, it's not a decision I consciously made. It just happens."

"Even so." He caught Gabe's arm, halting him again. "If you don't tell Catherine about the accident, I won't tell your parents."

The men shook on it.

We joined the others in the nook and accepted teacups from Professor Nash. Gabe and Alex gave Cyclops a detailed report on our interactions with Thurlow, and agreed that it wasn't clear whether the money lender knew about the untitled books.

To everyone's surprise, Daisy had another opinion. "It has to be him," she said. "He's the killer."

"Why?" Alex asked.

"Because it was his man, Billy Burgess, who was seen watching the bookbinder's shop late at night. Burgess is known for being rough and Mr. Littleproud died of his injuries."

"He died of a heart attack."

"Brought on by his injuries," she said tartly. "Also Mr. Littleproud was short on money and Thurlow is a money lender. It's simply a matter of putting the pieces together to form the whole picture."

"It's all circumstantial. It won't hold up in court."

"Can I not have an opinion?"

"That's not what I said."

She sniffed. Alex grunted. They both sipped their tea.

Cyclops watched his son sparring with Daisy with all the scrutiny of a detective surveilling a suspect. "Intriguing," he muttered into his teacup.

"We need to find Burgess," Gabe said.

"I have men looking for him."

"As is Murray."

The professor cleared his throat and pushed his glasses up his nose. "I don't like being the negative one, but what if he's dead? What if Thurlow killed him so that he wouldn't talk to the police?"

Having been in the motorcar rammed by Thurlow's men, I now knew how ruthless he could be. He'd tried to kill five people he considered a threat, including one he'd danced and flirted with mere hours earlier. If he saw Billy Burgess as a liability, he wouldn't hesitate to permanently stop him from talking to the police.

Cyclops warned us that it was too early in the investigation to focus on one suspect. "We simply don't have enough evidence to prove it was Thurlow. Until we find Burgess, or until Thurlow makes a mistake, we have to follow other lines of inquiry. Regarding that, I spoke to several other publishers of children's books yesterday. Unfortunately, none kept records of rejected manuscripts going back that far *unless* it was an author they already published, then it was noted on that author's file."

Gabe nodded. "That's what Mr. Woodhouse said, but they

had no record of Honoria submitting her subsequent manuscripts to them."

We finished our tea and headed downstairs. Daisy collected her bicycle from where it leaned against the wall and rode off along Crooked Lane. Alex pretended not to watch her and Cyclops pretended not to watch his son. Both sported small smiles that gave them away, however.

Once she was out of sight, Cyclops plucked his hat off the stand by the door. "I almost forgot. I spoke to my colleagues in Ipswich. They've found no one by the name of Folgate, but suggested we check the local Silversmiths' Guild for information about John Folgate if we believe he lived there up until his death in 1890." He slapped his hat on his head. "At least there's no need to worry that the killer could go after the family of the silver magician who made the corner protectors. Speaking of which, have you managed to narrow down the kind of magic in the books?"

Gabe glanced at me. "It's paper magic. If the corner protectors were made by Folgate the silver magician, it doesn't appear he put a spell into them, although without a silver magician to verify it, we can't be completely sure."

Cyclops left, and Gabe and Alex were about to leave, too, when the telephone rang. Professor Nash answered it then passed the receiver to Gabe.

"It's for you. A Miss McCain. She says your butler gave her this number when she telephoned the house looking for you."

I felt as though we'd conjured up the assistant to Mr. Woodhouse, the publisher, after discussing the company where she worked with Cyclops. It turned out she no longer worked there, however.

"She was dismissed yesterday," Gabe said as he hung up the receiver. "She's quite upset."

"I can imagine," I said. "She worked there for years."

"Why did she want to speak to you?" Alex asked.

"She wanted to tell me she remembered seeing Mr. Woodhouse in the archive room the day the murder was announced in the newspapers. She says he never goes in there, so it struck her as odd. When he came out, he was carrying an old piece of paper. She knew it was old because it had yellowed with age."

Alex scoffed in disbelief. "Why didn't she tell you this the day you called on the publisher?"

"Miss McCain claims she kept it from us because she knew it would reflect badly on Mr. Woodhouse and she didn't want to lose her position. Now that she has lost her position anyway, she no longer feels any loyalty to him."

"She didn't feel a great deal of loyalty before now," I pointed out. "She was rather scathing towards Mr. Woodhouse the younger when we called at his office."

"Whatever her motive, we need to follow it up." Gabe reached for his hat on the stand. "Coming, Sylvia?"

* * *

Mr. Woodhouse's new assistant was younger than Miss McCain by a few decades. The pretty brunette stood over a crate beside her desk, a pile of periodicals in her arms. She perused the title of each before discarding them into the crate.

She set the rest aside to greet us with a smile but became flustered when Gabe said he was with Scotland Yard and needed to speak to her employer. She checked the appointment book several times. "I don't see your name here, sir."

"That's because we don't have an appointment."

"I see. Would you like to make one?"

"Is he in his office at the moment?"

"Oh. Uh." She scanned the appointment book again. "He doesn't have anyone with him now. Would you like to go in?"

"That would be ideal. Thank you."

She knocked on Mr. Woodhouse's office door then opened it upon his invitation. "Mr. Glass and Miss Ashe are here, sir."

"I don't wish to see them now."

The assistant's face fell. She didn't want to be rude to us but she wanted to obey her employer. In the end, Gabe made the choice for her. He strode into the room and held the door open for me, then thanked the assistant again.

She gave him an awkward smile in return, but it withered upon seeing Mr. Woodhouse's scowl. She hurried out, closing the door behind her.

His scowl became a tight smile as he reluctantly invited us to sit. "How is the investigation coming along?"

"We're making progress," Gabe said. "We have one more question for you. You were seen removing a piece of paper from the archived file of Mrs. Honoria Moffat-Jones."

Mr. Woodhouse stilled. "Who told you that?" When neither Gabe nor I answered, he added, "It was Miss McCain, wasn't it? You can't believe a word that woman says. She's disgruntled because she had to be let go from her position here. The company is taking a new direction, you see. We want fresh faces, new ideas, and energetic staff."

"We're not here to criticize your employment policy. We simply want to know why you removed a piece of paper from Mrs. Moffat-Jones's file shortly after the murder. What was on it?"

Mr. Woodhouse's jaw firmed. "Unfortunately, Miss McCain has sent you on a wild goose chase. Naturally she saw me leaving the archive room with a piece of paper. I come and go from there all the time. But it wasn't from Mrs. Moffat-Jones's file." He leaned forward and clasped his hands on the desk. "A word of advice, Mr. Glass. Don't listen to vindictive former employees with an axe to grind."

Gabe straightened. "I have a word of advice for you too.

Don't lie to Scotland Yard. It will get found out, and when it does, it will make you look guilty."

"I have no reason to lie, Mr. Glass. Now, if you don't mind, I have a lot of work to do."

Gabe rose and placed his hat on his head. "The piece of paper you removed from Mrs. Moffat-Jones's file was the submission note written by the assistant to her editor, wasn't it? It won't be difficult for us to find the name and current address of the editor or assistant to ask if they remember."

Mr. Woodhouse sat back with a satisfied smile. "They've both passed away." The smile vanished as he realized how cruel it made him look. "Sadly."

We saw ourselves out. His assistant smiled at us as she continued to discard periodicals one by one into the crate. Gabe smiled back, but the contents of the crate caught my eye. I removed what at first glance appeared to be a magazine, and showed the front cover to Gabe. It was the most recent edition of an auction house catalog. The same catalog that listed Honoria Moffat-Jones's untitled books on page four.

Mr. Woodhouse *had* lied. He knew the manuscripts existed before our first visit.

# CHAPTER 14

"*Y*ou're throwing these out?" I asked the assistant.

"Mr. Woodhouse said I could. He doesn't want them."

I showed the latest issue of the auction house catalog to Gabe. "You need to ask him again."

He refused to accept the catalog. "You should ask. It's your discovery."

"But..." I caught sight of the young assistant, watching me with curiosity and even a little admiration. She might have been employed by Mr. Woodhouse because of her pretty, youthful looks, but that didn't mean she was inept or unwilling to learn. I couldn't defer to Gabe now.

After drawing in a fortifying breath, I marched into the office without knocking and tossed the catalog on the desk in front of a surprised Mr. Woodhouse.

He spluttered some nonsensical syllables before finally getting a full sentence out. "I say, what's the meaning of this?"

I opened the catalog to page four and stabbed my finger on the entry for the books. "You saw this before or last visit.

You realized how valuable manuscripts handwritten on magic paper by a popular author would be, and you wanted them. Did you confront Mr. Littleproud before he sold them, or after? Did you believe your company owned them because you published Honoria's first book? Did you murder the bookbinder to get them?"

"Steady on, Miss Ashe."

Perhaps I got carried away a little, but I didn't think a soft approach would work. Mr. Woodhouse was a ruthless businessman. He wouldn't respect me if I tiptoed around him.

Perhaps he was a ruthless murderer too.

Mr. Woodhouse stood and picked up the catalog. "This belonged to my father, not me. He had all the catalogs sent to him. You can check with my assistant. There'll be a record of him receiving these every quarter."

"That may be so, but your father retired eighteen months ago, and this was sent here. It's conceivable that you saw it. You realized how valuable the manuscripts were and decided you wanted to get your hands on them. When Mr. Littleproud wouldn't sell them to you at a good price, you decided to steal them from him, not realizing he'd already sold them. You attacked him, but he died before he could reveal who he sold them to."

"No! Good lord, your accusation is outrageous! I'm not a killer, Miss Ashe. I never met the bookbinder, let alone murdered him." He tugged on his cuffs and didn't meet my gaze.

"What aren't you telling us, Mr. Woodhouse? What are you hiding?"

He looked up sharply. "Nothing. I didn't *need* to murder that fellow as at least one of those manuscripts is ours to publish. No other company can. It says so in Mrs. Moffat-Jones's contract."

"Under what clause?" Gabe asked.

"The option clause. Mrs. Moffat-Jones was contractually obligated to offer her follow-up manuscript to us before she sent it to any other publisher."

"You had the first right of refusal."

"Precisely. It's standard practice in all publishing contracts to include that clause and hers was no different. If you don't believe me, you can read it for yourself. Since Woodhouse and Collins owned at least one of those stories, I had no reason to murder the bookbinder. He, or the publisher who bought them, would have had to hand one over. They still do."

He was right, he had no motive given the contractual terms gave Woodhouse and Collins first right of refusal. But what if her manuscripts had been submitted and her editor *did* refuse them?

Gabe realized it at the same time I did. "Her husband was right. She did send them here, fulfilling her contractual obligation. Her editor read them but rejected them. His assistant noted that down and filed the note with her contract and other paperwork. *That's* what you removed the day Mrs. Moffat-Jones died. By destroying the evidence of her submissions, you can say she failed to comply with the option clause, giving Woodhouse and Collins the legal right to take one of her manuscripts."

He must have realized he couldn't bluff his way out of it anymore. He conceded with a heavy sigh. "All right. It's true. But it was my father's idea. He was ill, but his mind was still sharp, right up until the end. He saw the manuscripts in the catalog and asked me to check the archives to see if she submitted them to her editor. If she had, he suggested I destroy the evidence so we could stop whoever bought them from publishing them. We were going to put the original bound manuscripts on display here in our offices. The publicity surrounding them would have been incredible. The story of their discovery years after her death would appear in every newspaper. Journalists and the public would lap it all up, particularly given the gruesome nature of Littleproud's murder."

His callous greed rendered me speechless.

Not so Gabe. "Your plan would only have worked if another publisher purchased the manuscripts and had permission from Mrs. Moffat-Jones's heirs to publish them. But the buyer is a private collector with no such plans. You destroyed evidence for nothing. You lied to us for no reason. Unless you truly are the killer and are attempting to cover your tracks with this story about the option clause..."

"No! I'm not!" He pointed at the door. "Leave. Next time you want to speak to me, make an appointment. My lawyer will be present."

Gabe and I left. He touched the brim of his hat in farewell as we passed the open-mouthed assistant who'd heard every word of our exchange. Gabe seemed quite cheerful given the heated encounter.

"Do you really think he used the option clause and destruction of the filed note as a ruse to put us off the scent?" I asked.

"He's most likely innocent of the murder. But it was fun to watch him squirm."

\* \* \*

THE GLASS LIBRARY wasn't the usual place of quiet research and reflection that I was used to. Raised voices came from the ground floor reading nook. I recognized Willie's, but not the other one. It belonged to a man.

Professor Nash sat at the front desk, looking as though he

wished he could be anywhere else. "Thank goodness you're back, Gabriel. You too, Alex." He pushed his glasses up his nose. "Can you please tell Willie to put her gun away? She won't listen to me."

Gabe strode through the marble columned entrance to the library proper. The professor, Alex and I followed behind.

Willie stood in the reading nook, pointing her gun at a very large man with his arms crossed over his chest. He wore only one glove, and a small scar marked his cheek. He glowered back at her, daring her to shoot. He clearly didn't know her or he wouldn't have risked his life.

Murray perched on the edge of the desk, eating a slice of cake. He acknowledged our arrival with a lift of his chin but kept eating. Alex joined him and picked up a slice of cake from the plate on the desk. They might as well have been watching a stage show.

"What's going on here?" Gabe growled.

"Murray found Billy Burgess," Willie said. "He was hiding out in the back room at the pub where his brother works, like the coward he is. Before he confronted Burgess, Murray telephoned me to come get him."

Murray swallowed and brushed the crumbs off his fingers. "I telephoned you, sir, but Willie said you were out. I just needed someone with authority to come get him. I reckoned her gun ought to do the job. But he won't answer our questions."

"Only the guilty don't answer questions," Willie sneered.

"I didn't murder the bookbinder!" Burgess snapped. "But I know what the Old Bill are like. They'll twist my words to make me look guilty. I ain't going to jail for this!"

"We're not the police," Gabe said. "But I do have the authority to arrest you if you don't cooperate."

Willie waggled the gun. "Or shoot you."

Gabe put his hand on the barrel to lower it. "I'd rather you didn't. Not in here."

The moment she holstered the gun, Billy Burgess took off. He was fast for a large man, and he knew the best route to escape was past the weaker folk—the professor and me.

Unfortunately for him, my instincts kicked in. My mother's drills had paid off a few times in recent weeks, and they did so again. As Burgess shoved me out of the way, I extended my foot.

He tripped over it and crashed to the floor with such force, the overhead chandelier jangled. He groaned and rolled over. Blood streamed from his nose.

Murray and Alex grabbed an arm each and hauled him to his feet. "Nicely done, Sylvia," Alex said.

Willie raised her gun again and pointed it at Burgess. "Now you know why I got my Colt out."

Gabe touched my elbow and dipped his head to peer at me. "Are you all right?"

"Yes, thank you."

"That was impressive."

"It was instinct."

His hand moved from my elbow up my arm. "You're shaking. Come and sit down. Professor, can you bring Sylvia a cup of tea?"

He steered me to the desk chair while Murray and Alex forced Burgess onto the sofa. He shook each of them off before accepting the handkerchief Alex handed to him. Both men hovered, not risking Burgess trying to flee again.

Gabe joined them, and the three men plus Willie almost blocked my view of the thug. "You claim you didn't kill Littleproud," Gabe said. "Convince me and I'll let you go."

Burgess wiped the handkerchief across his nose and said nothing.

I cleared my throat. "Excuse me, may I say something?"

The men parted to allow a clear line of sight between Burgess and me. He looked like a typical thug employed by Thurlow, with muscles bulging on every visible part of him. He ignored me. He didn't even look my way. Perhaps he was embarrassed to have been thwarted by a woman of my size.

"I met your sons."

That got the reaction I wanted. "Don't go near my family."

"You mistake us for the kind of people you work for. Your family is lovely, Mr. Burgess. The boys are sweet, and I can see that you care for them very much. If you love them like I think you do, you should tell us the truth. Otherwise there's a real risk you'll be arrested for the murder and that would be a terrible outcome for your boys. They need their father at home, not in prison."

Burgess shifted his weight and looked down at the bloodied handkerchief in his lap. For a moment, I thought my tactic hadn't worked, but then he lifted his head. "I was hired to find the address of the bookbinder's silver supplier."

His admission was most unexpected. From the way Gabe glanced at me, I suspected it took him by surprise too.

Burgess mistook our confusion for ignorance about the process. "Bookbinders use corner protectors on covers sometimes. The most expensive kind are made of silver. The person who hired me wanted to know where he could find her."

"Her?" Gabe echoed. "He thought Littleproud's silver supplier was a woman?"

Burgess nodded.

Marianne Folgate. It had to be her. What other woman would have access to the silver corner protectors made by John Folgate? It seemed we weren't the only ones who knew of her existence.

"Who hired you?" Gabe asked.

"I don't know."

"Come now, Billy, don't treat us like fools. We know Thurlow regularly hires you."

"It wasn't him. This cove telephoned me at the pub. Thurlow would just come right up to me and hire me, face to face, but this one wanted to keep his identity secret. It was hard to hear him over the noise, but it was definitely a man and not a voice I recognized. He didn't give his name, just instructions. He left money for me in a designated drop point in the park."

"Did he want anything else from Littleproud's shop? Books, for example?"

"Just the address of the supplier. I watched the book-binder's shop a few times and worked out he sometimes stayed late. That suited me. I didn't want to confront him in the daytime. So I waited until he was alone and no one was around, and spoke to him. The man who paid me said I could rough him up to scare him. He said to do whatever was necessary."

"Do you know Littleproud died of his injuries?"

"It wasn't me! I didn't rough him up in the end! I didn't have to. The bookbinder was going to give me her address, no questions asked. He didn't care. Anyway, he told me the information wasn't easy to get to, that he had to move some things around." He shrugged. "I didn't know what he meant, but I had time. The man on the telephone gave me three days to get the address. So I went back to the shop the next night to collect it. That's when I saw the bookbinder's body. He was dead on the floor." He put up his hands in surrender. "It wasn't my doing. He was already like that, I swear. The place had been turned over, like the killer was looking for some-thing. It was a real mess, but that wasn't me, either."

"What did you do?" Gabe asked.

"I had a poke around and found the book that lists his

suppliers' names and addresses behind the counter. I copied the details for the silversmith. Rinehold. He was a him, though, not a her. I passed on the information to my contact and he paid me, just like he promised. Only, it wasn't the right supplier, so I found out later."

"He didn't want Littleproud's *current* supplier," Gabe filled in. "He wanted the previous one, from years ago. But you didn't know that. You thought you had the right one when you found Rinehold's details in the supplier's records, but Littleproud had known you were after an earlier one because you mentioned the untitled books from the auction catalog to him. That's why he suggested you return later, because he needed time to find the old information."

Burgess's employer wanted the one who'd supplied the silver corner protectors on Honoria Moffat-Jones's books. When we'd spoken to Mr. Rinehold, Littleproud's most recent supplier of silver corner protectors, he said someone had posed as a detective and telephoned about the ones with the engraved JF in the silverwork. That had been a mere two days before we made the same inquiry. The caller had to be Burgess's employer after Burgess gave him Rinehold's details. The man hadn't realized it was the wrong supplier until he spoke to Rinehold.

"Your employer must have been angry when he discovered Rinehold wasn't the silversmith he wanted," I said.

"Aye. He told me to go back to the bookbinder's and look around again, but I refused. The shop was a crime scene by then. Your lot were crawling all over it. I knew if I was seen, I'd be the number one suspect."

Alex offered Burgess a cigarette from his case then lit it for him. "You've been in hiding since."

"Not hiding. Laying low." Burgess drew deeply on the cigarette and blew smoke out of the corner of his mouth. "Can I go now?"

Gabe and Alex exchanged glances then Alex nodded.

Burgess rose and stepped closer to Willie. He pointed his cigarette at her holstered gun. "You ought to watch where you point that, little lady."

She slowly pushed back the flap of her jacket to reveal more of the gun. "Call me that again and I'll point it at a piece of you that'll turn you from a big man to a little one if I pull the trigger."

He gave an amused grunt around the cigarette butt.

Alex escorted him out of the library as the professor returned with the tea.

Gabe and Willie both finally relaxed as I filled the teacups. "So it ain't Thurlow," Willie said. "Damn it. I really wanted him to be guilty."

Gabe accepted the teacup from me but put it down before taking a sip. "Thurlow didn't hire Burgess, but he could still be the murderer. Littleproud was low on money, even after selling the books to Lady Stanhope. Either he hid the money she paid him somewhere and we just haven't found it, or he used it to pay creditors immediately after receiving it. Perhaps Thurlow was one of those creditors but the payment wasn't enough so he used force in an attempt to get more. What is now clear is that we have two possible motives for the murder. One: Burgess is lying about Littleproud already being dead when he entered the shop and he *is* the killer. The problem with that theory is I believe him."

"As do I," I said. "He had no reason to rough up Littleproud."

Alex returned and sat beside the professor on the sofa. "I agree. Not only is the motive weak, I also think Burgess is telling the truth."

"So the second potential motive is the books, not the silversmith," Professor Nash said. "The killer wanted them because they're valuable."

Gabe nodded. "But did he or she want them for the magic paper or the silver which was made by a magician?"

"Or for Honoria's stories?" I added. "I wouldn't discount Mr. Woodhouse yet. He's ruthless and a liar. He might have hoped to get the manuscripts through legal means, but worried that a buyer might not relinquish them so decided to steal them instead, only to find out he was too late and Littleproud had already sold them."

I'd assumed speaking to Billy Burgess would answer a lot of our questions, but instead it had led to more. Nor had we eliminated any suspects. It now seemed like we had another one, a secret one. All we knew about Burgess's employer was that he was a man and he knew the initials engraved on the corner protectors belonged to a little known silversmith magician, John Folgate.

Whether that man was also the killer remained to be seen.

Something in one of Burgess's responses intrigued me. When he'd asked Littleproud for the name and address of his previous silver supplier, Littleproud said he needed to move things around. "What do you think he meant by that?" I asked.

Alex shrugged. "That he'd archived the old supplier file somewhere, storing it away where he could get it if necessary."

"But it's an odd expression. Why not say he needed to fetch it, or get it out of storage or out of a box? Why 'move things around?'"

Neither Willie nor Alex thought it meant anything significant, but the professor agreed with me. It was an odd choice of words. "Words have meaning. Littleproud must have had a reason for choosing them. If he didn't say 'fetch' then it's likely the records are in the shop somewhere."

Alex wasn't convinced. "That place was well and truly turned over by the killer. Everything that could contain old records was opened. I looked through the drawers, cupboards, and boxes when I tidied up and I saw no other files or ledgers, nothing like that."

"But you didn't *move* anything," I pointed out.

Gabe lifted his teacup and pointed it at Alex. "Drink up. We have some furniture to rearrange."

\* \* \*

WILLIE CLAIMED she had better things to do than search the crime scene again, so it was just Alex, Gabe and me who returned to the Paternoster Row shop. The men removed their jackets and placed them on the counter. As they rolled up their sleeves, they surveyed the room to find the best place to start. Alex suggested they begin by moving the heaviest pieces, that way it would get easier as they progressed. Gabe thought it more likely that Mr. Littleproud would store old files under something he could move on his own, therefore they should start with small cabinets.

"What do you think, Sylvia?" he asked.

I'd been thinking of Gabe's forearms as he slowly revealed them. They were nicely muscled, the sort of arms a girl would like to be enveloped by.

"Sylvia?" he prompted. "Is everything all right?"

"Yes! Yes. Perfect. I mean, I'm fine. You should help him." I indicated Alex, considering how best to move one of the tables, then I quickly turned away before Gabe noticed my reddening cheeks.

I found myself facing a framed photograph of the shop with a young Mr. Littleproud standing behind the counter. Several books were on display, some stacked, others opened on special stands for customers to peruse his handiwork. To the right of the counter was the door that led to his private room where he slept when he worked late.

I frowned and looked around the room. The counter was in a different position in the photograph compared to its current location near the front door. It was near the back in the picture. The work tables were located where I now stood, the shelving unit behind. I could see why Mr. Littleproud changed the layout. Customers had to pass through the messier working area to get to the counter and displayed books. The current layout was cleaner, more aesthetically pleasing.

There was a good reason why it had once been laid out differently, however. A reason that wasn't clear until I saw the photograph. There was a trapdoor in the floor near the back. It was unobstructed when the photograph was taken, and easily accessible, but when Mr. Littleproud rearranged the room, he'd placed the shelving unit on top of it.

I removed the photograph from the wall. "Move the shelves two feet to the right."

Gabe checked the photograph then looked at the shelves. "He couldn't move that on his own."

Alex put his shoulder to it and pushed. It budged and he could have pushed it all the way, but he didn't want to scratch the floor. Gabe took the other end and they lifted it and moved it across until the trapdoor was revealed.

Alex pulled it up and we all peered inside. A set of stairs led into a basement storeroom, but we couldn't see much more than a few boxy shapes in the darkness.

I fetched an old oil lamp from under the counter and lit it. I handed it to Gabe. "You first."

He grinned. "I thought it was ladies first."

"I'm not going down there."

Alex took the lamp from Gabe. "Afraid of ghosts, Sylvia?"

"Afraid of spiders."

He hesitated then handed the lamp back to Gabe. "I

wouldn't want to deprive you of being the first one to discover a long-lost treasure."

The long-lost treasure consisted of nothing more than a few boxes of old files, some broken tools, and a chair with three legs. After Gabe re-emerged with the boxes, we sat at the tables and opened them. I breathed in the smell of old paper before lifting out a pile. Many had yellowed but they'd been protected in the boxes and were still legible. Thankfully there were no small creatures scurrying about.

We took a stack each and flipped through the papers. There was a whole file listing several of Mr. Littleproud's former silversmith suppliers. I easily found the name we wanted.

I turned the piece of paper around to show Gabe and Alex. "Marianne Folgate supplied only a small collection of silver corner protectors. She wasn't his regular supplier back then." The notes below her name described the batch along-side the quantity Mr. Littleproud purchased and the price paid. It also stated the corner protectors were made by her father, John Folgate, a silversmith from Ipswich. The word Deceased appeared in parentheses as well as a note that she inherited them from him.

"Littleproud wanted to know their provenance in case they turned out to be stolen goods," Gabe said as he read. "There's no address listed for Marianne."

I pointed to the date on the yellowed paper. "This is around the time she was living in Wimbledon."

"Whether she was living in the Wimbledon townhouse when she sold the corner protectors to Littleproud or not doesn't matter. We don't know where she went after she moved out of there."

We were back to square one in our hunt for Marianne Folgate.

As for our hunt for the killer, we seemed to have hit a

dead end there too. We found no money in the basement storeroom, no reference to a gambling or other debt.

Alex blew dust off another box then coughed as it billowed in his face. He waved the cloud away. "That trapdoor hasn't been opened in years. If he does have a recent debt, he won't have stored the information down there."

Gabe accepted a stack of papers from Alex and began to read the top one. After a moment, he lowered it with a shake of his head. "Why didn't Mrs. Littleproud tell us about the trapdoor and storeroom? She must have known about it."

"Perhaps she simply forgot it was there," I said.

Alex pulled out some old account ledgers from a box and passed one to me. I smoothed my hand over the first page. Water must have got to it at some stage. The ink had faded and the paper didn't sit flat. After a cursory glance, I closed the cover. It contained nothing more than some old customer details.

Continuing seemed rather pointless to me but I kept my mouth shut. I enjoyed touching the old papers, feeling their texture against my fingertips, even the smell. Huon Barratt had once claimed to know how ink was made, which ingredients it contained and the process used, even if the ink contained no magic at all. His father had taught him the skill, and as a magician, he had an acute awareness of his craft. If I'd been trained in the art of papermaking, I'd know how this paper was made, whether from trees or rags, by hand or machine. Now that I knew what magical warmth felt like, I was quite sure it didn't have any spells on it.

I set aside the ledger and reached for another at the same time as Gabe. Our fingers touched. Our gazes lifted, connected. The sensation that tingled my skin wasn't so different from how magic felt. The sensation causing my heart to skip wildly was something altogether unique, however. Only Gabe could do that to me.

Did he know?

Alex's voice jolted me back into the moment. "I found it. I found the record for Honoria's manuscripts. The name of the person who brought them in for binding is listed here. All five of them." He looked up at Gabe, shaking his head in disbelief. "It's a relation of yours."

# CHAPTER 15

abe studied the entry Alex pointed to. "A relation by marriage. I never knew him, although I've heard my parents and yours speak about him."

"And not in a good way," Alex said darkly.

I got up to read over Gabe's shoulder. "Lord Coyle. Willie mentioned him recently. He married your father's cousin, didn't he?"

"Hope Glass. My grandfather and her father were brothers. Her father was the previous Lord Rycroft, but he didn't have any sons so the title went to my father as the next male on the family tree. Hope was his youngest daughter. I haven't seen her in a long time."

"For good reason," Alex muttered.

When he didn't elaborate, I asked, "Because she's mad? Willie alluded to that being the case for Hope and her sisters."

Neither Alex nor Gabe knew the exact reason, only that they were told she wasn't a nice person. Her husband, Lord Coyle, had apparently been a thoroughly horrible fellow, but again, neither knew the full story.

"My father will know," Alex said. "And Willie."

I wondered if it was linked to the story about the paper cuts that Willie was so reluctant to discuss. If so, then she'd probably not want to talk about Lord Coyle either.

I leaned over Gabe, seated at the table. I had to get quite close to him to read Mr. Littleproud's small writing. His nearness meant it took me longer to focus. "The entry is dated 1891. Twenty-nine years ago. I wonder why Lord Coyle brought them in for binding and never collected them."

Gabe breathed deeply. I waited or him to say something, but he didn't.

"Gabe?" Alex prompted.

Gabe closed the book and placed it back into the box. "Let's call on his widow and see if she knows."

I indicated the fading light outside. "It's getting late."

"Then we'll leave it for tomorrow. I have to get their address anyway. Bristow will know it."

"*Their* address?" I echoed.

"Her and her son, Valentine, the current Lord Coyle."

Ah, yes, the son who Willie claimed looked more like the driver than Lord Coyle. I was rather keen to meet them. Gabe's English family must be very odd indeed if his American cousin called them mad. She was hardly the sanest person herself.

* * *

GABE TELEPHONED the library the following morning, inviting me to his place to meet his cousin, Lady Coyle. When he spoke to her the previous evening, she had insisted on visiting him, not the other way around, and offered her regrets that her son couldn't attend.

When I arrived at Gabe's house, Willie was only too

happy to tell me why. "She doesn't want us to know that Valentine's still in bed. Apparently he's a no-good lay about who drinks and gambles all night, and has no employment during the day."

Alex narrowed his gaze at her. "I don't think you're in a position to criticize anyone for that list of vices."

She folded her arms over her chest. "I ain't a lord with responsibilities. I don't have to support my mother or run a household. I never lost my father's estate because of my debts. I'm free. He ain't." She suddenly grinned. "It's justice, though."

"What is?" I asked as I sat on the sofa in the drawing room.

"Hope getting an idiot for a son. She doesn't deserve a good one."

"Is he an idiot, or is he simply trying to forget his war experiences?"

"He didn't serve. Apparently he's got a lazy eye or two left feet. Something like that. I reckon his mother had a liaison with a doctor who made up some ailment that stopped him from having to go."

Gabe hitched up his trousers at the knees and sat beside me. "That's enough, Willie. Let's try to keep this civil. Whatever Hope did in the past, it's finished. It's not like her life has been easy since her husband died. For one thing, she's had to suffer the speculation of people who believe her son is not her husband's." He arched his brows pointedly at her. "For another, they've lost everything."

She snorted. "Not everything. They ain't living on the street, Gabe. They had to sell off the country estate and the London townhouse to pay their debts and they now live in a small flat, but it's in a nice area. Besides, they ain't got nobody but themselves to blame. She and the idiot like to gamble and they spend money like its water. The father, too. He's got a nice shiny new Rolls Royce to drive his lover and son around in."

Gabe rubbed a hand over his face and groaned. "I don't suppose there's any chance you'll leave for this interview."

She threw herself onto an armchair and crossed her ankles. "Nope. I'm going to sit here and gloat about how good our lives turned out compared to hers."

"You'll do no such thing."

Willie's smug smile remained. I suspected it was going to take some convincing to wipe it off. She seemed to loathe Lady Coyle.

"What *did* she do to you?" I asked.

Willie's smile vanished. "It's a long story and it ain't all mine to tell." She patted her jacket pockets. "Anyone got a cigarette?"

"You've given up," Alex reminded her.

She swore under her breath and slumped into the chair. Her right foot started to tap lightly against the other, a nervous habit that reminded me of Gabe's thumb tapping. It was most unlike her. She was usually so cocky. Perhaps her earlier smugness was all an act, covering up her nervousness.

I was more intrigued by the Dowager Lady Coyle than ever.

It was something of a relief to find she was quite normal. She was nothing like Willie's description. I expected a *femme fatale*, but she was an ordinary looking middle-aged woman who, like most women of her generation, followed the pre-war fashions of flouncy dresses of layered lace over a restrictive corset. Unlike today's straighter lines, her outfit was designed to accentuate the feminine hourglass shape. Lady Coyle's figure may have once been an hourglass, but no corset could turn back time. She had a waistline that was indistinguishable from her bust and hips. The bloodshot eyes made her look tired, and the gray tinge to her skin aged her beyond her fifty-odd years. Her smile would have elevated her appearance if it wasn't so forced.

She glanced around the room, taking it all in. Her gaze, at least, was sharp. "India has changed a few things."

"I live here now," Gabe said. "My parents live at Rycroft Hall, although they're currently holidaying overseas."

"Yes, I heard. Your mother writes to my eldest sister, Patience, who occasionally bothers to write to me. She does love telling me every time one of her stepchildren has another offspring." Her gaze settled on me.

Gabe made the introductions. "Miss Ashe is assistant to Professor Nash at the Glass Library."

She put out her hand and I shook it. The lace glove was scratchy. "I remember the professor. He and that friend of his came to my house years ago to peruse my husband's library. They purchased a handful of tomes I was prepared to part with." She eased herself into the armchair with a wince of pain before replacing it with her false smile. "How are your parents, Gabriel?"

"Fine, thank you. And you, Lady Coyle?"

"Call me Hope. You're old enough now." Her smile softened into a genuine, somewhat wistful one. "You are so like your father. So handsome and tall. There is very little of India in your appearance. I believe you also didn't inherit her magic."

Gabe indicated the others. "You remember my father's cousin Willie, and my friend Alex."

"The son of the one-eyed pirate. How can I forget? So... distinctive." She turned away without extending her hand to him.

Alex rolled his eyes and sat.

Willie approached Lady Coyle, hands on hips. She seemed

rather put-out not to have been acknowledged at all. Knowing Willie, I suspected she would have preferred an insult to complete disregard. "I reckon you wish you could forget me."

"Actually, I remember very little about you. Were you around much in those days?"

The muscles in Willie's jaw worked, but no words came out. She stood there, quietly fuming at being all but ignored, then and now.

Thankfully Bristow entered carrying a tray. His arrival dispersed the tension and Willie resumed her seat. Gabe filled the interval with small talk as Bristow poured the tea, asking after Lady Coyle's health and that of her son.

"Valentine is well," she said through that forced smile of hers. "Now that life is getting back to normal, he's looking forward to picking up where he left off, so to speak."

Willie opened her mouth but shut it when Gabe shook his head at her. If she were a teapot, steam would have been billowing out of her nostrils and ears as she muttered something under her breath.

Lady Coyle accepted the teacup from Bristow and sipped. While she didn't look in Willie's direction, I got the distinct feeling she knew how much Willie wanted to retort. It was almost as if Lady Coyle was baiting her, knowing she was forced to stay quiet.

Lady Coyle set the teacup down. "How is your fiancée, Gabriel? She must be rather anxious for your parents to return so the wedding can proceed. I admit, I'm surprised they went away before your marriage. You young folk have had to wait so long already, and now you must wait even longer." While on the surface, she was all sweetness and sympathy, the undertone was unmistakable. She was accusing Gabe's parents of being selfish.

Beside me, Gabe bristled. "Ivy ended our engagement."

"Ah. Then your mother knew exactly what she was doing." She picked up her teacup. "I must say, your telephone call was quite unexpected. I wasn't aware you worked for Scotland Yard."

"On a consultancy basis only."

"And you, Miss Ashe? Where do you and the Glass Library fit in?"

"I'm assisting Gabe and Alex, since books are at the heart of this investigation."

"Gabe, is it?" She gave me a thorough inspection, as if seeing me for the first time. I suspected I came up lacking, if her barely perceptible huff of breath was an indication. "Have you met Matt and India, Miss Ashe?"

"No."

"When you do, you'll see what I mean when I say the apple doesn't fall far from the tree. Now, tell me all about this case."

That she would ask me and not Gabe was a sure indication she was trying to get my measure, beyond mere outward appearances. I often felt like I was being assessed when people saw me with Gabe, but no more so than now. Not even Alex's mother, Lady Rycroft's good friend Catherine Bailey, had tested me so blatantly. If Lady Coyle was close to her cousin, I'd expect the reason behind it was the protection a family member, but they were estranged.

It was unnerving. So much so that I stumbled at the first hurdle. "The books are magical."

She frowned. "What books? How are they magical?"

"They, er, were brought to the library where I work. They're not magical in themselves but do contain magic. The paper does. Or perhaps the silver."

"Silver? Good lord. They must be valuable indeed if they're made of silver." She laughed, pressing her hand to her bosom as it jiggled along with all of her chins.

"The books aren't made of silver, just the corner protectors. On the covers," I added. "The bookbinder had them."

"He's the one who brought them to you? I don't understand why. Are you a magician, Miss Ashe? Were you going to verify the magic for him?"

Her rapid-fire questions came at me like bullets. But it was the question about me being a magician that hit harder than the others. It completely twisted my tongue. All I could do was stare at her and say, "Um."

Thankfully Gabe came to my rescue. "A bookbinder by the name of Littleproud has been murdered. We believe that five unpublished manuscripts he bound for a client are at the center of the investigation. He had them in his possession for years, waiting for the client to collect them. Old records show they were brought in by your late husband."

"I see. And you would like to return them to me. How very thoughtful."

"The books are evidence."

"So they're currently with you? Or in Scotland Yard's evidence room?"

"I'm not at liberty to say."

"If the books belong to me, I have a right to know. How long before I can have them back, do you think?"

Gabe cleared his throat. "That's not why I asked you here today. Your husband died in 1891."

"Yes."

"That seems to be the reason they remained uncollected."

"Then the bookbinder should have contacted me, as the widow. He should never have kept them for so long. At least they'll be returned to me now. I am grateful, Gabriel." She turned to me. "Miss Ashe, please inform Professor Nash that the books will be for sale. As a favor to my cousin, Matt, I'll offer them to the Glass Library first."

I smiled weakly.

Willie piped up from her corner of the room. "The library holds books *about* magic, not books that contain magic."

"I shall speak to the professor myself. I'm sure he'd like to own them. If not, perhaps he can give me a valuation."

Gabe didn't mention Lady Stanhope. The ownership of the books was somewhat contentious and he wouldn't want to open that can of worms here and now. It was something for the two women to battle over after the investigation ended. They'd have to fend off competition from Mr. Moffat-Jones and Woodhouse and Collins Publishing, too.

"I take it you weren't aware of the manuscripts?" Gabe asked.

"No."

"Do you have any documents of your late husband's that might have mentioned them? We need to know how they fell into his possession."

"It's likely someone sold them to him. He was always collecting magical things, just to possess them. It was quite a ridiculous hobby of his, really. The value of several items in his collection decreased after magicians could practice their craft freely. Many were worth very little and I was forced to sell them for much less than he paid. But these books must be valuable or the bookbinder wouldn't have been murdered for them." She leaned forward. "How much, do you think, Gabriel?"

"I don't know. The records of your husband's purchases...?"

"I'm afraid I haven't kept any of that. When we moved into the flat, we had to throw so many things away." She set the teacup and saucer on the table beside her with slow, deliberate movements. "Since you have evidence that my husband owned them, the books clearly belong to Valentine and me. You will see that they're returned to us, won't you?"

"The books will be returned to their rightful owner the moment they're no longer required for the investigation."

She pushed herself to her feet, wincing a little before plastering the tight smile on her face again. "When you bring them around, telephone first so I can make sure Valentine is home. It's been a long time since the two of you have caught up and I know he'd like to see you again. You can discuss business. Valentine is an enthusiastic and creative investor. He doesn't limit himself to English investments. They're too conservative here, he claims. He looks for schemes with greater reward, like the one he's currently investing it. It operates out of America by an Italian immigrant named Ponzi. The returns are extraordinary. We'll have doubled our money in a month. Just imagine what that will be worth by the end of the year. When you bring the books, I'll have Valentine give you the details so you can take advantage too."

"I'm glad to hear things are going well for you both," Gabe said.

"Things are turning around after some difficult years. Losing the houses and letting the staff go has been trying."

"You kept your driver, though," Willie said brightly. "That must have made him happy. You and your son, too, I expect."

Lady Coyle's nostrils flared.

"Does he live in? Oh, wait, you just have a small flat now so..." She dug her hands into her pockets and shrugged oh-so-innocently.

Lady Coyle chose to ignore her once again. It was probably the only way to cope with Willie when she was in a taunting mood. Arguing with her would only lead to her raising the level of her taunts.

Gabe stepped forward, blocking Lady Coyle's line of sight to Willie. He smiled and took her elbow to guide her to the door. She limped a little. Either her knees or ankles pained her.

When Gabe returned alone, he sported a thoughtful frown. Despite being asked what caused it, he wouldn't respond. He simply shook his head and sat.

Alex got up and poured more tea for those who wanted it. He handed Gabe a cup. "Go on. You can tell us. What is it?"

Willie crossed one leg over the other knee. "It's on account of Hope looking so changed, isn't it? You can't get over how different she is now from the last time you saw her."

"That's not it," Gabe said.

Willie might as well not have heard him. She addressed me. "Hope used to be a beauty. She was the prettiest girl in every room. All the men wanted her, but she chose ugly old Coyle. He was rich and powerful and more than anything, she wanted to be rich and powerful, so it was a good match. But look at her now, as ugly as her late husband."

"That's not kind," Gabe chided.

"She doesn't deserve kindness. Anyway, it ain't unkind if it's the truth. Do you think she looks like a sack of old pota-toes because she drinks too much? Cocaine? No, that would make her thin. Must be drink, and sitting on her ass all day long." She strode to the escritoire and opened the top drawer. "Can I use some of your letterhead?"

"Why?"

"I want to write and tell India that Hope's aged as elegantly as a piece of old fruit."

"Willie!"

"You're right. India won't celebrate Hope's downfall. Nor will Cyclops or Catherine." She clicked her fingers and grinned. "Duke will." She sat and pulled out a sheet of letter-head from the drawer and bent to the task of writing.

"Is Duke the friend your parents are visiting in America?" I asked Gabe. I recalled his name being mentioned before as a close friend of Willie and Cyclops who'd returned to the States and settled down with a wife and children.

Gabe wasn't listening, however. When he failed to answer, Alex and I exchanged glances.

"What are you thinking?" Alex prompted him.

Gabe winced as he set his teacup down carefully. He wasn't in pain, however. At least not physical pain. I suspected it was his thoughts that troubled him. "I don't like saying this, as they're family, but we have to consider Hope and Valentine as suspects. I wasn't aware how desperate her situation was until today. It's feasible she knew about the manuscripts but didn't realize how valuable they were until she saw them in the auction house catalog. She and Valentine might have gone to Littleproud's shop to retrieve them only to find he'd already sold the collection. He died before they could find out who he sold them to." Even as he said it, Gabe shook his head. "I'm over-thinking this. Of course they wouldn't do that."

Alex agreed. "She didn't seem to know about the books' existence."

"She's a good actress," Willie said without looking up from her letter. "She's also ruthless, so don't go thinking she wouldn't send a big brute to beat Littleproud up. She's capable of anything."

It was clear that we needed to find out how the books had gone from Honoria to Lord Coyle, and Lady Coyle couldn't help us. Cyclops still had men assigned to the task of questioning London publishers, but considering the vast passage of time, it would most likely result in a dead end. But it wasn't necessarily a publisher who'd sold them to Coyle. We couldn't discount the theory that Honoria had sold them to him herself after every children's book publisher rejected them.

I suggested we ask Mr. Moffat-Jones if his first wife knew Lord Coyle. Even if he'd only heard of him by reputation, it would establish a link between Honoria and the collector and throw more weight behind the theory she'd sold him the manuscripts. It would mean we could stop chasing down publishers and focus our attention elsewhere.

Gabe and Alex agreed to head to the Moffat-Jones house next, while Willie was too busy writing to give an opinion.

After freshening up, I joined Gabe and Alex in the entrance hall along with Bristow. The butler held out a silver tray with a folded piece of paper on it.

"Mrs. Ling has asked if you could pass this recipe on to your landlady," he said with stiff formality. "It's one of Mr. Glass's favorite recipes, translated from the original by Mrs. Ling."

Ever since Mrs. Parry expressed interest in Chinese cooking, Mrs. Ling had corresponded with her, sending translated recipes from her native land. Despite having never met, Mrs. Parry told me they'd formed a bond, exchanging recipes, market news, and cooking tips.

I tucked the recipe into my bag. "Please thank Mrs. Ling on Mrs. Parry's behalf. And on my behalf, too. I do enjoy it when Mrs. Parry makes one of Mrs. Ling's specialties."

"I will. And Mrs. Bristow would like to pass on her regards to you, too, Miss Ashe." The butler opened the front door and saw us out.

Gabe gave me a curious smile as he held the Vauxhall's door open for me. "I think my servants like you more than they like me."

I laughed. "I doubt that."

"If you like Mrs. Ling's cooking so much, you should come to dinner. She'd relish the chance to cook a banquet of Chinese food for you." He took my hand to assist me into the motorcar. "I'd like you to join us, too. You've become a fixture around here."

"A fixture?" I teased.

He apologized. "I meant you fit in with this household. I

include Alex's family in that, since they're a regular fixture here, too. You have a civilizing effect on us."

The front door of the house burst open and Willie rushed out, waving her arms in the air. "If you don't wait for me, I'll put dead mice in your beds."

I raised my brows. "Civilizing?"

He chuckled. "No one can civilize her."

# CHAPTER 16

$\mathcal{T}$he maid shot Alex a flirtatious glance as she bobbed a curtsy. He didn't notice. Considering he was a consultant for Scotland Yard, he ought to be more observant. But he was rather oblivious to the effect he had on women. Gabe could be equally ignorant at times.

Both men were more interested in our host than they were in the maid. They exchanged small talk about the English cricket team while Eleanor Moffat-Jones poured the tea. I tried to engage her in conversation, too, but her one-word responses made it difficult. Nor would she meet my gaze. When she passed me the cup and saucer, some tea spilled over the rim.

"I'm so sorry, Miss Ashe. I'll pour another."

"It's quite all right. This one is perfectly fine."

She glanced at her husband, but he was more interested in hearing Alex's opinion of a new fast bowler than his wife's mishap.

Mrs. Moffat-Jones picked up a second teacup and saucer and offered them to me. "Take this and I'll use that one."

"No, really. It's just a drop."

Given that her hand shook slightly, the tea was in danger of spilling over the rim of that cup, too. She stared at it, not sure what to do. She knew if she held it much longer the tea would spill but she seemed frozen, unable to pass it along or put it down.

I took it from her and handed it to Gabe then picked up the others and passed them around. When I came to her husband, he accepted the teacup without a word.

Mrs. Moffat-Jones perched on the edge of the chair with her hands clasped tightly in her lap, the fingers interlocked. She watched her husband from beneath lowered lashes.

They were each other's opposite. She slight and anxious, he solidly built and self-assured. He drew attention simply by being present whereas she almost disappeared. Or perhaps she wanted to.

"Now." Mr. Moffat-Jones's booming voice made his wife jump. "Have you come to tell me you've cracked the case, Glass?"

"Not yet," Gabe said. "We have some more questions for you."

"Indeed? Well then, ask away."

"Do you know Lord Coyle?"

He shook his head. "Doesn't ring any bells. Is he the murderer?"

"He's the one who took Honoria's manuscripts to the bookbinder for binding."

"Is he a publisher?"

"He was a collector of magical artefacts."

"Was?"

"He died not long after taking the books in for binding. That's why he didn't collect them. We're trying to find out how he came to own them."

Mr. Moffat-Jones's teacup clattered down hard onto the saucer, making his wife jump again. "He never owned them, merely possessed them. I own them now. If a publisher sold them to this Coyle fellow, then he did so illegally, without my wife's consent."

"How do you know it was without her consent?"

"Of course it must have been. She submitted them to publishers and instead of publishing them, one must have seen the value in selling them to a collector of magical artefacts. Honoria wouldn't have sold off her manuscripts to anyone other than a publisher. What other explanation is there for this lord possessing them?"

"The link is what we're trying to establish."

Mr. Moffat-Jones nodded thoughtfully. "Yes, I see how establishing a link is vital to unearthing the killer's identity. Did you try Woodhouse and Collins? Honoria would have sent her manuscripts there before trying other publishers."

"We can't divulge that information," Alex told him.

"Well then, I suppose you need a list of publishers Honoria sent them to."

"The last time we were here, you said you couldn't tell us which publishers she submitted them to, beyond Woodhouse and Collins," Gabe pointed out.

"Let me have another look through Honoria's things. Perhaps Lucille, my eldest, will have some notes among her mother's belongings."

"Why didn't you offer to look last time? Finding a list of Honoria's submissions would save us a great deal of time and effort."

Mr. Moffat-Jones had claimed they had very few of his first wife's belongings, which was the reason he gave for wanting her manuscripts returned. Now he was claiming he might have her manuscript submission records after all. I wondered how long it would take to miraculously find the list, proving Honoria submitted her manuscripts rather than sold them. Probably about as long as it took to type it up.

I didn't voice my doubts. I didn't want to step on Gabe's toes. There might be a reason for not challenging Mr. Moffat-Jones. If I was being honest, I also stayed quiet because I didn't want to attract Mr. Moffat-Jones's attention.

He seemed to realize the knot he'd tied himself into without any of us having to say anything. He tried to explain away the discrepancy in his story. "I didn't realize how important those old records of hers were and didn't want to open up old wounds. The death of her mother is a difficult matter for Lucille, so I prefer not to talk about Honoria in her presence. But if locating those records can prove *we* own those manuscripts, well, dig them up we must."

I tried to gauge what Mrs. Moffat-Jones thought of her husband's excuse, but she gave nothing away. I couldn't even see her eyes, cast down as they were. Not even her hands moved. They remained clasped in her lap. Her tea was going cold.

Gabe thanked Mr. Moffat-Jones for his time. "Anything relating to those manuscripts that you can find will be a great help."

Mr. Moffat-Jones leaned heavily on his walking stick and pushed himself to his feet with some effort. "Of course, of course."

Mrs. Moffat-Jones suddenly came alive, as if she were an automaton that had been wound up. She brightened, smiling as she stood. "It was lovely to see you again, Miss Ashe, Mr. Glass. And it was a pleasure to meet you, too, Mr. Bailey."

There was nothing in her words or actions that was out of place. She said and did all the right things. Yet something was amiss. While she glanced often at her husband, he did not look her way. He treated her as if she wasn't there. She treated him as though he were a bomb about to explode.

For someone who'd seen her mother's interactions with men over the years, it set me on edge. My mother would observe men she was forced to interact with carefully, but only while they didn't notice her. The moment they looked her way, she pretended to be staring at something else. Most thought she was rude. But I knew it was a hesitation bordering on fear.

Mrs. Moffat-Jones's reactions bothered me for the rest of the journey back to the library. Her husband was outwardly friendly and polite, yet something about him was unnerving. I couldn't quite put my finger on what. He wanted the manuscripts, that much was obvious, but I couldn't blame him for that. They had both monetary and sentimental value for his daughter.

He ignored his wife, however. He also paid me very little attention. Again, those facts weren't unusual. That was how some men were with women. They didn't think we had anything of value to contribute.

In the end, I decided it was Mrs. Moffat-Jones's reaction to her husband that I found more unnerving than Mr. Moffat-Jones himself. Part of me wanted to shake her, tell her not to disappear into the background when in the same room as him. I wanted her to know she could have something of value to add to conversations, if only she found her voice.

The hypocrisy of someone like me wanting to shake sense into her wasn't lost on me. I rarely spoke out of turn, unless truly pushed to my wit's end, and she wasn't entirely dissimilar.

"You've been quiet," Gabe said as he walked along Crooked Lane with me. "Is something wrong?"

I considered telling him about my impressions of Eleanor Moffat-Jones but decided against it. It was irrelevant to the case. It would also reveal more of my own difficult relationship with my mother than I was prepared to share.

"Nothing," I said brightly. "I'm just mulling over the investigation."

"Let me know if you have any revelations because I can't see my way through." He sighed. "I feel as though we're missing something."

"Why do you say that?"

"Instinct. But instinct won't get us anywhere."

"I disagree most strenuously. You have excellent instincts, Gabe, and instincts can lead to seeking the truth. We'll work it out. We just need to unlock what those instincts are telling us, but they *will* unlock."

We'd reached the front door of the library. He opened it for me but didn't enter. "Thank you."

"For what?"

"For believing in me."

It was an odd thing for such a confident man to say that it quite took my breath away. That and the way he looked at me with those beautiful green eyes of his as he said it. It sent a jolt through me.

As did the way our hands touched as I slipped past him into the library.

It wasn't until later that I wondered if he'd deliberately reached for me.

* * *

BEING around books always had a soothing effect on me. I'd assumed it was because reading forced me to focus on the story and not my problems, but now I realized it must be because I was touching paper. The magic within me responded to the products of its craft.

That calmness allowed my mind the freedom to wander as I shelved books in the library. Given the investigation occupied most of my days of late, I expected it to wander in that direction. Instead, I thought about my mother.

Our relationship had been fine, on the whole, but I knew

now that it was because I always capitulated to her will. When she asked me not to stay out late, I went directly home. When she told me to avoid a particular man, I did. When she said it was time to move to a new city, I didn't question her. My brother did, in his teens, but even he stopped asking why the constant need to start over somewhere new.

My mother had been strong. She had to be, to raise two children alone without support. Sometimes that strength had turned domineering. It made her cold and difficult to love.

As I grew older, I realized that strength was borne from an abundance of caution. She was determined that James and I should be kept safe from a world she saw as cruel.

Her strength of character was different to Eleanor Moffat-Jones's meekness, yet I couldn't help thinking they were both fearful. My mother's reaction to her fears was to move to a new city, to keep her children close. Mrs. Moffat-Jones tried to make herself as small as possible.

The reason for their difference was clear to me now—my mother didn't live with the source of her fear. Mrs. Moffat-Jones did.

She'd not suffered physical harm that I could see, but there were many other ways her husband could frighten her, not all of them resulting in obvious bruises. Perhaps he bullied her or threatened her. Or perhaps she knew some-thing about him that scared her.

Perhaps she knew he'd murdered Mr. Littleproud.

I pushed a book into place on the shelf. The silver ring of my mother's that I'd taken to wearing caught the light. She would not want me to get involved in another's private busi-ness. If she was here, she'd advise me to stay out of Eleanor's life. She'd never once interfered. She'd never checked on an ill neighbor or invited a friend over for tea and cathartic chat. She'd never had friends.

I didn't want to be like her.

I headed downstairs to the front desk where the professor was reading a book.

He looked up and smiled. "Going home?"

I peered through the marble columns at the clock above the mantelpiece. The library closed fifteen minutes ago. "I need to make a telephone call first."

Gabe was not at home, but Murray said he was expected soon. I left a message for him to meet me outside the Moffat-Jones's house and then I left, taking the auction house catalog with me.

I waited on the pavement across from their house for an hour, but Gabe didn't arrive. Mr. Moffat-Jones did leave in a cab, however. All I needed was a few minutes alone with his wife to show her the catalog. He need never know I was there.

The maid answered my knock. "You again."

"Is Mrs. Moffat-Jones at home? I have a quick question I need to ask."

She glanced past me. "You're alone? Those handsome blokes not with you?"

"Mr. Glass should be here shortly. Is she receiving callers?"

"Martha?" came Eleanor Moffat-Jones's voice from the depths of the corridor. "Is someone there?"

"It's that woman from Scotland Yard again."

Eleanor appeared behind the maid, wiping her hands on her apron. It didn't wipe off all the flour. She'd been cooking, which accounted for the delicious smells wafting along the corridor from the kitchen. "Miss Ashe! This is a surprise. You just missed my husband, I'm afraid."

"It's you I'd like to speak to."

Her hands stilled. "Oh."

"May I come in? It won't take long."

"Of course. Please, come through. Martha, can you stir the gravy?"

Martha muttered something under her breath then stepped aside. I followed Eleanor to the sitting room.

She indicated I should sit then glanced behind her. "I apologize for Martha's abruptness," she said quietly. "I'd let her go but it's so difficult to find staff these days. The girls don't want to be domestics. Who can blame them? The wages are better in the factories."

I pulled the catalog out of my bag and handed it to her. "Do you recognize this?"

She took it from me and studied the cover before handing it back. "No, sorry. Why?"

I showed her the page with the entry for Honoria's bound manuscripts. "What about these?"

"No."

It was a disappointment but not a complete setback. Just because she'd never seen the catalog didn't mean her husband hadn't. "Now that Mr. Moffat-Jones isn't here, you can be completely honest with me."

She bristled. "I haven't been dishonest with you, Miss Ashe."

I apologized. "That came out wrong. I know you have to be careful around your husband and watch what you say. But now that he's not here, can you tell me...was he home on the night of Mr. Littleproud's murder?"

Her eyes widened and her lips parted with her soft gasp. "I...I suppose so. You should ask him." Her gaze lowered to her hands clasped on her lap. It was the same demure, meek pose she employed when her husband was in the room.

It gave me a reason to keep pushing. "I know he frightens you."

She suddenly looked up. "He doesn't."

I didn't believe her. Not when her eyes filled with tears

and she couldn't meet my gaze. I moved to sit beside her and folded her hand in mine. "I don't want you to be scared of him anymore, Eleanor. I want to help you, but you need to help me. Was your husband out on the night of the murder?"

"I don't know," she murmured. "We have separate bedrooms and I take laudanum to help me sleep. My God... do you think he did it?"

My heart sank. She couldn't give me the answers I wanted, after all. She didn't recognize the catalog and she wasn't aware if he left the house that night. Yet she *was* afraid of him. She would only be afraid if she had a reason.

"Tell me why you fear him," I said. "Don't deny it. I can see it in your eyes, your manner... He frightens you. Is that because you believe he murdered Mr. Littleproud?"

Her chin trembled as she tried to contain her emotions. She glanced over her shoulder at the door.

"He's not here, Eleanor. This is just between you and me." I gave her hand a slight shake. "Do you believe him capable of murder? Is that why you're scared?"

"I don't believe it. I know it. But not the bookbinder."

I frowned. "Who?"

"His first wife. Honoria. He killed her."

# CHAPTER 17

*E*leanor seemed as shocked as me to hear her accuse her husband of murdering his first wife. She glanced at the door again, as if she suspected him to enter at any moment and rage at her.

"Why do you say that?" I asked. "Do you have proof?"

"No." She kept her voice low, but she now seemed eager to speak. It was as if the admission had released a cork, allowing it all to spill out. "He told me, and I believe him. He uses it as a threat, you see, a way of keeping me in my place. Don't do anything to anger him or I'll end up like poor Honoria. Dead at the base of the staircase." Her lips trembled as the tears welled in her eyes. Eyes that implored me to help.

"I'll ask my colleagues at Scotland Yard to look into it."

She grasped my wrist. "No. He'll find out. He'll hurt me if he knows I told you."

"They'll be discreet. He won't find out. But perhaps you should tell your husband you're going away for a little while. Do you have someone outside of London you could visit?

She shook her head. "I can't. He'll be suspicious. I've never spent a night apart from him. And what if the police can't find proof? It's best if I stay here and carry on as if nothing is amiss." She glanced at the door again. "That way he won't suspect."

She had a point, but I loathed the idea of her staying a moment longer under the same roof as a murderer.

She would not be convinced, however, and I reluctantly gave up. I tucked the catalog under my arm and collected my bag. She rang a bell and Martha arrived to show me to the door. The maid paused in the doorway, frowning.

"Is something the matter?" Eleanor asked her.

"I think I burnt the gravy."

"Never mind. We can make more."

Martha showed me to the front door while Eleanor hurried along the corridor towards the kitchen. "I wasn't employed as a cook," the maid told me.

"Martha, do you live-in?"

"Yes." She folded her arms over her chest. "Why?"

"Did Mr. Moffat-Jones leave the house of an evening after his wife went to bed? This would be a little over a week ago."

"No."

"Is it possible you wouldn't know if he had?"

She shook her head. "I'm a light sleeper, and he's got a heavy tread. I'd hear him. He hasn't gone out at night in a long time."

I caught a cab to Gabe's house, but Bristow informed me that he was at Catherine and Cyclops's place with Alex. He gave me the address and suggested I try there if it was urgent.

It was, and Cyclops was the perfect person to speak to.

My nerves jangled all the way there only to finally settle once I was inside. Catherine Bailey instantly knew something was amiss and invited me into the parlor where everyone was gathered. At first I thought they were having a party, it was so loud, but then I realized it was simply their four children, Gabe and Willie all talking over the top of one another. For someone from a small family that never had friends visit, it was quite different from what I was used to.

I liked it. They were all very welcoming, inviting me to sit then placing a cocktail glass in my hand before I could even greet them all individually. Alex's sisters crowded around, each one firing a different question at me.

The eldest, tomboy Ella, wanted my opinion on what motorcar Gabe should buy next. Mae, the middle one, wanted to know where I'd bought my dress. When Lulu, the youngest at seventeen, asked if she could try on my hat, I handed it over.

Willie and Alex's voices rose over the lot of them. They were discussing motorcars, too, each giving a different opinion of what Gabe should purchase to replace the Hudson. Gabe appeared to be listening, while watching me with a small dent between his brows. I pretended not to notice, but heat prickled my neck and face despite my best efforts. I quickly turned away, to see Catherine talking to her husband by the door.

Cyclops nodded at something she said then Catherine plugged her fingers into her ears. Cyclops whistled shrilly and everyone fell silent. He pointed to his daughters. "You three, leave Sylvia alone. Alex and Willie, keep your voices down."

Only Willie mumbled a protest under her breath. The rest remained silent.

"Now, Sylvia," Cyclops said. "Catherine tells me something's troubling you which I assume is why you're here."

"What's wrong?" Gabe asked, approaching.

I drew in a deep breath before letting it out. As much as I liked the noise, it could also be overwhelming. Now that it had stopped, I needed to gather my thoughts again. "I've just come from the Moffat-Jones's place. Eleanor's behavior worried me this morning. She seemed anxious around her husband and I wanted to know why."

"You shouldn't have called there on your own if you had any concerns about him."

I bristled. "I left a message with Murray for you to meet me there. When you didn't arrive and I saw Mr. Moffat-Jones leave, I thought it would be safe enough for me to speak to Eleanor. Besides, I suspected she would respond better without you and Alex there."

Catherine sat beside me. "And? What did she say? Does she think her husband killed the bookbinder? Is that why she's anxious?"

I shook my head. "Not Littleproud. She says he murdered Honoria."

Alex swore under his breath, earning a glare from his mother and a giggle from Lulu.

"Does she have proof?" Cyclops asked.

"He admitted it to her, in a way. He uses it as a threat to keep her obedient. He'd tell her he'd kill her too if she did something that displeased him."

"Brute," Catherine spat.

Willie used a much cruder word, but no one seemed to mind.

"Cyclops, can you get Scotland Yard to reopen the case?" I asked.

He scrubbed a hand over his jaw. "I'll try."

"You have to be discreet. He can't find out you're investigating or she might be in danger."

"I thought you looked into Honoria's death," Alex said to his father.

"I did, but there was nothing in the original report to make me think it was anything other than a terrible accident. Moffat-Jones found his wife at the base of the stairs. Her injuries were consistent with a fall."

"He may have pushed her."

"He wasn't there at the time, so he claimed. I'll re-check his alibi and go over the other evidence again. Something might stand out to a pair of fresh eyes."

"Eye," Lulu said with another giggle.

Catherine took the girl's glass from her and sniffed the contents. "This is a martini. Willie!"

Willie had been sipping her own drink and spat the mouthful back into the glass. "I didn't give it to her. I'd give her whiskey or bourbon, not a martini."

Lulu blinked sweetly back at her mother. "It was just a little one."

"Little but strong." Catherine tipped the contents of the glass into a vase of irises. "We'll discuss this later."

"Speaking of things Willie is responsible for," Cyclops went on, "I had a visit from Lady Stanhope today. Apparently one of her magical manuscripts is missing. You wouldn't happen to know anything about that, would you, Willie?"

I clutched the stem of my glass and swallowed.

"Why would I?" she asked.

"Because you know Gabe and Alex needed it for their investigation and that she wouldn't let them borrow it."

"Then accuse them, not me."

"You also know how to break into a house without being detected."

"So do they."

"And you're also foolish enough to do it."

"You meant to say brave enough." She winked at me.

I sank into the chair.

Thankfully Cyclops didn't notice. "You've met Lady Stanhope. You know how difficult she can be. She demanded we recover it by the end of the week or she'd speak to my superiors."

"She'll get the book back tomorrow," Gabe assured him.

Willie rolled her eyes. "It'll miraculously turn up on a shelf where the maids will find it, and Lady S will wonder if it had been there all along. Now stop fretting, Cyclops, and top up my glass."

Alex poured another round of drinks, but I declined. Catherine invited me to stay for dinner since one more wasn't going to make a difference. It was a squeeze to fit around the dining table, but we managed it, although everyone was conscious of not extending their elbows too far.

We adjourned back to the parlor as soon as the meal was over. Gone were the days of men and women separating after dinner. While some households probably kept up the tradition, the Baileys didn't believe in stiff formality. Alex and Ella even sat on the floor.

It was late when I announced I was heading home. Gabe offered to drive me. Any hopes I held of being alone with him were dashed when Willie and Alex rose to leave, too.

We said our goodbyes and piled into the Vauxhall. Alex kept it idling while Gabe escorted me to the front door of the lodging house to collect Honoria's bound manuscript.

I used my key but Mrs. Parry was still up. She greeted us without a hint of admonishment in her voice, despite it being late and I'd not told her where I'd be. Gabe was already a favorite of hers, although I suspected that was because his cook passed on her Chinese recipes rather than his charming manner. I left them chatting and fetched the book from my room.

I held it to my chest as I returned to the entrance hall. Gabe smiled at Mrs. Parry and she bade us both goodnight.

"She must really like you," I said once she was gone. "She never leaves the gentlemen callers alone with her lodgers."

"I bribed her with more of Mrs. Ling's recipes."

I handed over the book, but he didn't take it straight away.

"Are you sure you can part with it?"

"Of course."

He accepted the book, but instead of leaving, he tucked it under his arm. I wasn't aware I was staring at it until he cleared his throat. I looked up to see him smiling sympathetically.

"My mother didn't know she was a magician until she was in her twenties. Her parents never said a word."

"It must have felt strange. Stranger than how I feel, I mean. She would have had to keep the discovery a secret in those days."

"It was difficult, more so because she didn't have anyone she could turn to. She told me she took it one day at a time, one discovery at a time. She described it as peeling back layers, each one revealing something new about herself or about magic. Once she understood how magic felt and how she needed to be near timepieces, she worked on them whenever she had the opportunity. She took them apart and put them back together, sometimes the same watch or clock, over and over. Even though she didn't place a spell in them, just working on them made them function better."

My gaze dropped to the book. "The process must have been a comfort, too."

"When I was young, she used to describe to me how it felt. She'd watch me closely as she spoke, to gauge my reaction. She was watching for signs of recognition in my face, of realization that I felt it too. There were no signs, of course, but she still got me to work on timepieces with her. I was nowhere near as good, but I can pull apart a watch and put it back together faster than most artless watchmakers." He laughed softly. "She said it would be a useful skill if ever my father's investments failed."

"Perhaps she was thinking of Lady Coyle's situation."

"Perhaps she was." He looked through the open door to

the motorcar, idling at the curb. It was too dark to see Willie or Alex, seated in the front. "Sylvia…"

"Yes?" I murmured.

"Why don't you want to talk about it? Your magic?"

"I don't know. I mean, I do, just…" I shrugged. He was right, I realized. I had been avoiding thinking about it as well as discussing it.

"I haven't told anyone, nor will I unless you give me permission. But I want you to know you can talk to me. I might not be a magician, but I understand magic. That was the point of my anecdote about my mother, in case you hadn't realized." He gave me a wry smile.

I didn't smile back. He might have thought mentioning his mother would comfort me, but all it did was show me how different our upbringings had been, how different my mother was from his. Lady Rycroft had nurtured her son. She was loving and accepting.

My mother loved me. I knew that in my bones. But she hadn't *shown* it. She wasn't *loving*. If she was from a magician family, as my brother suspected and as my magic now proved, then she deliberately hid it from us.

How would she react if I'd discovered I was a paper magician when she was alive? She wouldn't be as accepting as Gabe's mother. I suspected she would have ordered me to keep it a secret. If I'd told her I wanted to seek out other paper magicians, she would not have supported me.

It was why my brother never spoke to her about his suspicions but tried to find out more on his own.

Gabe touched my chin, raising my gaze to his. It wasn't until then that I realized I'd been staring at the book again. He smiled tentatively. "Talk to me, Sylvia."

"There's nothing to talk about. Goodnight, Gabe." I took a step back.

He took a step forward and opened his mouth to speak, but Willie's shrill voice stopped him.

"Hurry up, Gabe! We ain't got all night."

He sighed. "I'd better go before she wakes the entire street." He headed for the door but doubled back. He held out the book. "Keep this. Lady Stanhope can do without it for a little longer."

I accepted it without realizing I was reaching out. I hugged it to my chest and watched him go, my heart thudding louder in protest with every retreating step.

* * *

I TOOK the book with me to the library. My time with it was limited so I wanted to keep it close for as long as possible before I was forced to give it back. Professor Nash brought me a cup of coffee and a trolley full of books to catalog. They'd come from his attic.

"I was going to suggest you get started on these, but you look tired." He lightly grasped my shoulders and steered me in the direction of the reading nook. "Why not sit down with your coffee and rest awhile. Perhaps you could read a book."

It sounded like heaven. But there was only one book I wanted to read. I removed Honoria's manuscript from my bag and took it with me to the sofa. I'd looked through it before, of course, but I wanted to read it this time.

It was another fairy story, about a little girl who turned into one after eating a mushroom in her garden. While it was a charming tale, it was somewhat derivative, reminding me of several I'd read while growing up. Every time I turned the page, I stroked it to feel the magical warmth. It was just as the Petersons described. A tingling sensation, an awareness deep inside, of the magic calling me.

But halfway through, I suddenly stopped. The page felt

different from the others. I flipped back and forth, stroking several more pages, but they were all the same. The one in the middle was different. The magical sensation was still there, but it felt odd, like a rippling, churning pool where the magic on the other pages was flat, uniform.

The Petersons hadn't felt it because they hadn't touched *this* page. I thought about returning to their factory to ask what it meant, but another idea struck me. Indeed, it was something Mr. Peterson mentioned in passing that suddenly threw a new light on the case.

If I was right, then the killer could be identified on these pages.

I didn't need to speak to a paper magician to confirm my theory, however. I needed to speak to a magician specializing in another magical discipline altogether.

I closed the book and raced to the front desk. "I have to see Gabe," I told the professor as I grabbed my bag. "Is that all right with you?"

"Of course. Go!"

I caught a cab to his Mayfair house only to be met by a yawning Willie at the front door. She was dressed in a gentleman's dressing gown, her tangled hair tumbling around her shoulders in a mess that looked inviting for nesting creatures.

She informed me that Gabe wasn't at home. "Bristow says he and Alex have gone to the Moffat-Jones's house. They want to try to convince Eleanor to go somewhere safe until this all blows over."

I clicked my tongue. "Drat."

She narrowed her gaze and peered at me. "What's wrong? Why the urgency?"

"What do you know about combining spells?"

She stepped aside to let me in and closed the door. "Not much. India explored it years ago, and I reckon other magicians have since experimented combining their spells with others." She shrugged. "Why?"

"I need the name of a graphite magician. I hoped Gabe could look up his parents' list to see if there are any in London."

She folded her arms over her chest. "I can look it up, but not before you tell me why you need one."

"Mr. Peterson, the paper magician, told Gabe and I about paper magic and graphite magic combining to create invisible writing, if done in pencil, of course." I removed Honoria's untitled book from my bag and opened it to the page that felt different from the rest. "This page contains paper magic and one other kind. I think it's graphite but won't know unless a graphite magician can confirm it. I also don't know how to make the hidden writing visible again. I hope he or she does. I think whatever is written here will lead us to the killer."

"Huh. Well ain't that interesting. Go wait in the drawing room. I'll check the list." She headed off only to stop again. "How do you know there's another spell combined with the paper one?"

"I can feel it." I hugged the book to my chest. "I've just learned that I'm a paper magician."

She snorted a laugh. When I didn't join in, she said, "Huh," again. "Does Gabe know?"

"Yes."

Her lips flattened. "Paper, eh? My favorite kind." Her sarcastic mutter implied otherwise.

She returned to the drawing room fifteen minutes later dressed in her usual attire of buckskins and old jacket. Her hair was up, albeit still messy, and she was tying a red and black checked handkerchief around her neck. "I found a graphite magician who works in a fancy stationer's shop not far from the Glass Library." She removed a piece of paper from her pocket and flicked it with her finger.

"Thank you, Willie." I reached for the address but she held the paper out of my reach.

"I'm coming with you. We have to get a cab on account of Gabe having the only motor."

"That's not necessary. I can go alone."

"I'm coming."

She seemed determined so I didn't bother to protest. Arguing with Willie was a hopeless cause.

I thought the drive would be quiet, but she peppered me with questions the moment we slid into the backseat of the cab.

"So where does the paper magic come from in your family?"

"I don't know."

"Do you know any spells?"

"No. I don't need to know any. I don't manufacture paper."

"Good."

"Why good?"

"How did you find out you were a paper magician?"

"It was a realization that came to me over time. I suppose I just knew, deep inside."

"What did Gabe say when you told him?"

"Not much."

"Why didn't he tell me?"

"He was leaving it up to me to announce."

"Who else knows?"

"No one."

"So I'm the second person you've told?"

"Yes."

That was met with a grunt, the meaning of which I couldn't decipher.

The fancy stationery shop, as Willie called it, sold everything from paper and notebooks to maps, travel planners, writing implements, desk accessories, and gift sets. A selection of pencils was artfully displayed in fans and wheels on the counter. While we waited for the assistant to finish serving a customer, I inspected the monochrome artwork on the walls. All were done in pencil and signed P. Conway.

The customer left and the assistant approached us, smiling.

"Are you Victoria Conway?" Willie asked.

"She's my mother and the owner of this shop, but she isn't in today. My name is Petra Conway. And you are?"

Willie introduced us and outlined the reason for our visit, leaving out the part about me being a paper magician. The pretty dark-haired assistant's eyes gleamed at the mention of invisible writing.

"How interesting," she said. "I've heard of this from my mother, but never seen an example of hidden writing before. May I see the book?"

I passed it to her, deliberately not opening it to the relevant page. I wanted to see if she could find it. It would give me an indication of how strong her magic was.

She flipped slowly through the pages, passing her hand over each one. "I can sense the magic, but it's not graphite. Are you sure it's paper magic, not ink magic?" She tapped her finger on a word. "Only a specialist in each discipline would know the difference."

"A paper magician has confirmed that it does contain paper magic," Willie said.

"And an ink magician says it doesn't contain ink magic," I added.

Petra continued to turn the pages. "A reliable one, or Huon Barratt?"

I couldn't help smiling at that. "You must know him."

"Oh yes," she murmured. "I know Huon."

"You don't think he's reliable?" Willie asked.

"He's usually drunk these days, so I hear. I haven't seen him since before the war so I can't say for certain. I'll admit he is a strong magician. Pity he's an arrogant turd."

I grinned. "You really do know him."

She looked up and smiled ruefully. "I've known him all my life."

"Your families are friendly?"

"Ink and graphite? Good lord, no. Our families have been rivals for generations. But that's not why I dislike him. I dislike him because he thinks he's the bee's knees. Just because he's good looking and wealthy, he expects everyone to gravitate towards him. Mind you, some do, but only those who are as shallow as him."

Willie quite liked Huon, but wisely didn't try to defend him. She wasn't going to win against an opinion that had been nurtured over centuries. Besides, we needed Miss Conway on side. "Do you think you can help us?"

She stopped at the page that I suspected held the graphite magic. She placed her palm against it. "It's here." She caressed the page and breathed deeply. "Glorious."

"Do you know a spell to make the pencil visible?" Willie asked.

"I don't need a spell. I can see it."

Willie looked over her shoulder. "Where?"

"Everywhere on this page. The story written in ink sits over the top of it, but I can read it clearly enough."

Willie squinted at the page. "I can't see a thing."

"That would be why it's known as invisible writing."

Willie grunted. "What does it say?"

"It's a letter addressed to a Mr. Pryce. There is very little in the way of an introduction, and the tone is quite abrupt. I would describe it as businesslike, but there's an undercurrent of panic. The first line states that the writer has performed his task as requested and the money is now in the account. Then there's a number which I assume is the account number referred to." Miss Conway's finger followed the invisible writing across the page as she read. "It goes on to say that the police asked him some questions, but he doesn't think they suspect him. He assures Mr. Pryce that he did not bring his name into it but warns him that he will probably be the main suspect. The writer urges Mr. Pryce to leave the country at his earliest convenience, but if he is caught, he must keep his word as a gentleman and not implicate his accomplice. He wishes him well. It's signed Angus."

Considering the contents of the letter and who the paper originally belonged to, the name came as no surprise. Angus Moffat-Jones. It all made sense now. He'd not committed a single crime. He'd committed three.

# CHAPTER 18

$\mathcal{W}$illie swore as she hailed a passing cab, earning a glare from an elderly couple who promptly crossed the road to avoid us. "Gabe and Alex are at the Moffat-Jones house now. They could be in danger."

"They won't be," I said. "There's two of them and one of Moffat-Jones. Besides, they've probably already left. We should return to Park Street."

The cab pulled up and we clambered in. But instead of giving the driver her address, she told him to go to Crooked Lane. "It's closer," she told me. "We'll telephone Gabe from the library, then telephone Scotland Yard. Cyclops can send his men to the Moffat-Jones house." She indicated the book I clutched tightly to my chest. "He mentioned Moffat-Jones was questioned in relation to a fraud committed at the bank where he worked years ago, but just in passing."

"He wasn't a suspect, but this letter proves he *was* involved. If the police had seen this, he would have been arrested as an accomplice. Moffat-Jones and the Pryce fellow must have communicated with invisible writing."

"Ingenious," Willie said.

"Diabolical," I countered.

Professor Nash greeted us amiably, but quickly sobered upon seeing our grim faces. He pushed his glasses up his nose and offered to make tea.

Willie telephoned the Park Street house, but Gabe still wasn't home. She slammed the receiver down on the hook before picking it up again and handing it to me. "You call Scotland Yard. I'm going to the Moffat-Jones house." She hurried towards the door. "If Gabe and Alex are still there—"

The door was shoved open from the other side. It smacked into her, knocking her over. She hit her head on the edge of the desk as she went down.

She did not get up.

Mr. Moffat-Jones filled the doorway. Sweat dripped from his brow and his face was brick-red. A thick vein throbbed above a collar that seemed too narrow for his neck. His gaze took in Willie, unconscious on the floor, then shifted to me and finally fell on the book. "Give that to me, Miss Ashe." He'd dispensed with politeness altogether which meant he knew we were onto him. He could probably read it on my face.

Or he'd encountered Gabe and Alex. Where were they now?

If he'd caught them helping Eleanor escape…

*Oh God.* "My friends…where are they? Are they all right?"

His lips twisted with his cold sneer. "Give me the book and I'll tell you."

Was it a lie to get me to hand over the book? I couldn't tell. All I knew was that with one swipe of his fist, he could knock me unconscious too.

I picked up the book. It felt heavy in my hand, weighing me down. I studied it. The silver corner protectors gleamed in the light, the green leather cover felt a little roughened from age. But it was the paper inside that grabbed my attention and didn't let go. I rubbed the book's open edge with my thumb, and a jolt echoed inside me. The magic in the pages called to me. It hummed through my veins, filling me from head to toe.

Mr. Moffat-Jones stepped closer. "If you don't give it to me, they'll die."

I drew in a steadying breath.

He smashed the end of his walking stick into the floor. "It's mine!"

When I didn't move, he stepped closer and reached for the book.

I swung it, smashing it into his hand with such force, the blow wrenched his arm backwards. He grunted but it didn't stop him. He raised his walking stick and brought it down to strike me.

I dove out of the way, kicking as I did so, landing my foot on his right knee.

With a howl of pain, he collapsed to the floor.

Willie came up beside me and cocked her gun. "Stay there or I'll shoot."

The door opened and Gabe stopped dead upon seeing the situation. His gaze quickly swept up from Mr. Moffat-Jones to me. "Sylvia? Are you all right?"

Alex bumped into him and peered over his shoulder. "Seems the women have it in hand."

Willie holstered her gun. "Course we do. Call your father, Alex. Tell him we solved three crimes for him."

Both men skirted Mr. Moffat-Jones, whimpering on the floor as he clutched his knee. Alex moved to the desk while Gabe clasped my shoulders. His thumb caressed the underside of my jaw.

"Are you sure you're all right?"

I nodded. "Although Willie fell unconscious there for a moment."

She touched the back of her head. "It was nothing." She showed us her fingers. "No blood or brains. I'll live."

I blew out a long, steadying breath. "What about you and Alex? Did he cause you any problems?" I nodded at the murderer. He looked harmless, seated on the floor, unable to get up without assistance. But he was a ruthless man who knew how to use his size to intimidate and hurt. Fortunately, I knew how to use his size against him.

"We never saw him," Gabe said. "We tried to convince Eleanor to leave but she refused. We probably spent too long trying to change her mind."

"He must have arrived home while you were still there and overheard."

"We didn't hear him enter. The only other person in the house was the maid." The moment he said it, we both realized how Mr. Moffat-Jones had known we were onto him.

"Martha slipped out and alerted him," I said. "She also told him about the catalog I brought around yesterday. She recognized it. Did she collect your mail and give it to you before your wife saw?" I asked Mr. Moffat-Jones.

He didn't answer.

"You must have been paying her well," Gabe said.

Mr. Moffat-Jones snorted. "She's no fool, that one. Martha knows how to get what she wants, and what she wants is money. Greedy little whore."

Professor Nash's footsteps sounded on the stairs. "Tea?" He stopped on the second last step and took in the scene with all the lack of surprise of someone who had witnessed many strange events in his time. "I'm going to need more cups."

Alex hung up the receiver and joined us. "You said three crimes have been solved. Honoria's murder, Littleproud's murder, and...?"

Willie reached up and clapped him on the shoulder. "You

have to wait for Cyclops to get here. We ain't explaining it twice."

By the time Cyclops and his men arrived, the professor had made a lot more tea. He even offered Mr. Moffat-Jones a cup but received a sullen glare for his efforts.

"So go on then," Alex said. "We're all here now. What are the three crimes?"

"Fraud, murder and murder," Gabe said, brows raised in question.

I nodded. "I was looking through this book this morning and remembered something Mr. Peterson had said about invisible writing." I explained about the combining of spells for Alex and Cyclops's benefit, and how Willie and I had called on a graphite magician who read the hidden words to us.

"But how did you know that page had a graphite spell on it?" Alex asked.

"That's another story," I said. "Miss Conway told us the invisible writing was a letter written by Mr. Moffat-Jones to a Mr. Pryce."

Realization dawned on Cyclops's face. "The bank manager suspected of fraud. You worked for him. You were a witness in the investigation. No one suspected you."

Mr. Moffat-Jones rubbed his knee. "I was clever."

"If you were clever, you would have asked for more money. Pryce stole a fortune from the bank. He disappeared and the money was never recovered, but it was obvious that he did it. What made you and Pryce decide to communicate with invisible graphite?"

"His wife was a graphite magician and told him that combining her spell to make graphite strong actually worked counter-intuitively when combined with paper that also had a spell on it to make it strong. The pencil marks became invisible. In those days, it wasn't easy to find magicians. They were still in hiding. But Pryce knew some through his wife. He gave me a stack of papers with magic already infused through them."

"Do you know the name of the paper magician he purchased them from?" Gabe asked.

"No."

"How did you read his letters?"

"Pryce told me where to find a graphite magician who could see the invisible writing. The same fellow used his spell on the pencil I used to write my letters on the magic paper. That was the only the second one I wrote." He lowered his head. "I shouldn't have bothered. I never sent it in the end."

"Why not?" Gabe asked.

"I wrote it to warn Pryce not to implicate me if he was questioned. But he disappeared before I sent it. Then I forgot about it for a few months until I read an article in the newspaper. Someone thought they'd seen him in Australia. It was probably a hoax, but it reminded me of my unsent letter. I thought I should destroy it and went looking for it. When I couldn't find it, I asked Honoria and she told me she'd used the paper. She'd already sent her stories off to several publishers but couldn't remember who had them. She was dim-witted sometimes."

"You became angry with her," I said. "You've got a hot temper and you lashed out at her. You pushed her down the stairs."

"I wasn't even there. Check the original police notes."

"I have," Cyclops said. "This morning, I checked out your alibi again. You lied to the police, Mr. Moffat-Jones. The only reason you'd lie is to hide your guilt. You pushed her, didn't you?"

"It was an accident!"

"You were angry with her. You couldn't control your temper."

Mr. Moffat-Jones's nostrils flared and his jaw hardened.

"Your temper is why Eleanor is afraid of you," I said. "It's also why you accidentally killed Mr. Littleproud. After Honoria died, she became quite famous. Her published story sold many copies. The publisher who had her subsequent manuscripts at that time realized how valuable they were. Perhaps he was a magician himself and could detect the magic in the pages. He sold them to a collector named Lord Coyle who took them in for binding, but died before he could pick them up from the bookbinder. Years later, when Mr. Littleproud decided to sell them, he contacted an auction house. They featured them in their catalog before the scheduled auction date. Do you regularly receive the catalog?"

"A friend posted it to me after seeing Honoria's stories in there," he muttered. "I knew one of those books contained my letter to Pryce."

"You had to get it back," Gabe said. "You couldn't risk a magician discovering the hidden text. It implicated you not only in the fraud, but also in Honoria's murder if a detective connected the two incidents. So you called at Littleproud's shop after hours and asked him to hand over the manuscripts. Littleproud told you he'd sold them. You demanded to know who purchased them, but Littleproud refused to tell you. Your temper came to the fore again and you beat him up. Littleproud's heart couldn't cope with the trauma and he died before he could reveal where the books had gone. Did you then turn over the shop just in case they were there after all?"

"I was looking for a bill of sale."

"When Sylvia and I showed up asking questions about the books, you saw an opportunity to find out who bought them. You pointed out several times that they belonged to you, that Littleproud had no right to sell them. You frightened your wife into lying to Sylvia for you. She told Sylvia that you were home that night."

I shook my head. "That was Martha. Eleanor sleeps in a different room to him and takes laudanum, so couldn't account for his movements that night. But Martha the maid knew he was out. She lied to keep his secret and throw us off the scent."

"Earning herself a nice little bonus in the process," Alex said wryly.

Cyclops ordered his men to take Mr. Moffat-Jones back to the Yard for processing. It required two burly constables to haul him to his feet, while a sergeant held the door open.

Gabe pushed off from the edge of the desk. "Wait. I have another question. Does the name Folgate mean anything to you?"

Mr. Moffat-Jones shook his head.

"Did you impersonate a Scotland Yard detective over the telephone when speaking to Littleproud's silver supplier?"

"No!"

The constables escorted the limping Mr. Moffat-Jones out of the library. Once the door was closed, we all expelled a collective breath. The professor suggested we retreat to the reading nook for tea and sandwiches. Cyclops had been about to leave, too, until food was mentioned.

Now that it was all over, I was a little shaken. While I'd never felt in any danger during that encounter, there were other times when the situation could have ended differently. Not realizing Martha was spying for Mr. Moffat-Jones was a mistake.

Gabe clasped my elbow. "Are you sure you're all right?"

"I am, thank you."

Although my reassurance did nothing to dim the concern in his eyes, he released me and helped the professor pour the tea.

I sat beside Willie. She seemed very pleased with herself. "Been a while since I solved a murder," she said.

"*You* didn't solve it," Alex pointed out.

She slapped a hand on my knee. "How does solving your first murder feel, Sylvia?"

"First?" I pulled a face. "I hope there won't be more."

"We work for Scotland Yard. There are always more murders."

"*You* don't work for Scotland Yard," Alex said.

"Course I do. They just don't pay me."

Cyclops chuckled. "The commissioner would love more staff like you."

"That so?" As she turned to look at him properly, Willie's elbow lifted the edge of her jacket, revealing her holstered gun.

"On second thought, maybe not."

Gabe handed Willie a cup of tea. "Are you sure your head is all right?"

"It's too thick to crack," Alex quipped.

Willie lifted her teacup in salute. "Amen to that."

The professor returned with a plate of sandwiches. He offered them around, only to pause when he reached Gabe. "What I don't understand is how Moffat-Jones and the murder are linked to the silversmith, Folgate, and his corner protectors."

"They're not," Gabe said. "The person who hired Billy Burgess to find Littleproud's silversmith supplier had nothing to do with the murder. The only link is that both he and Moffat-Jones saw the untitled manuscripts in the auction house catalog. While Moffat-Jones wanted the books for one particular page, Burgess's employer didn't want the books at all. He just wanted to find out who sold the corner protectors with John Folgate's initials engraved on them to Littleproud. Presumably he's looking for the Folgate family."

"Or Marianne specifically," I added. "Any word from your solicitor about the owner of the Wimbldeon house where she lived?"

"Nothing yet." His gaze softened. "Don't worry. We'll get to the bottom of this mystery."

"It probably doesn't matter, after all." I cleared my throat and waited for everyone to look at me. "It would seem I'm related to paper magicians, not silver."

Professor Nash, Alex and Cyclops all lowered their teacups and stared at me. Cyclops was the first to recover his voice. "Have you discovered which paper magician family you're related to?"

"Not yet."

His gaze connected with Willie's.

"There are a few around the country," Gabe said. "I'll write up a list based on my parents' information."

We heard the front door open and close, but by the time I reached the marble columns, the newcomer was passing through them. Lady Stanhope strode past me without so much as a good afternoon, straight up to Cyclops, sipping his tea.

She pointed at him. "Why aren't you out searching for my book? The longer it's missing, the harder it will be to find."

Cyclops looked like he wanted to sink into the armchair. "Ah..."

Gabe picked up the book from the sofa. I'd carried it to the reading nook with me, not having put it down after I used it to smack Mr. Moffat-Jones's hand away. "He was just on his way to return it to you."

She inspected the front and back cover, satisfying herself that it was undamaged. "Who is the thief?"

"It was returned anonymously to Scotland Yard."

Lady Stanhope's gaze shifted from Gabe to Cyclops.

"How convenient." Her narrowed gaze moved on to Alex then Willie.

Cyclops sipped his tea.

Gabe offered her his arm to escort her back outside. As they walked off, he asked if she was free the following day. She gazed up at him with wonder and enthusiastically invited him to luncheon.

"He didn't have to bend over backwards," Willie muttered. "She believed him about the book."

Alex scoffed. "You must have hit your head harder than you think if you believe that."

\* \* \*

Daisy arrived at the library the following day before closing, wheeling her bicycle with a cart attached to the back. Her face was flushed and her shirt clung to her frame. She removed her neckerchief and dabbed her forehead with it. "I need a drink after dragging this thing all the way from home."

"I'll fetch you a glass of water," Professor Nash said.

"I don't want water, Prof." She flipped back the canvas cover on the cart to reveal bottles of gin and vermouth. "We will need glasses and ice."

"Olives?"

She tucked a bottle under one arm and removed a jar of olives from the cart. She shook them and grinned.

I peered into the cart. "What's in that briefcase?"

"It's a box not a briefcase. There's a portable Decca gramophone and some records inside."

I pulled out the heavy wooden box by its handle. It was battered and scratched, and one of the wooden side panels had a hole in it. "Did you find this in the rubbish?"

"I bought it off the widow of an officer who died in '17. She says he took it with him to the Front and would play records in the trenches when his men needed cheering up. It still works."

The hole must have been caused by a bullet.

Daisy led the way up the spiral staircase. "I was in the mood for a party, and since you said the others are coming after closing, I decided this was as good a place as any. The prof doesn't seem to mind."

I suspected Professor Nash liked having everyone gather in his library. He certainly never complained.

"I wasn't sure if he had enough gin and vermouth, though, so I decided to bring my own. And I didn't think he'd have a gramophone. Oh, and I invited some more friends."

"Who?"

"Huon Barratt, and Gabe's friends, Juan, Stanley and Francis. If we're going to celebrate, why not make it a proper party?"

I set the gramophone down on the desk and opened the lid. "I'm not sure celebrating the solving of a murder is in good taste, but I admire your *joie de vivre* nevertheless."

"I'm not celebrating you solving the murder. I'm celebrating my change of career. Ah, here's the professor." She opened a bottle of gin and accepted a glass from him. "I have absolutely, positively decided not to pursue an acting career. The moving picture business is full of unscrupulous players. The casting directors and producers expect the actresses to sleep with them, and the women are catty towards each other because they're all rivals for the limited number of parts. Going to their parties is like walking into a hive full of angry bees without the reward of honey." She plopped an olive into the martini and handed me the glass. "So I'm going to be an author."

Professor Nash beamed. "Good for you. It's wonderful to see you young people following your dreams."

I wasn't sure encouraging her to follow every single dream was a good thing to do, but on the other hand, Daisy had a little money to keep her going before she became desperate for an income. The professor was right. It *was* good to see people follow their dreams after the war had ended the dreams of so many.

She poured each of us a martini then raised her glass in a toast. *"Chin chin."* She sipped and glanced at the clock on the nearest shelf. "Does anyone know what time the others are arriving?"

"Waiting for someone in particular?" I asked slyly.

"If you mean Alex, then certainly not. Why would I? He's rude and arrogant. Not to mention he doesn't believe in me. Just because he's a man and his life is mapped out for him, doesn't mean the rest of us have to be like that."

"You mean be like men?" I teased.

"I mean know what we want in life." She sipped again and glanced at the clock. "So when will they get here?"

Alex, Gabe and Willie arrived five minutes later at the same time as Huon Barratt, Francis Stray, Stanley Greville and Juan Martinez. Gabe placed the satchel he was carrying on the desk and accepted a martini from Daisy. He smiled at me over the top of her head and raised his glass. Daisy continued to hand out more cocktails.

Alex sidled up to me. "Where did she get Juan's number?"

"She must have asked him last time she saw him. Or he gave it to her."

We watched as Juan put out his hand to her. She accepted it and together they twirled and gyrated to the music. Juan incorporated some traditional Spanish moves into his performances which necessitated getting close to his partner. Daisy giggled and reached up to place her hands on his shoulders.

Alex turned away.

"You should ask her to dance," I said.

"I have two left feet."

"Then she can teach you."

Willie, standing on Alex's other side, jabbed him with her elbow. "If you want her, you got to say something. A girl like that won't wait around for you."

"I don't want her," he muttered. "I'm not her type."

"Did she say that?"

He nodded at the dancing couple, falling over one another with laughter as the tune came to an end. "She doesn't have to."

I joined Huon at the desk where Daisy had arranged the bottles and jar of olives. "I met someone who knows you yesterday."

He added a large dose of gin to his empty glass. "Friend or foe?"

"Definitely a foe."

"Now I am intrigued. Who was it?"

"Petra Conway."

"Petra? I suppose she called me all sorts of names and now you think I kill puppies in my spare time."

"She did tell me all about the fierce rivalry between your families. Ink versus graphite?"

"An epic tale." His eyes gleamed, but I wasn't sure if that was because he was amused, or he'd consumed his first drink too quickly. "Did she tell you she tried to kiss me?"

"No, but you're going to."

"It was ten years ago, at a trade exhibition. Our parents had booths next to one another. The organizers clearly didn't know that ink magicians and graphite magicians have never gotten along. We're fierce rivals. Our crafts simply can't co-exist happily." He shrugged, as if it were an obvious fact that couldn't change. "Petra and I were both young at the time. I was terribly handsome, of course, and she was quite pretty. We were both rebellious, precocious teens so ignored our parents' warnings to stay away from the other. We met up for a clandestine encounter behind the maintenance shed."

"How very Romeo and Juliet."

"Not quite as tragic. We shared our first kiss then got into an argument about which was better, pen and ink or graphite pencils. That's when I discovered she was self-righteous and pompous."

"Perhaps she's different now. Perhaps you are."

"Oh, I know I am. I'm far more handsome than I was in my gawky teens, and far less selective when it comes to the female sex. Even so, I'd never lower my standards that much. Self-righteous, pompous women are not worth the trouble." He plucked an olive out of the jar and pointed it at me. "I heard she's practically running the shop now. I'm sure there's not a thing out of place. She was always so prim and proper."

For a couple that seemed to dislike one another so intensely, they seemed to know a lot about each other's life.

"You should go to the shop yourself and see," I said, blinking innocently at him.

"Perhaps I will. I do need some stationery items."

"Pencils?"

He gave me an arched look. "You are wicked."

He walked off and Gabe took his place. "Making another drink?" he asked, nodding at the bottles.

"Not yet. What about you? You're not drinking?" He hardly seemed to have touched his martini.

"Perhaps later." He looked up at the armchair on the mezzanine walkway above our heads. "Come with me. I need to tell you something and it's too loud down here."

It wasn't altogether quiet up there either, but at least we were alone. The smallest of the library's reading nooks, positioned on the narrow mezzanine, was bathed in the bronzed light of dusk streaming through the large arched window. I clutched the stem of my glass tightly and smiled up at Gabe.

"I spoke to my father's lawyer today. He received a letter from an archivist at the Ipswich Silversmiths' Guild. The letter was in response to the lawyer's questions about the Folgate family. It gave their last known address and detailed the family's history. Apparently the archivist had been researching silversmith magicians ever since the guilds changed their rules and were forced to accept them back in '91. That's when he became aware of the Folgate family. He discovered they were the last of their kind in the whole country. The archivist traced the line back to a silver magician who was taken from the Ottoman Empire by the Medicis."

I gasped. "The magician who made the silver clasps on the Medici manuscript most likely came from the Ottoman Empire. So *he* was a Folgate?"

"He had a different name then, but yes, he was a distant ancestor of Marianne Folgate. The Folgate ancestor who moved from Florence to England changed the family name to be more English. The archivist listed every Folgate down the line, all the way to Marianne. He didn't know if she'd had children, nor could he find any reference to her after she left Ipswich. There was no reference to the Wimbledon house where my parents last spoke to her. It looks like she married a Mr. Cooper shortly before she moved to the house with him, but since there's no record of her in the London GRO, it's likely they married elsewhere."

"So we're no closer to finding her."

"No, but the lawyer found out something else about that Wimbledon house. Something...unexpected. At the time the Coopers lived there, it was owned by a company. The company was set up by lawyers acting on behalf of Lord Coyle."

"Hope's late husband?"

He nodded. "Apparently their son inherited the house but it was sold years ago."

"That is unexpected," I murmured. "Do you think it's a coincidence? Or did Lord Coyle lease the house to the Coopers because he knew them?"

"Most likely the latter. Coyle collected magician-made objects, and Marianne was a rare silver magician. It's likely he bought some pieces off her, particularly if she was selling off the pieces she inherited from her father after his death."

"Like she'd sold the corner protectors to Littleproud."

He nodded. "The connection seems as innocent as any other business arrangement. Coyle bought some things from her and he discovered she needed to rent a house, so he suggested she and her new husband lease a property he owned."

I was still considering the connection and what it meant, when Gabe offered up more news.

"According to the archivist at the Ipswich Silversmiths' Guild, someone else made inquiries recently about the Folgates. He didn't leave his contact details, but telephoned back the following day. The archivist told him everything he'd learned about the family. He identified the caller as a male."

"That must be the man who employed Billy Burgess, the one who impersonated a detective on the telephone to Mr. Rinehold." We'd thought as much but now we had confirmation. Someone else wanted to find Marianne Folgate. "Do you think we should speak to Lady Coyle about the Wimbledon house?"

"I doubt Hope can help us. She said she threw out a lot of her husband's papers, and it's unlikely Lord Coyle discussed his business with her."

"True. Anyway I'm not a silver magician, so it no longer matters. All of this research into the Folgates is interesting, but irrelevant to me now. I'm not related to Marianne."

"Your brother thought he was a silver magician."

"Perhaps he was mistaken."

"Were *you* mistaken when you came to the conclusion you were a paper magician?" He had a point. "And then there's your name: Sylvia."

It was too much to take in all at once. There'd been so many revelations in the past week, so many things to think about. I couldn't cope with discovering I was related to silver magicians on top of finding out I was a paper magician.

Gabe seemed to understand perfectly. "Don't worry about that now." He took my hand and stroked his thumb over my knuckles. "Come downstairs with me. I have something to show you."

"Oi!" Willie shouted from down below. "What are you two doing up there?"

My face heated and my tongue tied so that I couldn't respond fast enough.

Fortunately, Gabe was as quick-witted and smooth as ever. "Turn the music off. I want to make a toast to Sylvia solving her first murder."

Going by the confused faces below, they thought Gabe's toast was an odd one, too. The professor lifted the needle off the record and the music stopped.

Gabe cleared his throat and raised his glass. "To Sylvia!"

Everybody sipped although I couldn't contain my smile.

"Stop smirking," he muttered into his glass. "It was all I could think of on the spot."

"Speech!" Huon shouted.

It was Gabe's turn to smirk at me. "Yes, Sylvia. What would you like to say?"

I wasn't going to back down from his challenge, although I did require some fortifying first. I drained my glass and handed it to him. "Thank you, Gabe, and thank you all for coming to this...post-murder-solving party. Putting Angus Moffat-Jones behind bars was truly a team effort." I lightly applauded Gabe, Alex and Willie. "My only regret is that Thurlow didn't receive his comeuppance. If anyone deserves it, he does. But it would seem his criminal enterprise lives to cheat others for another day."

"Thurlow might still be at large," Willie bellowed. "But he's a miserable pigswill now without his girl at his side."

"Jenny?" I asked. "Why? What happened to her?"

Huon pointed his glass at Willie. "You seduced her, didn't you?"

"I helped her escape to the States," Willie said. "She left last night on a steamer. He'll wonder for the rest of his days what happened to her."

"You sneaky thing," I said. "You never mentioned you were helping her. When did you even meet her?"

She grinned up at me. "I sought her out after you said she was miserable with him. I offered to pay her ticket and gave her Duke's name and address. He and his wife will help her get on her feet when she arrives."

"That's where you've been these last few nights?" Alex huffed. "I thought you were out finding your next husband."

"Another husband! Nope. Not me. I ain't never getting married again. Husbands just up and die on me, and I can't go through that again."

Daisy put her arm around Willie's shoulders. "You have been unfortunate in that regard."

"I reckon it's because their hearts can't handle being so in love with me. I'm just too much, you see." She raised her glass above her head. "Here's to having lovers only from now on."

Seeing as it was the time for strange things to toast, Francis added another. "And here's to no more kidnapping attempts."

Beside me, Gabe nodded. "I'll drink to that."

Daisy waved at me. "Come back down, Sylvia. Dance with me."

Professor Nash put the record back on, and Daisy and I danced in the limited space of the reading nook. Huon and Juan danced with us on occasion, while the others talked. Only Alex glanced at us from time to time, a small frown on his brow, and Stanley remained apart from the others. He watched on in silence. Anyone would think he was an outsider, not a good friend of Gabe's.

Gabe tried to encourage him to join in, and Stanley moved closer a few times, but he always gravitated away again eventually. It dampened Gabe's mood.

When I took a break from dancing, I placed a hand on his arm. "You've tried."

"I wish I could do more to help him."

I sighed. I didn't have any answers that would make Stanley happier. I wasn't sure anyone did. What he'd experienced and how those experiences affected him were things he had to get to grips with in his own way and in his own time.

Gabe suddenly clicked his fingers. "I almost forgot. I have something for you." He set down his glass. "Come with me."

Instead of leading me out of the reading nook, he led me to the chair behind the desk. He picked up the satchel he'd placed there and opened it. He removed one of Honoria's books and handed it to me.

"I got this for you."

I gasped as I opened it. The magic spilled out from the pages, warming my fingertips before rushing along my veins. "Lady Stanhope sold it to you?"

"It was more of a trade."

I tilted my head to the side and regarded him. "You gave her one of your mother's watches."

He shrugged. "It was an old one, with no sentimental value."

"Would your mother agree?"

"She would agree that I did better from the trade than Lady Stanhope." He indicated the book. "Do you like it?"

I hugged it. "Very much." I stood on my toes and kissed his cheek. "Thank you, Gabe. I'll cherish it."

"Good. But will you put it down long enough to dance with me, or should I bow out and concede defeat?"

I pretended to consider his options. "It's a tough decision. I mean, the book won't step on my toes."

He laughed.

I put the book down and turned back to him, grinning. "I'll risk the sore toes."

"I'm honored."

We danced until our feet hurt and most of the others had left. It felt good to dance with him and laugh after the grim investigation we'd just completed. But I was under no illusions that our relationship would develop into something more than friendship. He made his feelings and intentions clear by keeping me at arm's length as we danced.

I accepted it. Indeed, I'd come to terms with it.

If only my heart would listen to my head and accept it too.

**Look For:**
THE DEAD LETTER DELIVERY
*The 4th Glass Library novel*

Did you know the Glass Library series is a spin-off of the Glass and Steele series? Go back to where it all began with book 1, The Watchmaker's Daughter by C.J. Archer.

# ALSO BY C.J. ARCHER

## SERIES WITH 2 OR MORE BOOKS

The Glass Library

Cleopatra Fox Mysteries

After The Rift

Glass and Steele

The Ministry of Curiosities Series

The Emily Chambers Spirit Medium Trilogy

The 1st Freak House Trilogy

The 2nd Freak House Trilogy

The 3rd Freak House Trilogy

The Assassins Guild Series

Lord Hawkesbury's Players Series

Witch Born

## SINGLE TITLES NOT IN A SERIES

Courting His Countess

Surrender

Redemption

The Mercenary's Price

# ABOUT THE AUTHOR

C.J. Archer has loved history and books for as long as she can remember and feels fortunate that she found a way to combine the two. She spent her early childhood in the dramatic beauty of outback Queensland, Australia, but now lives in suburban Melbourne with her husband, two children and a mischievous black & white cat named Coco.

Subscribe to C.J.'s newsletter through her website to be notified when she releases a new book, as well as get access to exclusive content and subscriber-only giveaways. Her website also contains up to date details on all her books: http://cjarcher.com

Follow her on social media to get the latest updates on her books:

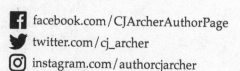

facebook.com/CJArcherAuthorPage

twitter.com/cj_archer

instagram.com/authorcjarcher